MW00577878

FAREWELL,
AMETHYSTINE

NONFICTION

FAREWELL, AMETHYSTINE

AN EASY RAWLINS MYSTERY

WALTER MOSLEY

MULHOLLAND BOOKS

LITTLE, BROWN AND COMPANY

NEW YORK BOSTON LONDON

Mulholland Books / Little, Brown and Company
Hachette Book Group
1290 Avenue of the Americas, New York, NY 10104
mulhollandbooks.com

First Edition: June 2024

Mulholland Books is an imprint of Little, Brown and Company, a division of Hachette Book Group, Inc. The Mulholland Books name and logo are trademarks of Hachette Book Group, Inc.

The publisher is not responsible for websites (or their content) that are not owned by the publisher.

The Hachette Speakers Bureau provides a wide range of authors for speaking events. To find out more, go to hachettespeakersbureau.com or email hachettespeakers@hbgusa.com.

Little, Brown and Company books may be purchased in bulk for business, educational, or promotional use. For information, please contact your local bookseller or the Hachette Book Group Special Markets Department at special.markets@hbgusa.com.

ISBN 9780316491112 (hc) / 9780316578868 (lp)
LCCN 2024934371

Printing 1, 2024

LSC-H

Printed in the United States of America

For Sonia Sanchez,
the shining light
of literature and love

FAREWELL,
AMETHYSTINE

1

"Naw, naw, man. Shit no. They wanna kick her outta that school because she a Black woman want the Constitution to practice what it preach. All kindsa white revolutionaries and, and, and activist teachers up there at UCLA and they don't make a peep about them."

"But, Raymond," Tinsford "Whisper" Natley rumbled, "they say she's a Marxist, a communist."

"So? It's a free country, ain't it?" my friend challenged.

Raymond Alexander, Saul Lynx, Whisper, and I were sitting around the conference table in my office at the back of WRENS-L Detective Agency.

Mostly on Monday mornings we got together to discuss events in the news. Monday was a good day because the rest of the week you couldn't trust that we'd all be around. At the top of the week around 9:30, 10:00, my partners would migrate back with paper cups of bitter coffee in hand.

For the past couple of months, Ray, also known as Mouse, had shown up for this informal meeting every other week or so.

This was an unexpected wrinkle. Saul and Tinsford had once asked me to keep him away from our workplace, because Raymond was a career criminal who practiced everything from racketeering to first-degree murder. But that request changed on a Wednesday morning in the late fall of '69.

I was out, going around a few SROs in Inglewood, looking for a missing husband, while Saul was at Canfield Elementary School because his son, Mo, had gotten into a fight. That morning, as every morning, Niska Redman occupied the reception desk and Whisper was in his office.

Somewhere around 11:00 my friend Mouse dropped by. Niska brought Raymond to LA's best detective's cubbyhole of an office. There she introduced the man who needed no introduction.

Weeks later Whisper told me that he said, "Easy's not here, Mr. Alexander."

"I'm not here for him, brother," was the heist man's reply. "It's you need to hear what I got to say."

Without even sitting down, Raymond told Whisper that a man named Desmond Devereaux was planning to kill Natley because he got DD's brother arrested for a killing in Oxnard.

"And how would you know about that?" Whisper was a small man, even smaller than Ray, but he was someone you knew to take seriously.

"He sent a guy ovah to ask me about you."

"Why would he ask you?"

"Because e'rybody knows I know Easy and that's just one step away from you."

Tinsford sent Niska home, left messages for me and Saul, and then went out with the deadliest man I knew, to take care of business.

They were gone for two and a half days, after which they never spoke about DD again. I hadn't heard another word about the man anywhere.

Ever since then Raymond has been welcomed into our Monday morning talks.

As usual it was a rollicking conversation. Each of us had a favorite story in the day's newspaper. We laughed at the rumor coming from the Turkish countryside: some people there thought that the newest flu epidemic was somehow caused by the moon expedition. The U.S. had similar issues with Russian spy satellites. White parents in Mississippi had a sit-in complaining about even just the word *integration*. But it was Angela Davis and UCLA's attempt to oust her from her teaching position that got Raymond and Tinsford riled.

"But," Tinsford complained, "the communists want revolution."

"So did Thomas Jefferson." Raymond wielded the name as if it was a weapon. For the past few months, he'd been spending his spare time reading heavy tomes of history about politics and race.

But Tinsford had been reading his entire life.

"Jefferson was influenced by the French Revolution, not Karl Marx."

"Angela was influenced by the Frankfurt School," Raymond said. I knew right then that he was going to be a whole new kind of threat in the coming decade.

"What school is that?" Saul asked.

"It's these college professor guys from Germany," Mouse said. "This guy Herb Marcus, somethin' like that, works with them. They want things to change, and Angela does too. That's why the trustees tryin' to fire her."

"Mr. Rawlins?" Niska Redman, our office manager, was standing at the door.

"Yeah?"

"That woman, Miss Stoller, the one Mrs. Blue wanted you to talk to. She's here."

Niska was tallish for a woman at that time, maybe five nine, and brown like the lighter version of See's caramel candy. She usually tried to be serious because of her job, but you could tell that she was always ready to laugh.

"Well, guys," I said to my friends, "I guess it's time to get back to work."

And that was it. Saul and Whisper went to their offices. Mouse left for a world of bad men, bank robbers, and bloodletters.

Niska backed up into the hall, allowing the men to file by, then she returned followed by a woman two shades darker than her.

"Amy Stoller," Niska announced.

The potential client was wearing an ivory-colored dress that had a high collar and a knee-level hem that flared just a bit as if maybe responding to an errant breeze.

Already standing to see my friends out, I took a step in the potential client's direction and held out a hand.

"Easy Rawlins," I said.

"Nice to meet you." She obliged the gesture with a firm grip.

"Have a seat," I offered, motioning at the three chairs set before my gargantuan desk.

I'd started WRENS-L Detective Agency with a quasi-legal windfall I'd come upon years before. Saul and Whisper came in as partners, but they made me take the big office. I'd accepted the allocation with only mild trepidation. I wasn't humble among friends or clients. But as an orphan in Houston's Fifth Ward, I'd learned that, in the world at large, if people knew you had something, they were liable to take it.

I made it behind the desk. Ms. Stoller waited for me to sit down before she settled in. This struck me along with something else about her, a subtle scent she wore that was reminiscent of the bouquet of some ancient forest, welcoming but having hardly any trace of sweetness.

She was in her mid- to late twenties with satin brown skin and amber eyes on a face that was wide and unusually sensual. Her mouth was also wide, promising a beautiful smile. Stoller's eyes being lighter than her skin meant something that I couldn't put my finger on. But that wasn't a bother, not at all.

"It's a very nice office," she said. "Kind of like the master bedroom in an apartment, or even a house."

"The whole building used to be a rich man's home till the furniture store downstairs bought it."

She let her head tilt to the left and gave up half a grin.

I knew that this was a very important moment but had no idea if it would be for the good or not.

2

"How do you know Jewelle, Ms. Stoller?"

"I work for her and, you know, she treats all the women in the office kinda like they're family."

There was an aura of unconscious elegance surrounding her. This brought a question to mind.

"Is Amy your given name or is it short for something else? Amanda? Amelia?"

Smiling she said, "Amethystine."

I was, unexpectedly, enchanted by the name. It seemed somehow...perfect. For a moment I didn't know what to say and she had nothing to add. This quietude didn't bother either one of us. We sat comfortably in the expanding silence.

"So, um," I stammered. "How'd you come to work for Jewelle? You study business or real estate at school?"

Showing more of her left cheek than the right she said, a little shyly, "I was working for her husband at the insurance company P9, and she told him that she wanted to meet me."

"What you do for Jackson?"

"You know Mr. Blue?"

"I knew Jackson back in the biblical days when he robbed Peter and then robbed Paul too."

That got me the broad grin I'd been searching for.

"I went to P9 to apply for a job in statistics and they gave me a test. I guess I did pretty good on it because the human resources lady sent me to Mr. Blue's office."

My eyebrows rose a bit.

"What?" she asked.

"Jackson's the highest-ranking vice president of P9. I can't even think of a reason why he'd want to meet an entry-level applicant. Did he know you or somethin'?"

"We had met. He's the one told me about the kind of jobs they had. But I didn't tell him that I was applying."

"Then why would they send you all the way up to the thirty-first floor?"

"I asked him that very same question," she said. "You know what he told me?"

"What?"

"He said that those white people in personnel don't never hire Black people and so he asked the president...ummmm." She snapped her fingers a few times trying to remember the name.

"Jean-Paul Villard," I said, filling in the blank.

"Yeah. Jackson asked Mr. Villard to tell human resources to send the colored applicants to Mr. Blue if they did well on the written test. And it was a good thing they did."

"Because he hired you?"

"Not only that. You see, they ask you about your education before getting the transcripts, and I lied, sayin' that I graduated from USC with a business degree."

"That must'a tickled Jackson."

"Yeah. He said that he didn't make it past the fifth grade in school."

"And he failed the fourth grade."

We were having an excellent time.

"But then Jewelle got involved," I prompted.

"Yeah." She seemed a little bit shy again.

"You don't have to explain that one. Jackson is a genius by nature and a dog by nurture. He's been kicked more times than he's been kissed. I know exactly what happened."

"There was never anything inappropriate between us." Amethystine's words bordered on anger.

"I believe ya. What happened was one night Jackson probably said at the dinner table that he had a Black woman working in mathematical predictions, what he calls statistics. And in that moment Jewelle heard that little twang of excitement Jackson gets when a girl strikes his fancy."

"Mmm," was her reply. She nodded, signaling, maybe unconsciously, that we should get down to business.

"So," I said. "What can I do for you, Ms. Stoller?

"Miss Stoller."

With a smile I said, "What can I do for you, Miss Stoller?"

"I used to be Mrs. Fields, wife of Curt Fields. That's why I'm here."

I waited patiently.

Then, a bit hesitantly, but with no discernible shyness, she said, "Curt and I were married soon after we met. When he proposed to me, I thought that I'd never meet a man as good again. I said yes and we were doing really well, really happy, you know?"

"I've been there," I said. Our eyes met and connected.

"I was very happy," Amethystine Stoller averred, "and then, well, I got bored. So I left him."

"You got divorced?" Maybe there was a hopeful little quiver in my chest.

"Yes. But...we're still friends. I liked him and, I think, he was hoping we'd get back together again. I told him that I wouldn't do that; I wouldn't do that to him. I mean, he deserves somebody who would love him like a woman does a man, you know?"

"Yes, I do."

"But even with all that, when I got into a kind of a jam, he helped me without askin' for nuthin'. So I feel like I owe him."

"What kind of jam?"

"That doesn't have anything to do with why I'm here."

"Okay. Why are you here?"

It was work getting at what she wanted, but less like pulling teeth and more like plucking apples from the upper tiers of a golden tree. There I sat, in the gilt-green dome of my imagination.

"You're very patient," the young woman observed.

"I don't have all the time in the world, but you got an hour penciled in on the calendar."

Amethystine studied these words a moment or two and then said, "I still feel very kindly toward Curt, and so when his parents called me yesterday I knew I had to do something."

"What did your ex-in-laws want?"

"The Sunday before last he told them that he was going out with some friends."

"He lives with his parents?"

"No. He makes a good living and has his own place. He's just a good son. Tells his mother everything. You know...boring."

"So," I encouraged. "He called and said he was going out."

"And nobody's heard from him since."

"Black kid."

"White...man."

There was nothing this woman said that I did not like. Her sentences were pithy, like a combat general's orders in the heat of battle.

But she didn't look military. The dark skin under her pale dress made her seem, somehow, vulnerable.

"Okay," I said. "A missing person. Gone a week. Tell me about him."

Amethystine Stoller smiled at me like a refugee seeking passage at a foreign border. The emigrant had shown her papers and now she was being ushered through.

"Curt's a forensic accountant. He works mostly for courts and lawyers, prosecutors and, if they can afford it, the defense. He uses computer files, libraries, three part-time research assistants, and a newspaper clipping service that works out of Chicago. He goes after hidden wealth, the movement of money, and what Curt calls *false fronts*."

I was finding it hard to concentrate on the words she was saying. This because she reminded me of a woman named Anger. Anger's mother was a Black woman named Angel, her father a high-yellow killer called Shadow Lee. A dark-skinned, sharp-eyed young woman, Anger worked the back rooms of whatever job she was hired for. And she only did jobs that were in opposition to whatever law there was. For a long time, she worked for a small warehouse that bought and sold stolen goods off Black dockworkers employed at the Galveston port.

When I was fifteen, and nearly a full-grown man, Anger was seventeen and had been on her own at least half a dozen years.

*   *   *

"I feel guilty," Amethystine said, shocking me back to the present.

"Guilty about what?"

"About leaving him. He was pretty useless when it came to dealing with anything but numbers. Numbers and long hours at work."

Also boring, I thought.

In a bizarre turn of mind, I got the urge to ask her if she was going to get me killed. But instead I said, "I'm gonna need his parents' information, and his."

"You mean like their names and addresses?"

"Yes."

"I don't know Curt's new address. I mean, I don't see him very often because, because he needs to get over me."

Nodding, I pushed a yellow legal pad and yellow No. 2 pencil across the desk.

While writing she said, "Mrs. Blue told me to come see you, but she didn't tell me what it would cost."

"Jewelle and I work on an old-school monetary system."

Looking up, Amethystine asked, "What's that?"

"We trade in favors."

"Trade?"

"Back and forth like two tennis players in hell."

"Is there some favor you need from me?"

"No, at this point all I need is information."

She worked the pencil across the blue-lined yellow sheet with intensity. It was then that I noticed she was left-handed.

"Do you have any idea of where Curt might be?"

"No."

It was the first lie she uttered. That's when I decided, for sure, to kick the tires on her missing person case.

"Does he have any enemies?" I asked, as PI protocol demanded.

"I couldn't say. I mean, he doesn't run around with a bad crowd or anything, but he's kind of innocent, know what I mean?"

"Maybe, but why don't you explain?"

"He's a soft touch, gives away money on the street to anybody who says they need it. He believes that people mostly tell the truth and keep their promises. He's a white man but I don't think that ever, even once, he thought there was anything unusual about us being together."

"You don't share his beliefs?" I teased, mildly.

"Do you?"

"Your number on that paper?" I asked in reply.

She took up the pencil once more.

3

For quite a while after Amethystine had departed, I stared out the window at our backyard neighbor's picnic table.

Not long before, a quintet of hippies lived there, growing marijuana in a jury-rigged greenhouse. They escaped capture by the LAPD because I had warned them of the threat, and now a young couple lived there with their toddler son.

Anger Lee and I were walking down a dark Galveston alley late one Wednesday night. I was smitten with her even though she treated me like a little brother.

I'd just gotten off from my job as a dishwasher at an upscale bordello on Rent Street. Halfway down the alley a big Black man jumped out, slapped me, and then pulled out a jagged-looking black-bladed knife.

"Bitch! You comin' wit' me!" the attacker yelled at Anger.

Fifteen-year-old man that I was, I jumped up and tried my best to demolish our attacker. Instead, I was laid on my back with a knife wound in my left shoulder and a concussion that lasted nine days. Even though I was outmanned, my attack was a success because it gave Anger the chance to pull out her long-barreled .41-caliber pistol.

"Back it up, suckah!" she yelled.

Then there was a shot.

"Mr. Rawlins?"

Niska was standing at the door, her words a beacon set on leading me out of a nightmare.

"Yeah, baby?" I said, speaking words in the language of a long-ago life.

"Can we talk?"

"Come on in."

She crossed the threshold.

One of the many things I liked about our office manager was that, whenever she was nervous, it showed in her gait.

Stiffly she moved to the central visitor's chair. We then sat in unison.

"What can I do for you, Niska?"

The differences between our office manager and Amethystine were many.

Niska was open and aboveboard, a churchgoer, and careless about things that did not matter.

"I've been here over two years," she began. "Before that I worked for Mr. Natley."

I nodded.

"That's a long time," she added. "Since I was sixteen."

"It is."

"I like this job and, and I'm pretty good at it."

"And now you want a raise," I said with absolute certainty.

"No. You pay me more than most kids my age get. It's just that I don't want to be an office manager forever."

"That's why you're going to college, right?"

"I want to be a PI like you."

These words created a vacuum in my mind. I didn't see Niska as a detective. As a matter of fact, I had never met a woman PI. In my experience, back then, women only did *men's jobs* if they worked on a farm or if the men had gone off to war.

"What do you think about that?" Niska wanted to know.

Searching for the right words, I asked, "You talk to Whisper 'bout this?"

"Tinsford treats me like he my uncle or sumpin'. He always comes and picks me up if I ever work after nightfall and if he's out of town he gets somebody else to do it."

"But you drive your own car," I argued against the man not there.

"They walk me to my car."

Her look was plaintive, and I could understand why.

"I can see why a man like Tinsford would think he had to protect a young woman," I said. "That's just the world we come from."

"But it's not the world we live in, Mr. Rawlins," she complained. "Just as much as a man, a woman has to follow her dreams. She has to be able to take care of herself too."

"And your dream is to be a private detective?"

"Uh-huh."

"But why? I thought you were studyin' business or somethin'."

"You remember when I told you about the guy I met at the TM retreat a few months ago?"

"Yeah."

"He's a patrol cop and wants to be an investigator one day. When he found out that I worked for two Black detectives he was so excited. It made me realize how good and important your job is."

"You're a big part of this job, N."

"I know. I mean I know that I help. But you're out there in the world making sense out of things that are hidden, secrets. Reggie wants to do that, and while he was saying it, I realized that I did too."

"Reggie's a Black man?" I asked, realizing how often that kind of question came to mind.

"Yeah. And he wants to be like you and Whisper."

"And you do too?"

"Yeah."

"Why?"

"Because this work makes more sense than book learning does. Human sense."

I was impressed.

"What do you think?" Niska insisted.

"The first thing is you have to talk to Tinsford. You can tell him that I support you and that I'll be part of your education. But he has to agree. I won't go against a partner like that."

Niska gave me a long, soulful look and then nodded.

"You're right," she said. "If I want something like this, I have to stand up for myself. Thank you, Mr. Rawlins."

She stood up, held out a hand for me to shake, and then walked out with confidence and aplomb.

After Niska was back at her desk, my mind wandered for a while. There were many thoughts swimming around up there. Mouse talking revolution, Niska wanting to put her life on the line. And, most important, Amethystine Stoller, who somehow reminded me of a woman named Anger with a smoking gun in her hand.

I nodded to myself and picked up the phone.

* * *

"Commander Suggs's line," informed a woman's voice that was weathered by age.

"You sound sad, Myra."

"Oh. It's you, Mr. Rawlins." Her words seemed to be coming up off some dismal memory like mist from a stagnant lake. "Can I help you?"

"He in?"

Without Myra Lawless saying another word, the phone made three loud clicks and then another line began to ring.

"Captain McCourt." The answering voice was not only deep but also musical.

"Anatole?"

"Who is this?"

"Easy Rawlins."

"What do you want?" I was not Mr. McCourt's favorite person.

"I was trying to call Melvin, got Myra, and she passed me along to you, I guess."

There was silence for a beat.

"Commander Suggs is away on vacation," Anatole McCourt said as if reading the words off a cue card. "He'll be back in a couple of weeks."

I'd seen Mel only five days earlier. He'd told me then that he was going on vacation to Paris with Mary Donovan—his live-in girlfriend who was born and breastfed on the other side of the tracks.

Mel and I were having breakfast at Tony's Bistro Diner on Flower Street. We liked going there for our now-and-again morning meetings because Mary had him on a forever diet and I'd always get the strawberry waffles.

"Last time I was in Paris was during the Allied occupation," I'd said. "When you goin'?"

"May, before it gets too hot."

Mel took a four-week vacation once every two years; that was a hard-and-fast rule. So Anatole was lying, but that didn't matter. Conversing with liars was my bread and butter.

"Well then, maybe you could help me, Captain."

"What do you need?"

"I've been asked to look for a missing person. A man named Curt Fields."

"Negro?"

"White."

"What's he done?"

"Disappeared."

"And who is the client?"

"His wife. Mrs. Fields."

The cop went silent, but my mind did not wander. I was trying to read his thoughts over the phone.

"Okay," he said at last. "I'll look into it. Why don't we meet at Clifton's around one?"

I knew then that whatever was going on with Mel, there was something wrong with it. McCourt saw me as the Element and himself as the Cure. We'd traded information from time to time, but never had he asked for a meet.

I called Mel's home phone but there was no answer. This was strange because Mel was one of the few people I knew who had an answering machine.

Next I flipped through my Rolodex looking for the card containing the number for Pink Hippo #3. After eight rings, an answering machine did engage.

"Nobody's here right now," a man's deep voice proclaimed. "If you want somethin' then leave a message and somebody might get back to you."

When the beep sounded, I said, "Easy Rawlins," and then hung up.

4

Clifton's downtown cafeteria was replete with twelve-foot-high grotesque tiki sculptures carved from redwood tree trunks, bamboo-themed furniture, and women servers in tight-fitting, calf-length, white silk dresses that had bright-green blades of grass emblazoned on them.

It was a buffet-style place with long cafeteria lines where you filled up your tray with whatever food you wanted. Cashiers awaited payment at the ends of the long aluminum tracks.

There were fifty or more patrons sitting at tables or walking down the line, pushing dark trays and studying the offerings — which were anything but Hawaiian.

"Can I help you, sir?" a woman asked.

She stood at the host's podium. Her name tag read DAISY but she was Asian, probably Chinese, slender, with a forlorn look in her eyes and a smile on her lips. She was in her mid-thirties, an age that was kind of a DMZ dividing youth from adulthood. Her face was long; maybe that's why I felt she was sad.

"I'm meeting someone for lunch," I said.

"Do you see them?"

She wasn't being short or rude. Clifton's was a busy place with three floors of dining space and no waitstaff except for drinks.

"No," I said. "Maybe he left a note or something for me at your desk."

"I don't think—"

"His name is Anatole McCourt and he's quite tall."

Daisy's head moved back maybe two inches, the kind of reaction any mammal might have when they catch the odor of something unexpected.

"Oh," she said. "Yes. Follow me."

She led me through the first-floor dining room to a stairway that wound upward past the second level to the third. We walked down a slender hallway that had hanging framed oil paintings of flowers every four feet or so. Finally, we came to a curtained doorway. This she gestured for me to go through.

On the other side of the beaded green blind was a solitary balcony that looked down onto the second-floor dining room. The table there could have seated four easily, but Anatole McCourt was there alone.

When I realized that he had arrived before me I considered walking away and taking my own unplanned vacation.

Anatole McCourt was tall and beautiful by masculine standards. He followed the law to the letter and was chivalrous to women. All that and he'd never so much as shaken my hand. Now I was invited into his private booth. And he was early, which meant that he was hungry for something other than teriyaki chicken thighs.

"Private balcony, huh?" I said, taking the seat across from him.

"You want a drink?"

"Do I need one?"

"Up to you." He was almost chipper.

"Maybe later."

"You hungry?" the cop offered.

"Sure. Wanna go down to the line?"

"No."

He pressed a black button set on the balcony's upper banister shelf. Immediately, a short mustachioed man came in through the beaded curtain.

"Yes, Captain?" the swarthy Caucasian inquired.

"Bring us out some appetizers and two of the regular."

After the waiter was gone, I wondered aloud, "I didn't know they had table service at Clifton's?"

"They do for me."

It's funny how we, men in America and probably around the world, can compete over anything at all.

"So," I said, "why we got to meet here instead of your office?"

"The man you're looking for has been identified as a possible part of a numbers scheme being run by a man named Shadrach."

"What part of the scheme is Fields?"

"We don't know. He is almost certainly helping them hide the proceeds, but he may also have something to do with planning."

"Racketeering?"

"They aren't sure. But they'd like any information you have."

"I don't know anything. Woman, sayin' she was his wife, came to my office and said he was missing, that his parents went to the police, but they didn't find anything."

"And what have you found out?"

"Mel was the first person I called."

The curtain parted and the mustachioed man came in with a

tall Black waiter carrying a pupu platter that was overflowing with skewers of teriyaki beef, stewed chicken, and butterflied shrimp, along with sweet pork ribs, chicken wings, fried rice balls, and cracked cold crab claws.

After the platter was installed at the center of the table, they brought in two meat-loaf plates with side dishes of mashed potatoes and short-cut wax beans.

"Anything else?" the head waiter asked Anatole.

"Yeah, bring me a Laphroaig."

"Right away, Captain."

He departed, leaving us to feast.

I could feel my heart working. Anatole McCourt was not the kind to share police information, not to mention their resources, with a man like me. A Black man, a fake cop, a friend of the notorious Raymond "Mouse" Alexander—I was everything a man like McCourt despised.

The waiter must have had the drink waiting because he returned with it just that fast. He put the peaty liquor down in front of McCourt and bowed his way out again.

"Okay," I said. "I give."

"What do you mean?" Anatole savored the first sip.

"Look, man, you don't like me. You never did. You wouldn't even talk to me if it wasn't for Mel. So, you got me here to talk about somethin' specific."

"Yes. Of course. I was asked by the men investigating Fields to get you to share what you know and what you find."

"No."

"No, you won't share?"

"No, that's not why we're here. You never work with people like me. It's against your nature. You'd rather let killers and rapists get away than be in debt to me. You think that you'll catch the bad guys later, on some other beef. No. What is it we really doin' here, Anatole?"

The beautiful Irishman downed the rest of his double shot. He'd savored the sip but needed that gulp to keep him from throwing me off the balcony. He could probably count on one hand the number of times he'd had to come clean with someone like me.

"We're looking for Mary Donovan," he admitted. The tops of his perfectly sculpted earlobes were tinting red.

"What for?"

"That's police business."

"Mel's a friend'a mine. I thought he was your rabbi."

"We're not asking you about Commander Suggs."

"I once asked Mel how he explains his relationship with Ms. Donovan. You know what he told me?"

Anatole didn't say anything, but I could feel his attention magnify.

"He said that she was his one external organ."

"So, you refuse to help?"

"What's goin' on with Mel, man?"

The juggernaut cop's face twisted. He wanted to hurt me. After maybe half a minute he stood up from his chair and said, "Finish your food, Rawlins, it might be your last meal as a free man."

That was an exit line, but McCourt paused, thinking that maybe I'd be afraid enough to fold.

I looked up at him, considering the threat. Anatole was a brawler, a bad man with his fists. There was no question that he could have beaten me to death right there and then.

But I had just turned fifty. The average life span of Negro men in that year was sixty. He had more to lose than I did, and besides, Melvin Suggs was my friend.

When he saw that I wasn't going to cave, the cop stormed out of our meeting place.

I devoured two wings and one rice ball, then made my way down the stairs to the basement toilets. Between the men's and women's doors was an old-fashioned phone booth with an upholstered seat.

My adopted son, Jesus, pronounced *Hey Zeus* by those who knew him, answered, "Hello?" on the first ring.

"Hey, Juice," I hailed.

"Hi, Dad."

He'd been sexually molested before his third birthday and had no idea of where he was from or who his people were. He had the features of Native Americans mixed in with a touch of Spanish blood. Raised till the age of five with a Mexican family, Jesus then came to finish off the sentence of childhood with me.

Deep-sea fisherman, long-distance runner, husband, and the father of my granddaughter, Essie, Jesus was a better man than I at less than half my age.

For a few years he and his wife, Benita Flagg, had lived in northern Alaska. Jesus, whom we mostly called Juice, owned his own fishing boat and made good money. But a couple of days before Melvin Suggs went missing, he and his family came to stay with me and Feather in Brighthope Canyon. Essie had grown into a toddler and Juice had a fairly fresh wound on the right side of his jaw.

*   *   *

"How you doin', son?" I asked from the basement of Clifton's.

"Good. It's twenty below in Alaska and I'm in a T-shirt."

"Thought you liked the cold."

"I liked the people, the salmon when they ran. But the cold up there would kill you if you let it."

"What you guys up to?"

"Feather and Benita makin' dinner. A couple of Feather's girlfriends comin'. You gonna be here?"

"I don't think so. I got this job."

"Okay. We'll be around. Wanna talk to Feather?"

Over the few moments of silence that it took Feather to pick up the receiver, I ruminated on how lucky I was to have a family at all.

"Hi, Daddy," Feather said with great exuberance.

"Hi, honey, how are you?"

"Mr. Fenton, the English teacher, said that everyone should say exactly what they felt and Lonnie Laughton said that Mr. Fenton was a bastard for not lettin' people study communists and stuff like that. And, and, and then Mr. Fenton kicked Lonnie out for usin' foul language but that wasn't fair because he said that we could say whatever we felt..."

She went on for two minutes or so, slowly shifting from one subject to another. She was going to be in a swimming competition and she kind of liked bad-boy Laughton. She wanted to take the PSAT early and graduate a semester or two before schedule.

"How are you, Daddy?" she asked, surprising me some.

"I'm gonna be kinda late tonight, baby girl."

"What you doin'?"

"Looking for people who aren't there."

5

That was back in the last few years when Santa Monica was still almost a village. I drove to an address on Maritime Lane that sat across the street from a nameless garden park. If you had the inclination, you could walk through the park, descending past the lawns and shrubs across an asphalt bike path and, finally, to the beach.

Matchbook houses painted in pastel colors perched there on the rise looking out over the Pacific, the largest continuous expanse on the face of the earth.

Toward the center of the block there was a wood-frame California bungalow painted pale pink behind the barest strip of lawn. The front porch was one step up and the two chairs on the deck were covered with windblown leaves under a thin crust of silt.

Approaching the front door, I stopped for a moment. It had been a big day and the sun hadn't yet set. There I was, driven forward by just a name from a woman whose mere presence plowed up my earliest adolescent memories.

The front door of the house was eggshell white behind a green screen. I considered walking away from there. I might have done so if the muted door hadn't swung inward.

"Can I help you?" asked a small woman.

She was white and stout like some elf or sprite from a German fairy tale. Her head was large, covered in coiffed gray, and her eyes, behind crystalline glasses, held on to a strong blue.

"Hi," I said. "My name is Ezekiel Rawlins."

Those blue-stained orbs asked, *And?*

"I'm a private detective. A woman named Amethystine Stoller retained me to help you with the disappearance of your son, Curt."

The little elf-woman's mouth opened slightly, and she took a step backward, becoming partially submerged in the shadows of the house.

Then a man, the same height as the woman, stepped forward—from nowhere, it seemed.

"What's that again?" he asked me.

Where the woman was solidly built, her male counterpart looked as if life had eaten away much of the substance of his manhood. Once blue, his eyes were now gray, and his shoulders were sharp under the drab green T-shirt.

I repeated word for word what I had said to the woman.

"Amy?" he replied.

"Yeah."

The three of us stood there for a moment, almost as if the conversation was over.

Then another man, shorter, older, and more slender still, emerged from the oblivion of the interior.

"What's your name?" he asked in a stronger voice than either of the others.

"Ezekiel Rawlins. They call me Easy."

The newest cast member of our improvised scene was smiling and friendly, wearing a sporty buff-colored suit, dark-brown shirt, and true-yellow silk tie. He pushed the screen door open and said, "Come on in, Easy. You need something to drink?"

The living room was twelve by twenty feet with a low, eight-foot ceiling and a thin tan carpet made from some grainy, synthetic fabric.

There were two short burgundy couches that were set together to form an el. I took the settee facing the front door while my three hosts fit easily onto the other sofa.

We sat there for a moment. The front door was still open, the Pacific Ocean lounged under slowly darkening blue.

"I'm Harrison," the oldest of the family piped. "Harrison Fields."

"Curt's father?"

"No," the other man murmured as he shook his jowls. "I'm Curt's father...Alastair. And this is Curt's mother, my wife, Winsome."

"Winsome Barker-Fields," the woman added. "You say that Amy hired you to look for Curt?"

"Amethystine works for a friend of mine, and she, my friend, suggested that your ex-daughter-in-law call me. I do this kind of work for a living."

"We don't have any money," Alastair claimed. He was leaning forward, elbows on knees and hands clasped.

"That's all taken care of, sir."

"Where'd Amy get money like that?" he demanded.

"This is a favor for the woman she works for."

"Are you a real detective?" Winsome asked.

Instead of trying to explain, I leaned over, dug out my wallet from a back pocket, and produced my detective's license. She read it closely and then tried to hand it to her husband, but he waved it off. Harrison took it instead.

"You've already done more than the Santa Monica PD," the elder Fields said, standing up and leaning over to hand back the ID. "We had to go down to the station and all they did was have us fill out a form like a fucking application for a job."

"Harrison!" Winsome said sharply.

"I'm just sayin'."

"You don't have to curse."

"I'm sure the police are doing their job," I said. "But it's always good to have extra eyes on the lookout."

"We don't have any money," Alastair said again.

"I understand that, sir. Amethystine and my friend have covered all costs."

Alastair nodded, but it didn't feel like he understood.

"Amethystine..." I began.

Winsome grunted when I said the name.

"She told me," I continued, "that she'd heard from you that he was missing and wanted to help."

"She could have helped by leaving him alone in the first place," Winsome said.

"Don't listen to them," Harrison declared, somehow sounding friendly. "You know, we're farming stock from rural Ohio. People back home don't trust anything new or different. But you're right, an extra pair of eyes will see things that others don't understand."

I nodded slightly, accepting and agreeing with his words.

"What I don't understand is why you're here in the first place," Alastair said.

"I went to talk to the police in Los Angeles..." I began.

"Why?" Alastair challenged.

"What do you mean why?" Harrison asked his younger brother. "Curt works in LA. He lives there."

"I asked the man why he's here," was the younger brother's answer.

"The LA police said that your son was doing some kind of business with guys that were, um, suspicious. Did he tell you about any of the people he was working with?"

Three little white faces turned toward me. They seemed like children then. I could almost understand why Amethystine got involved with her ex's disappearance.

"No," Winsome replied. "Curt never talked too much about his job."

"Are the people he's working with crooks?" Alastair wanted to know.

"I don't know," I admitted.

"What do you need from us, Mr. Rawlins?" Harrison asked.

"Anything useful. Friends, clubs, sports he might play or go to watch."

"When he was a kid he liked to play checkers," Alastair pulled out of memory.

"He has a baseball card collection in his room," Winsome added. "And, and, and he has a Japanese pen pal."

"What's his name?"

The parents thought really hard on this question. Every once in a while, they'd toy with a syllable or two, but with little progress.

"Damn," Harrison said. "It's Eiko Ishida. Don't you two ever listen to Curt?"

"Where does this Eiko live?" I asked.

"In Japan," Alastair said in a tone that called me fool. "Where else you gonna find a Jap?"

Raised on a steady diet of white mouths saying nigger-this and nigger-that, I was half-ready to walk out of that matchbook of a house. I might have done it if Winsome hadn't spoken up.

"Be quiet, Al," she said. "Can't you see the man wants to help?"

"He wants my money, that's what he wants," her husband replied.

"Do you have Curt's current address?" I asked anyone.

"He's out in Culver City, but we don't know the street address," Winsome admitted.

"You don't know where your son lives?"

"We never drive far, and he comes to see us. He only moved out a few months ago."

"He moved here after divorcing Amethystine?"

"Yes," Winsome said. "Of course. Why wouldn't he?"

"House seems kinda small for four people."

"The bedrooms are small but there's four of 'em back in that rabbit warren," Harrison said, pointing at a door at the back of the living room.

"We have his phone number," Winsome added.

"That wouldn't help me. But maybe you have the numbers of some of his friends."

"No, no. We never called his friends. Maybe I could remember some of their last names."

"What about Giselle?" Harrison suggested to his sister-in-law.

"Who's that?" I asked.

Looking both distressed and distracted, Winsome stood up from the red sofa and walked toward and then through the doorway that Harrison had said led to a warren.

There was silence among the men for a few moments, and then...

"How could you make a living doing work for nuthin'?" asked Alastair.

"I usually charge seventy-five dollars a day."

"A day!" the penny-pinching farmer complained. "A day?"

"Plus expenses. That way I can afford to do work pro bono now and again."

"Seventy-five a day. Most I ever made was two fifty a week. And I'm a white man."

You certainly are, I thought.

From the corner of my eye I could see Winsome coming through the rabbit door. She was holding a slip of paper in her left hand. She stared at the note until reaching me. Then she held it out away from her body as if she wanted to be free of it.

"Here," she said.

"What's this?" I asked, taking the offering.

"Giselle's number, of course."

"Who is she?"

"Some woman Curt knows. He told us if he didn't answer his home phone we were to call this one."

"And did you call her?"

"No."

I wanted to ask why not, but there are some mysteries not worth solving.

Turning my attention to the phone number, I saw that Winsome's handwriting was lovely. There was the first name and the number rendered in loving cursive.

"What's Giselle's last name?"

"I don't know," Winsome said. "We never met."

Alastair's wife was standing in front of me. I realized that she wanted me to leave.

"Is she a Black girl?" I asked, brandishing the paper.

"I have no idea."

I stood up then and the lady took three steps back, almost to the wall.

"I'll walk you out, Mr. Rawlins," Harrison offered. He levered himself up by putting one hand on his brother's shoulder.

Alastair looked at me and said, in wonder, "Seventy-five dollars."

I was parked down the block from the Fieldses' house. Harrison walked me all the way to the driver's side. When I opened the door, he put a hand on my left biceps.

"Curt's been doing some gambling out in Gardena," he confided. "His parents don't approve so they don't know. I don't know about the people he worked with, but there's some guys he gambles with sometimes."

"You know any of their names?"

"Just two. One's named Shadrach. Shad works for a guy named Purlo, he manages the poker club."

"What's the name of the place?"

"I don't really know. Might not even have one. It's the kinda place you have to know to go there."

"What do they look like?" I asked. "Shadrach and Purlo."

"You know, white guys. Tall like you. One a little less and the other an inch or so more. Um, uh, yeah... Purlo has a little scar over the left side of his mouth."

"A noticeable scar?"

After a few seconds' consideration Harrison smiled and then nodded.

I liked him. He was a familiar type.

"So, you've been to this place?" I asked.

"Yeah. Once or twice. Curt took me because he knew I wouldn't criticize or tell his parents."

"What's the address?"

"It's on South Normandie Avenue around 166th Street, but that won't do you any good."

"Why not?"

"Cops busted it some time ago and, and I don't think it opened back up."

"You know anyplace else Curt might be?"

"Not really."

I handed him my business card and said, "Thanks anyway. If you think of anything, you could reach me at this number. And tell your brother that I'll never charge him a dime."

"I'll tell him," the old man said on a laugh, "but he'll never believe it."

The nearest gas station was at the northeast corner of Lincoln and Pico. There I checked the oil and topped off the tank. After that I drove to the southeast corner of the lot and availed myself of the phone booth.

"Hello," she answered on the fourth ring.

"Miss Giselle Simmons?" I asked in my most courteous neutral voice, what white southerners call a northern accent, while Black folk call it a white voice.

She was quiet for a moment.

"You must have the wrong number," she said finally. "I'm Giselle Fitzpatrick."

"Oh, Lord," I improvised. "My name's Jack Farmer. I offer magazine subscriptions over the phone. You know, they give me a list of names and numbers and I make cold calls to see if you ladies might like a cheap subscription to *Redbook*, *Glamour*, or *Vanity Fair*. They must have mixed up your first name with somebody else's last."

"Well," she said clearly. "I don't need any subscriptions."

With that she hung up, leaving me standing there, receiver in hand, and looking at the rotary dial. I took out another dime and rolled out a number I hadn't called in a very long time.

"Hello?" she answered.

"Hey." The word was almost a grunt.

"Mr. Rawlins?"

"Yes, it's me, Karin."

"Is everything all right?"

"Can I come by?"

"Of course," she replied without hesitation.

Exiting the booth, standing there in the late twilight, and feeling the chilly sea breeze—I realized that I was no longer just gathering information. I was now committed to the case of the missing ex.

6

I drove to an address on Orlando Drive, up near Melrose. The entire block was made up of tiny houses. The one I approached was even smaller than the rest and smaller still because it had been subdivided into two discrete units.

There were two front doors on the porch. I was about to knock on the portal to the left when it opened inward, revealing a young woman. She was tall, five ten, with hair that was neither brown nor blond but somehow both colors, supple and in waves. Her skin was pale brown, very pale. And her eyes were the color of melted butter that was just turning dark over a high flame.

Karin Vosges. Young and handsome, between races, and almost perpetually bemused by a world that made no sense to her. She wore a shapeless light-blue peasant dress that had not gone out of style in Bavaria since before there was a German nation.

"Hi," she greeted, pulling her chin in slightly.

"Hey."

We stood there, appreciating that private moment like two very old friends at the end of their days, rather than a fifty-year-old man and a young woman half the way through her twenties.

"Is she in?" I asked.

"Yes."

Something about her delivery threw me back into her pre-
history.

It was 1945 and the war was over. By that time I had seen thou-
sands of men, women, and children—dying, mutilated, and
dead—and I had killed at least twenty-six of them up close
myself. Albert Grimes, corporal first class, came into my tent
some minutes before 3:00 a.m. I was asleep, and not asleep, a
state that being a participant in war had imparted to me.

"What?" I said to the shadow standing in the open flap.

"Sarge, it's me, Albert."

"What's wrong?" I was fully awake then, sitting up, reaching
for the pistol on the trunk next to my cot.

"I need help."

"Somebody after you?"

With World War II just over, Black soldiers, once again, had
to worry about our primary enemies—white Americans. They'd
seen us slaughtering white Germans. They knew we were bed-
ding German, French, English, and Italian women. They understood that there might well be a reckoning on the horizon.

"No," Albert said. "I'm in trouble and I don't know what to do."

We were bivouacked on the outskirts of Nuremberg, waiting
there in case there was any need to *pacify* German citizens who
thought that Americans belonged in America and Russians in
the USSR.

I lit the kerosene lantern next to my bed. Albert hunkered
down to face me.

He was the color of a copper penny that hadn't been shined in
a while. Twenty-eight, prematurely bald, and no more than five

seven, he was stronger than almost anyone in our squad. He was also very religious—that rare Negro who was more aware of being a Christian than he was of being Black.

"What kinda trouble?"

"Woman trouble."

"What you do?"

Unable to answer me right off, he fell back on his butt.

"I try and be a good man, Sergeant Rawlins. I do. I don't drink. I never take satisfaction in another man's pain. On Sundays, even when we was in battle I tried to read a few verses from my Bible."

"So, what's wrong?"

"Penelope Vosges."

"What you do to her?"

"The worst thing."

"Killed her?"

"Might as well have."

"Raped her?"

"She's pregnant with my child." The bald soldier wept.

"You sure?"

"Yes. The doctor said so."

I stood up from the cot and started putting on my fatigues.

"What you doin', Sarge?"

"We gonna go see the mother of this child."

Getting out of the camp at night wasn't much of a problem. I always kept a fifth of bourbon whiskey to trade for favors among the men. The sentry accepted the offering with a smile and a handshake.

In a borrowed jeep, Albert drove me to a run-down rooming

house on the south side of Nuremberg. We entered through a side door that led to the basement of the ramshackle structure.

The large cellar was lit by a few dozen candles. It smelled of burning wax. There was a huge bed in a far corner. Upon the bed lay a young, preternaturally thin German woman. When we approached the divan, she sat up.

"Albert," she said, not necessarily in greeting.

I recognized her immediately. She was one of the camp girls who sold themselves for rations and cigarettes, mostly to the Negro soldiers. Her face was plain and yet distinctive because of the intensity of her eyes. When I'd first seen her, laughing with the men at a beer hall, I thought that those eyes had witnessed more than most.

"Hey, Penelope. This here is Sergeant Rawlins."

"Why is he here?"

"I told him about our situation. He said that he wanted to come talk to you."

"You are a doctor?" she asked, telling me with that question everything I needed to know.

"No, ma'am. Albert told me on the way over here that he was afraid of what the Germans would say about you and his child. He's worried for your safety and wanted me to help get you out of Germany... with him."

If her question was an essay about the state of her pregnancy, the look on her face when she heard about what the pious corporal wanted was a whole novel of the convergent passions imprinted on the hearts and souls of the survivors of that terrible war. Albert was one of the few innocents I was aware of in that conflagration. For the great majority of us, innocence and goodness were liabilities. Penelope did what she needed to do in order to survive. Anything for a loaf of bread or a few lumps of coal. She would have committed murder to latch onto a man like Albert.

Young Karin Vosges stepped out onto the porch and took the two steps to the other front door. She knocked once and then again, cocking her head as if maybe she heard something. At least she thought so, because she used her key on the door and we entered the other unit.

The front room was lit by a dozen candles encased and magnified by hurricane glass lamps. Seated in a huge chair was the near-starving woman I'd first met in 1945. She was now four times the size of that undernourished waif.

"Mama," Karin said. "It's Mr. Rawlins."

The fat woman turned her broad, doughy face toward the sound of her daughter's voice.

"Guten Abend, Mr. Easy," the blind woman said.

"Guten Abend, Frau Vosges," I replied, trying my best to affect the right accent.

"Sit. Sit."

I sat on a padded wooden chair to her right.

Leaving us to our adult business, Karin went back out.

"You want a drink?" Penelope asked, her face turned in my general direction.

"Not yet. You?"

"Yes, please. You know where it is."

The small kitchen was illuminated by electric light, with a two-burner stove, a table already set for breakfast the following morning, and a squat Frigidaire refrigerator that was almost as old as I. There were two cabinets. The one on the left contained a brown glass bottle of vodka and the one on the right held two tumblers.

I placed the glass of vodka between Penelope's gathered hands.

Sitting next to her I was silent, not exactly sure why I was there. She didn't mind the silence. It gave her time to sip.

"Why you got all these candles, Pen?"

"I'm not completely blind," she whispered into the drinking glass. "Only mostly. I see shadows and those shadows dance by firelight."

That room reminded me of the war. The woman did too.

I brought Albert and Penelope to the company chaplain, Ferdinand Blythe. He was a white guy, but, like Albert, he was more interested in Jesus than he was in the color of a man's skin.

Albert was quiet before the man of God because he felt guilty about what he believed he'd done to Pen. She was quiet too. So, I explained to the military minister the problem the young couple had.

"...they need to be married so that Albert can get furlough and bring her back home," I was saying.

Blythe studied the young couple.

"Do you love him?" the chaplain asked Penelope.

"Very much." This probably wasn't a lie. She'd seen more death than I had and lost more than I could even imagine. If Albert wanted to save her, she was willing to love him.

Albert was crying.

"Why are you here, Easy?" his wife asked me twenty-five years later.

"Maybe I should have that drink," was my reply.

I went out to the kitchen to escape Penelope's blind scrutiny. I poured myself a stiff one, took a drink, poured a little more, and then made my way back to the room of dancing shadows.

Albert brought his bride to Los Angeles a few years before I got there. They lived in a walk-up apartment on Florence. There she bore Karin while Albert worked two jobs. Then, one day, at an amusement park in the Valley, two policemen stopped them . . .

The police said that he reached for a gun. Albert didn't die right off. Pen cared for him and once again plied the trade she'd learned in Nuremberg.

Karin was eight years old when her father finally passed on. I was godfather.

Later that night I brought the bottle in from the kitchen.

When she was drunk, Penelope told bawdy and sometimes heartbreaking stories. We drank and she sang. We talked war.

Late into the night she told me of the first time she saw a Jew stomped to death on the main street of Nuremberg, in front of his own store.

"I thought I had gotten away from all that until they killed sweet Albert."

"There's only one escape," I said.

"My heart aches for Karin," Pen lamented. "Albert was so, so loving to her and to me."

"And what about you?" That was part of the question I had come to ask.

Pen turned to me as if she could see.

"I don't know if she is his blood," she said. "But she is his daughter, and I am his wife. Is that what you came to ask me after all these years?"

"I'm not sure, Pen. I mean, I never knew a man who loved like Albert did. His love was so strong."

"Yes. He could make you into something more than you are. You, you saw that in him. You saw it in that basement."

"Yeah."

"Is that why you came?"

"I guess so. I mean, I was thinking about what somebody might do for love and then I remembered that I hadn't seen you guys in a while."

The smile on Penelope's lips was another part of the answer I'd come for.

The softest of knocks came on the door.

"Kommen," Pen said, her naturally husky voice an octave higher.

The door opened and Karin came through. She was still wearing the ankle-length blue frock.

"Just seeing how you two are doing," the dutiful daughter told us.

"We are having a most wonderful time," Pen said, as if making a public announcement.

"Yeah," I added.

"Your father's friend can drink like the people from my mother's village," Pen went on. "Back then alcohol was pure, wine tasted like the grape."

"I better be going," I said.

I stood up okay, but I had to take a few extra seconds to achieve balance.

"Thank you for a wonderful visit," Penelope said to me.

"Danke."

Her smiling teeth were somewhat tarnished, but they were still strong.

7

Karin walked me toward my car, parked across the street. When I stepped off from the curb, I guess I forgot that my foot had to go down so far. Balance failed and suddenly I was falling. But before I could hit the ground Karin bear-hugged me from behind and somehow held me up. I grabbed for the side of a car parked there and managed to stand again.

Walking me across the street she said, "You can't drive, Uncle Easy. You had too much to drink."

I gazed into the somber face of the pale brown youth and nodded.

"You can take my bed and I will sleep with my mother," she offered.

"I got to get home. Maybe I'll call a cab."

It was late and we both knew that a taxi driver, in that part of town, might refuse the fare when he saw my complexion. After the Watts riots, white people were more cautious of Blacks.

"I could drive you and come back in the morning," she offered.

"Your mom wouldn't mind?"

"No. I'll just go tell her."

"Say that one of the guys who guards the mountain will bring you back tonight."

She smiled, nodded, and then skipped her way across the street to deliver the messages.

I leaned against the hood of my car and took a deep breath.

It was near midnight in Los Angeles on a Monday. At that time the city was populated by workingmen and -women, and school-children—all of them at home in their beds. Now and then I could hear a car whooshing down Melrose, but the Vosgeses' block was silent and still.

I closed my eyes and thought about Mississippi-born Albert Grimes, a Black man, the grandson of slaves, who went to Europe, killed white men, and married a white woman who had had it even harder than he had.

I heard the car driving up the street. I wasn't concerned, even when it stopped; after all, there was always someone working late.

"Excuse me, sir," an unrepentant man's voice declared.

Opening my eyes I saw the two young white men, barely older than Karin.

"Evenin', Officers."

They flanked me and I remained motionless, propped up on the hood with both hands visible.

"What you doin' here, son?" the young man on the left asked.

I breathed in deeply, found that I couldn't talk with that much air in my lungs, exhaled, and then said, "Waitin' for my god-daughter. She's gonna drive me home."

"You live around here?" the right-standing cop asked.

"No."

"Where do you live?"

"Over on Forty-Second near Central," I lied.

"You been drinking?"

"Two shots with Karin's mother."

"Why don't you stand up and show us some ID?" the left cop suggested.

"Uncle Easy," she called from behind my inquisitors.

Both cops turned to see who it was. I realized that I was scared because I had to suppress the urge to run.

Using these few moments, Karin crossed the street.

"Good evening, Officers," she greeted. "Is something wrong?"

"Do you know this man?" asked the cop on the right.

"Of course I do. He's my godfather."

While they talked, I played out the probable scenario in my head. Karin was light-skinned but that didn't matter; a Black woman was a Black woman in America's eyes. She was young, but her race trumped the presumption of innocence. They would have to make sure she lived there. They'd go to Penelope's house, and she'd give them a tongue-lashing...

"You live in that house?" a cop, I'm not sure which one, asked.

"Yes."

That one word was like a stress crack in thawing ice. The cops looked at each other and, silently, the decision was made.

"Are you driving him home?" my right-side cop asked.

"Yes. He's tired and asked me to."

They weren't friendly to us. They would most certainly have arrested me for standing drunk next to my car. But they decided to believe Karin, that she lived there and wasn't burgling the tiny house. The world was changing in increments so small you'd have had to be a victim to feel it.

"All right then," the same cop said. "Drive safely."

* * *

"You're a good driver." I was sitting in the passenger's seat while Karin tooled up La Cienega toward Sunset.

"Been driving Mom since I was sixteen," she bragged. "I love it."

"Makes you feel free, huh?"

"Sometimes I go all the way out to Joshua Tree National Monument and just sit at one of the picnic tables until the sun goes down. In the night there are more stars than you can believe."

"I remember when I bought my first car," I said. "I asked the dealer how fast it could go."

"What did he say?"

"Not fast enough."

That put a damper on the next few minutes.

"The turnoff's just about half a mile up on the right," I instructed.

"I know. I came up there one time to swim with Feather."

"Oh yeah."

She made the turn and drove until we passed the last driveway.

Even though there were no electric lights, the three-quarter moon made everything visible. No houses at that point on the path, just shrubs and grasses, a tree now and then.

After we turned on the one-and-a-half-lane road that led to my mountain home, the tenor of our conversation changed.

"Uncle Easy?"

"Yeah?"

"Were you afraid when those policemen stopped to talk to you?"

"I can't say that I was actually afraid, but just aware that there was trouble. I mean, you'd have to be a fool to feel good up against men with batons and guns. But it's happened enough times that I can tell pretty quickly what's prob'ly gonna go down."

"The police murdered my father."

"That they did."

"He was the kindest man in the world." There were tears in her voice.

"He was that."

"We went to church every Sunday, just me and Dad. Mom said that she couldn't come with because she lost God in the bombing of Nuremberg."

"Albert loved you so much," I said. "Sometimes he'd come visit me and talk about how smart and pretty and kind you were. He loved it that you were there with him at church every week."

"I haven't gone since he died."

While we talked, the paved road turned into a dirt lane.

"You know what my mother said when I told her you had a ride back for me?" Karin asked.

"What?"

"She said that I didn't have to come home."

"She was angry about you drivin' me?"

"No. She wants me to marry you."

I wanted to make light of this ridiculous request on the part of Penelope Vosges but couldn't find the words.

The rest of the drive took about twelve minutes, no more than that. Trees had begun to fill out the desolate landscape and we'd started up a mild incline, finally reaching a natural cul-de-sac at the foot of the sheer side of a mountain. There were nearly a dozen cars parked on the left side of the turnaround. I recognized all but one of them.

At the foot of the mountain was a small wooden structure just large enough to hold a table and two chairs. Behind this shack stood an iron gate.

"Good evening, Mr. Rawlins," said a man with strongly accented words.

He was an inch shorter than Karin and hirsute in the extreme. His skin was Caucasian-dark and his eyes, I knew, were blue like the Mediterranean Sea. You could tell by his broad shoulders that he was a man of exceptional strength.

"Hey, Cosmo. This is my goddaughter, Karin."

"I remember. She throws the javelin and loves numbers."

"Hi, Cosmo," Karin said shyly.

"She needs a ride home."

Moving his chin up and down in a curt, almost military, nod, the night watchman turned and went back into the sentry's hut. There he got on the wireless system that his whole Longo family used to protect the mountain. On the air he spoke in gruff and guttural Italian.

"I always meant to ask you," Karin said. "Who are Cosmo's people?"

"Sicilians. Four sons and a father who had to leave home over some century-old feud."

While I spoke, a loud mechanical sound arose. That was the funicular used to ferry guests and residents up and down the mountainside.

Cosmo came out and used three big keys to unlock the metal gate.

"It's beautiful out here at night," my goddaughter said, maybe to herself.

"Yeah," I agreed. "Cavemen and dinosaurs would look up at that same sky."

The funicular reached the gate and Gaetano Longo emerged. Big and bearlike, the elder brother of the clan came out smiling.

"Easy," he proclaimed. Then with joyous surprise: "And Karin."

"Hi, Gaetano," she said softly. "Can you give me a ride?"

"Anywhere."

He walked off toward the small car park and Karin kissed me on the cheek, near my lips.

"We love you, Uncle Easy," she said.

"And I you."

I watched them get into the family pickup truck and drive off. Seeing the back lights disappear into the wilderness of my last home made me melancholy. That's when I remembered how drunk I was.

"Mr. Rawlins?"

"Yes, Cosmo."

"You have a guest."

"Who?" I turned and saw her standing in the doorway of the guard shack.

8

Mary Donovan stood five five with hair a little lighter than my goddaughter's. She was slender and deadly, brilliant and broken, a good ally to have at your side but no one you'd share your secrets with. Seeing her standing there almost sobered me.

"Hi," I said.

"You got a good poker face," she replied. "I'll give you that."

We hugged briefly and I stood back to look at her again. Mary D was like a great novel—just one read-through was not enough to understand what it means.

She wore a little black dress with its hem at her knee. She also had a satiny black shawl for the cold. No heels or jewelry, no makeup, not even a purse that I could see. This meant that she was flying under the radar—all business.

"You like what you see, Mr. Rawlins?" she challenged.

I noticed that Cosmo had retreated to his hut.

"I like to see lions in the zoo," I said. "But when they roar, they scare me to death, in spite of the bars."

She smiled, indicating with her hands that there were no bars between us.

I took a moment more and then, realizing that she was truly inscrutable, I said, "Wanna come up?"

She walked through the open gate and Cosmo came out. We entered the external elevator and the Sicilian gatekeeper closed us in. The mechanism engaged and we started to rise.

Late at night, ascending the mountain was always magical. Half the way up you could see as far as the Pacific, a vast darkness that dared you to perceive farther. Mary brought her face close to the glass in the door, appreciating the view that I loved.

The vertical railway arrived at the top of the mountain, a bowl-shaped depression that we called Brighthope Canyon. When the back door of the elevator opened, Mary and I exited onto an asymmetrical concrete platform studded with semiprecious stones and iron discs imprinted with the silhouettes of dozens of wild creatures both mythical and real.

"It's so beautiful here," Mary said on a calculated breath.

"Yeah."

We walked down a blue-brick path that shimmered grayly in moonlight.

There were only six homes in Brighthope. All of them owned by Sadie Solomon, the richest woman west of the Mississippi River. Sadie gave ninety-nine-year leases to certain people who had done right by her, and others who had that potential. I was both.

We arrived at the home where my daughter and I lived. Roundhouse we called it. Four stories high and cylindrical in shape, it was white even by moonlight.

I ushered Mary into the first floor, a grand sprawl with no separate rooms. We stayed there because my family resided on the upper levels, and I didn't want to disturb them with our noises.

We sat close to the outer balcony on rose-colored love seats that faced each other. Below, Los Angeles spread out under a carpet of electric light.

"You wanna drink?" I offered. It felt like the first move in a chess match.

"No, thank you, Easy. I need to keep my mind clear."

"Okay. Why you here?"

"You called me."

"Yeah," I admitted. She was Pink Hippo #3. "I tried to call Melvin, didn't get his machine, and then the cops gave me the runaround. I hooked up with Anatole and he said that he wanted to talk to you."

"Did you give him my private number?"

"No."

She studied my face a moment and then pulled her legs up on the divan.

"Mel's in trouble," she said.

"What kinda trouble?"

She bit her lower lip to indicate that whatever the problem was—it was bad.

"Somebody's got something on me, a fingerprint, maybe. They told Melvin that they'd let it lie if he got somebody out from under a prosecution."

"What they have on you?"

Giving a smile that might have been sexy she said, "There are some things that a girl just can't talk about."

Knowing a brick wall when slamming into it, I asked, "Where's Mel?"

"He took off a day or two before Underchief Terrence Laks was gonna fall on him."

* * *

I remembered Underchief Laks. A neatly dressed prig. He had four senior officers take me into custody on a Sunday afternoon when I still lived in LA proper. We were having a barbecue, my whole family, Jesus and Feather, Essie and Benita. The cops barged into the backyard, threw me on the ground, hog-tied me with chains, and were in the process of dragging me off. Jesus hefted a hot poker but I yelled at him to stand down.

"No, Juice! Make the call."

They brought me downtown and sat me in a chair before Terrence Laks. He was wearing a midnight-blue three-piece Wilkes Bashford suit that was tailored to his slim build.

"Mr. Rawlins," he said with a smile that would have worked well on a cartoon snake. "So nice to see you."

"What am I doing here?" I asked one of the few cops who outranked my friend Melvin Suggs.

"It's your turn, Easy. That's what they call you isn't it? Easy."

"My turn for what?"

"A man named Forman, Guillory Forman, was shot dead in his pawnshop last night. He was killed before he could testify against a man known as Paul Dustman."

"So?"

Laks turned to one of his minions, who, in turn, put a legal-length printed sheet in front of me.

"So, when you sign this confession you will be charged for his murder."

"I didn't kill him," I said with steely conviction that I did not feel.

"I know where you live, Rawlins."

"Why me, man?"

"We have a numbered list of Los Angeles's top criminals. One by one we choose them and make sure that they pay . . . for something."

Sounded like the plot of a bad James Bond movie. Seven out of ten of the city's white residents would have said it couldn't happen—not in America. Out of the remaining three, two would have said that I could have beaten the false charges in court.

Eleven out of nine Black Angelenos would have known that I was destined for a lifetime behind bars or a seat in the gas chamber.

"Hand our prisoner a pen," the underchief commanded.

My hands were uncuffed and somebody slapped a transparent Bic pen down before me. I considered that blue ballpoint. It was a weapon. If my life was over I should have been able to take at least one of these criminals with me.

"Hurry up, Rawlins," Laks said. "I have a dinner date with the mayor."

I looked up from the writing/killing instrument into Laks's eyes. A patina of concern passed over his smug stare. Maybe he was thinking of all the men and women I knew who could retaliate. Maybe he suddenly realized that it was a man he was trying to demolish.

Whatever it was, that thought was broken by a loud ringing.

He turned his attention to the phone, wondering, it seemed, who would be calling his office on a Sunday afternoon. After six rings he picked up the receiver.

"Yes?"

Surprise was followed by amazement; this wonderment turned his eyes to me.

"Um, well, yes. Of course, sir. No. No. Nothing like that. Yes."

He put down the phone gently. Then for a long moment he stared at his desk. After that meditation Laks looked up at me through knitted eyes. Before that moment I had been a disposable utensil in the prig's tool chest. Now I was the object of true hatred.

"Let him go," he said to his underlings.

"What, sir?" one of them uttered.

"Let him go."

"How'd Mel know that Laks was after him?"

"Somebody warned him," Mary said with a shrug.

"Laks had me in his sights one time. I thought I was dead but my son called Mel and he did some magic."

Mary had nothing to add to that.

"Where'd Mel go?" I asked.

"I don't know."

"You here 'cause you want me to find him?"

"No. I want you to find a man named Tommy Jester."

"Who's that?"

"He used to be an actor, but nowadays he does this and that."

"This Jester have something to do with Mel?"

"Not directly."

"You're not giving me much."

"I don't have a lot."

"Any idea where I could find the actor?"

"Not a one. We lost touch some years ago. Will you do it?"

"Will it help Mel?"

"I hope so."

"Okay."

"Let me give you a better number to call."

* * *

Not long after Mary had gone, I fell asleep on a rose-colored love seat.

I hadn't had many dreams in recent years. Life was good. I had family and friends, money and a safe place to live. I had a real profession that gave satisfaction.

In the dream I felt again the searing pain of the injury to my shoulder. I was laid up on a wadded cotton mattress while Anger Lee cleaned and dressed my wound; now and again she leaned down to kiss my lips.

I was hurt and bleeding, but at fifteen my dick was hard too.

"Did he hurt you?" I asked for the second or third time.

"Naw. He wanted to but you stopped that shit."

"I tried to stop him but he put me down."

"You just a boy, Easy, and still you the best man I ever known."

After saying this she pressed down on my shoulder and I grunted.

"That hurt, baby?" she asked.

"Little."

"You want me to make it feel bettah?"

"Uh," I said.

She pulled down my pants and mounted me. I was oozing blood, hurting, frightened, and feeling more like a man than I ever had in all the years of my life — before or since.

"I love you, Easy Rawlins," Anger Lee whispered in my ear.

At that moment everything was right in the world. I wasn't a poor orphan without a pot to piss in. I was a man. It didn't matter that I hurt or bled. It didn't matter that one day someone would kill me. The only things that counted were that my blood was red and Anger Lee loved me.

9

As a rule, Brighthope Canyon was subject to a stiff morning breeze. That wind was rattling on the glass doors to the outer balcony at just a little past 5:00 a.m. It was still dark outside, and, despite my age, I felt the excitement of a new day.

I rarely experienced hangovers, so getting up was no problem.

After changing in the upstairs bedroom, I went to the kitchen and set about making breakfast. Homemade sausage, grits, hotcakes, and hot peach, strawberry, and rhubarb compote.

"Grandpa?"

She was standing on the bottom step of the curved stairway. At five Essie was beautiful and brown, Buddha-like and forthright.

"Yeah, baby?"

"You makin' pancakes?"

"Yes, ma'am."

She giggled and scaled one of the high stools that sat at the dining ledge attached to three sides of the overlarge stove.

When she looked down on all that bounty she asked, "Can I have some?"

"We have to wait for everybody else."

After a moment of great concentration, she climbed back down and ran half the way up the steel stairway that was molded to the curved wall.

"Mama! Daddy! Breakfast!" she cried.

Back atop her stool she stared greedily at our morning fare.

Within a few minutes Jesus, Benita, and even Feather made their ways down in various states of morning dress.

"Mornin', Dad," Jesus said. He wore silken black pajamas that Benita got him for their honeymoon. He looked good there next to Ms. Flagg in her fluffy pink robe. Feather wore jeans and a T-shirt, every day, every day.

As I served them breakfast a conversation slowly arose. Feather asked Benita if she ever went salmon fishing with Juice.

"Lord no, girl," the onetime delinquent answered. "Wind so strong out there it like to blow you right off the deck."

"So you could fly, Mama?" Essie asked.

"Fly right into a shark's mouth."

Essie's eyes went as big as plates, her mouth a perfect O.

My mind at that time was mostly in turmoil. I couldn't have explained it. It didn't make sense that I'd be hankering after my younger days with empty pockets and trouble around every corner. It didn't make sense because nothing made me happier than my little family. I would have died for any one of them without hesitation.

I mostly listened while the tribe gabbed and ate. Feather asked questions that revealed her deeper nature.

"How long you guys gonna stay?" she asked Benita.

Benita glanced at my son.

"We're staying," he said.

"You are?" That was me.

"Yeah. Bennie wants Essie to know her family and there's some good fishing down here."

"You could stay with us," Feather offered.

Essie cheered.

"I wanna go to France this summer with the American Institute for Foreign Study, so there'd be even more room. I mean there's room anyway but there'd be more space."

Realizing that she might have gone too far, Feather turned to me and asked, "Right, Daddy?"

"They can stay as long as they want," I agreed. "I'm goin' upstairs to smoke my cigarette."

As a rule, I smoked one cigarette a day. This on the flat and circular roof of Roundhouse, where I fussed over twenty-seven rosebushes planted in generous terra-cotta pots.

That morning I had another task to accomplish. In a locked box on the windswept rooftop, I kept a special phone that could not be bugged or traced.

After three rings a groggy voice complained, "What the fuck is it?"

"Raymond?"

"Easy? Hey, man. What's up?"

"Not much. You know, workin'."

"With that fine young thang broke up our conversation yesterday morning?"

"Maybe."

"You still got some dog in ya, Easy."

"What was that German shit you was talkin' yesterday, Ray?" I asked to veer away from the topic of Amethystine.

"Frankfurt School, brother. Jackson was talkin' to me 'bout 'em. Niggahs want everything to change. Everything."

"Black professors?"

"You don't have to have black skin to be a niggah, man. You know that."

"Yeah, yeah, right. Just wanted to make sure you not talkin' fiction."

"What's goin' on, Ease? I was tryin' to sleep."

"I need to talk to Lynne Hua."

"Got some kinda itch need scratchin'?"

"I ain't runnin' after your woman, Ray. Don't worry."

"I only got one woman, brother. That's Vu Von Lihn."

Almost as long as I had known Mouse, his one and only true love was EttaMae Harris. I wanted to ask him about what was going on with them but I knew it would just turn him sour—and when darkness gathered around Raymond Alexander there was always danger in the offing. Even though Ray had become a reader, that did nothing for his sanity.

"I just wanna ask Lynne if she knows somebody."

"Okay." Mouse didn't ask questions if the answers didn't help in some way—help or make him laugh. "Let's meet at the regular place around two."

"You still have that problem?" My question was a response to the circumspection he used.

"Like a stone in my shoe."

"Okay, yah, see ya then."

I checked out the rosebushes, making sure that there were no aphids, then leaned over the edge of the four-foot brick wall of the roof wondering about Mouse.

Federal marshals were surveilling him because they wanted to get to a man he did work for sometimes. Ray's *work* was being a heist man on big jobs anywhere on the North American continent. If it was anybody else, I'd be worried that he'd soon be in prison—or dead. But Mouse was a wild card in any man's game.

"Pop?"

Jesus was standing at the doorway to the stairs.

"Hey, boy."

When he walked up to me, I studied his face.

"Cut's healing pretty good," I commented.

Touching the still reddish wound he said, "I had a fight with a guy up in the Northern Territory. He was messin' with a native and I didn't like it."

"You kill him?"

"I don't think so."

Jesus wasn't a talker. He watched, listened, and kept his own counsel. He told me as much as he knew, and so I left it at that.

I clapped his shoulder and said, "Good to have you home, boy."

"You need anything?"

"Naw."

We looked out over the wall for a few minutes and then he headed back downstairs. I took out the phone again and dialed a three-digit number.

"Information."

"Yeah. I'd like the phone number and address of Giselle Fitzpatrick in Culver City."

The phone number I already knew, and the operator told me that the address was 501½ Dragg Street.

Some years after that they stopped giving out people's addresses, but 1970 was still a time of trust.

*   *   *

I left the house of laughter and youth feeling hopeful if not actually confident. It was a fair winter's day in LA, the sun shone brightly, and all I needed was a thin green cotton sweater.

There were only two tools that any Angeleno needed to have: one was a car and the other a road map. I wound my way down to Robertson Boulevard and from there into Culver City. Dragg Street was only three blocks long, terminating in a dead end at a freeway overpass.

The last house on the left, as you approached the barricade, was a cobalt-colored bungalow. That address was 501 and so I figured Giselle's house was behind.

I climbed out of my brown Dodge, a junker from the early sixties, and walked down the driveway toward the back of the property. Part of a coral-colored structure could be seen past the dark blue of the front house.

"Excuse me," a man called out in a clear tenor voice.

Coming from the front of 501 was a well-built forty-something white man in drab gray cotton pants and a red-and-cream long-sleeved work shirt. I turned and he stopped maybe a yard and a half away. There was a black-handled ball-peen hammer in his left hand.

Idly, I wondered if he was left-handed.

"Can I help you?" he asked, his blue eyes looking me up and down.

"I'm going to see Miss Fitzpatrick at five oh one and a half," I said without stutter or impediment.

"And who are you?" His chin was darkening from stubble that had probably grown since his early morning shave.

I noted that he had a tight grip on the blunt tool.

"Who are you?" was my insolent reply.

The man's head pulled back as if he had been slapped. The hammer hand rose a few inches.

"This is my house," he stated with emphasis on the personal pronoun.

"Which one?"

"This house right here next to you."

"That don't have nuthin' to do with me, brother," I said, noticing the slippage back to the tongue of my upbringing. "I'm headed for the place behind yours."

"For what reason?"

This last question, added with the hammer, gave me pause. I realized that I was spoiling for a fight for no reason. Yes, this man was probably confronting me because a Black man walking down his driveway was, to say the least, a novel event. But having him swinging that hammer or, worse, calling the police, would not be in my client's interest.

"I'm here to ask Miss Fitzpatrick a few questions that are private. My name is Ezekiel Rawlins, and I don't mean anyone any harm."

"Why should I believe you?"

"Why would I lie?"

This last question stumped Bluechin. Maybe it would have been his answer to the same question.

"I'll go with you," he said.

So, we went down the driveway, entering a fair and wide lawn that stretched between his cobalt and her coral.

He knocked on her door and then turned his head toward me, prepared to tell me that I had failed his test.

The door opened. A woman of pale-skinned, raven-haired, and zaftig beauty stood there behind the screen, wrapped up in a seersucker teal bathrobe.

"Mr. Beaumont," she said in a reserved tone.

"Do you know this man, Giselle?"

She gazed at me a moment or two, then shook her head.

"Well?" Beaumont asked me.

Ignoring him I said to the lady, "Excuse me, ma'am, my name is Ezekiel Rawlins and I've been asked by Winsome and Alastair Fields to look for their son—Curt."

"Oh," she said in surprise. "They think he's missing?"

"That's what they tell me. I'm hoping that you might be able to point me in the right direction."

"What do you have to do with Curt?" Hammerhand Beaumont asked.

"What do you have to do with anything?"

"What?" he asked in a voice that might have been tuned to a midsize dog's bark.

"It's okay, Mr. Beaumont," peacemaker Giselle said. "I know what Curt's parents are talking about. Just, um, just let us talk."

It's hard to make blue eyes look wild, but Beaumont managed it. Things were not turning out like he expected them to. I was supposed to be as unwanted by Giselle as by him. There was a certain propriety to the world that he imagined, and I was the contradiction to that particular credo.

"Please, Mr. Beaumont, give us some time to talk."

"Yeah," I added.

Giselle pushed the screen door open and said, "Come in, Mr. Rawlins."

After I'd crossed her threshold, she closed the door on Beaumont.

* * *

The living room we entered was small, made smaller by outsized and garish furniture. The front window covered the entire wall, but the curtains were drawn. The dense, fluffy carpet was a natural hue of red, like that of a dusty apple.

"Have a seat," she offered.

I plopped down on a couch the dimensions of a queen-size bed.

She sat on a cushioned throne that was as purple as a Concord grape.

"What's this about Curt?" she asked.

As she spoke her left hand rose to her chin. There, on the ring finger, was an impressive emerald embedded in a thick, at least twenty-carat, gold band.

"You guys engaged?"

"We were."

"What happened?"

"I don't know," she claimed, shrugging her left shoulder, her head listed in that direction. "Saturday before last he told me that it was over. When I asked him why, he said that he wasn't happy. He gave me some money and told me to keep the ring. He's probably getting back with that girl he was married to before."

"Why you say that?"

"He had a picture of her in his wallet and he talked about her a lot."

"What'd he say?"

"You should know."

"Me?"

"She's Black too."

"My only job is to find Curt for his parents." It wasn't really a lie.

"He just talked about her, that's all," she said. "She was so smart and so hardworking. She had it hard and everything. I mean, a lotta people got it hard. You don't have to be Black to be poor."

"No," I agreed. "That's for sure. Um. Was Curt having trouble with anyone?"

"What do you mean?"

"No one has heard from him. His parents said that he called home almost every day."

"You mean would anybody try and hurt him?"

"Maybe he's keepin' his head down. They say he worked court cases sometimes."

She took longer with this suggestion, going over her memories like a low-flying airplane.

"No," she said, slowly swinging her head from side to side. "He wasn't even working any criminal cases...that I know of. Mostly just divorces and corporate bankruptcy cases."

"He talked about his work a lot?"

"Not really. He said it was pretty boring."

"So, he broke up with you on Saturday and went off anybody's radar on Sunday. He hasn't called you since then?"

"No."

"And you don't have any idea where he is?"

She searched my eyes then. This led me to think that she was the kind of person who naturally believed in themselves, their ability to understand what they were seeing.

I appreciated the respite. It gave me time to consider the man I was looking for.

Giselle was lovely. Elegant and poised, despite her broken

heart, she was somebody I'd try to get to know—all other things being equal. It was a rare event for me to identify with the taste of white men. I wondered how our similarities might help me find Curt.

"He said that he'd been hired to do a job that would get him some good money."

"Good money," I repeated. "His words?"

"Yeah. I never heard him say anything like that before. He told me that he was going out of town for a couple of weeks, and he didn't want to string me along."

"What kind of work was he hired to do?"

"Accounting, I guess."

"Anything to do with gambling?"

"No. Definitely not. Curt never gambled. I always wanted to go out to Vegas and he said he had no interest."

"Did he ever mention a man named Purlo?"

"Yes. One of the people he was working with was named Mr. Purlo. Who is he?"

"I'm not sure. His uncle, Harrison, mentioned the name."

"I don't know what to tell you, Mr. Rawlins. I don't really know much about his work. But you're right, he did call his mother every day."

"I guess when he broke up with the wife he moved in to live with his parents for a while."

"He did," she confirmed. "I'm not like that at all. My mom lives in Pasadena, and I haven't seen or talked to her in a month."

"I asked his mom if she knew his address, but she didn't."

"He's here in Culver City, over on Longerville Road. Three sixty."

At least that was something.

It was time for me to stand.

"Well, Miss Fitzpatrick, thank you. I'll try to make some sense out of this." I handed her my business card and added, "If you hear from Curt, my number is here. He can call me, or you can."

"You want my number?" she asked. "I mean, I'm mad at Curt but I wouldn't want anything to happen to him. Maybe you could call me when you find out where he is."

"I already have the number. I got it from his dad. But I'll do you one better and get him to call you."

I walked up the driveway and out to my car. Driving off, I could see Bluechin Beaumont standing behind his own screen door—making sure the threat was gone and, probably, cursing the road I'd be traveling.

10

Three sixty Longerville Road was a largish lot surrounding a small whitewashed California bungalow, set way back from the street behind a large green lawn. I walked up the concrete path to the open porch and pressed the doorbell. After an appropriate wait, I knocked. I found myself hoping that the young man would answer his door. I didn't want him to have come to harm.

I didn't want to slip my BankAmericard down past the bolt of the door either. But I did. There was a slim chance that someone would see me, but it was unlikely. This was a working-class neighborhood and there wasn't a postman in sight.

Another tiny home. The living room had a small couch and matching chair. The carpet was barely green and quite worn. Everything was in its proper place and there wasn't even a magazine on the coffee table.

From there led a small hallway that took me to a kitchen painted yellow and white. Again, there was little of the personal to the room. The young man's solitary existence was made apparent by the two plates in the cupboard.

The bedroom was small too. A single bed, unmade, and a

bookshelf over a blond-wood desk. The books on the shelf were science fiction, accounting reference manuals, and three volumes about Japan. There was a *Playboy* magazine, three comic books, and a stack of typewriter paper in the side drawers. The pencil drawer had three pencils, one fat pink eraser, and a Bic pen.

The small night table next to the head of Curt's bed was the only truly revealing thing in his house. There was a small package of three Trojan condoms, a nearly empty half-pint bottle of Night Owl whiskey, a prescription bottle of benzodiazepine, and, in the little drawer, a personal diary. There was only one sentence written on the first page.

I want to be better and what I write here will be my plan to achieve that end...

There was also a phone on the night table.

"Proxy Nine, how can I direct your call?"

"Jackson Blue's office, please."

"He's the senior vice president," the young man explained patiently.

"Uh-huh."

"What is it that you want, sir?"

"I want Jackson Blue's office."

"I'm not sure if he's in today," the operator stipulated.

"But I bet Monique, his receptionist, will know."

"Um... well, I guess... hold on."

The phone went silent for two minutes by my whiteface Gruen watch. Then there were a few clicks that led to another ring.

"Jackson Blue's office, Monique speaking."

"Hey, Mo."

"Mr. Rawlins!" I could imagine her berry-black heart-shaped smile. "How are you?"

"Fine. Yourself?"

"Good. I'm about to have a baby and P9 is giving me three months' maternity leave. Can you believe that?"

"Sounds great. By then you'll be so bored you'll probably want to be back on the job."

"I guess," she said with more than a little skepticism. "Jackson's not here. He's up in Seattle at a tech conference about transistors or somethin'. You want to leave him a message?"

"Naw. I'll just call him later. Congratulations."

"Thank you, darlin'."

The next call was to Mofass Enterprises. Their switchboard operator didn't try to hold me at bay. Instead, she put me right through to the president.

"Hello?" Mrs. Blue answered.

"Hey, Jewelle."

"Easy." That one word was friendly and inviting. "How you doin'?"

"Workin' hard and feelin' fine."

"Feather said that her brother and his family are with you."

"Yeah. It's good to see 'em."

"Are they gonna stay down here?"

"Looks like it. How's your li'l family?"

"Everybody's fine."

"I called to ask you a couple'a questions."

"Okay. Go on."

"First, what's Jackson doin' way up in Washington?"

"He says that there's natural resistance in most transistors and he was wonderin' if in the delay...What did he say?...If the resistance could be used to predict and control multiple currents of data."

"Smart as a whip and still superstitious."

"My hero," she agreed. "You need his number up there?"

"No."

"Then what?"

"I was gonna ask 'im what he thought of Amethystine."

"Why call Jackson? I'm the one sent her to you."

"She said that she worked for him first."

Jewelle laughed and then said, "Yeah. He didn't even know he was schemin' on her, but I did."

"So, what's her story?"

"She's like a cowboy outta the Wild West, Easy. Been on her own since her parents abandoned her and her little brother and sister. She did anything and everything she had to, to keep them kids fed and protected. She kinda reminds me of Jackson in one way. I mean, she's more or less self-learned. In another way she reminds me of you."

"Me how?"

"She ain't scared'a squat."

"How come she came to work for you?"

"That's a hard question. On one hand, she knew that I wouldn't let her keep workin' with my dog of a husband, and, on the other, she wasn't afraid of me at all. But in the end I think she just likes bein' around women on the job."

"You trust her?"

"Honey, I don't trust Jackson...but I love him."

"Okay, let me put it like this, can I believe what she's saying?"

"Oh, yeah. Amy don't play. She might not tell you everything, but whatever she does say you could take to the bank."

On the way down Central, headed for Watts, I took a left on Florence, almost on a whim. Two blocks down, on the south side of the street, stood a bright-green three-story building with yellow trim along the windows, front door, and edges. A big sign across the top floor read BOOKS AND THINGS.

Parking in front of the unique structure, I walked up the four concrete stairs to the entrance. A small sign on the yellow portal said COME ON IN.

The first floor was the bookstore proper. To the right were ten floor-to-ceiling shelves, each of which contained at least five hundred books. At the back of the room were magazine racks and shelves that had everything from *National Geographic* to *Spider-Man*.

The left side of the room was furnished with three long tables having six chairs and one long bench for each one.

There were five youngsters sitting at various tables either reading, writing, or both reading and writing.

Paris had told me that he wanted to set up an area in his bookstore for young scholars: local kids who had things to learn and needed a place to concentrate.

"Yeah, Easy," he'd said, years before, in the old bookstore that used to be across the street. "I wanna give 'em a place that's quiet, that don't have no TV or radio. A place where the only chores they got is sharpenin' they minds."

Between the bookshelves and the study area stood a high podium-desk, where Paris was installed.

Seeing him sitting there, looking upon the neighborhood intellectuals from on high, I remembered another thing he'd said.

"I'm'a sit on 'em like a mother hen, makin' sure they keep their minds on their work."

"Hey, Paris," I said, walking up to the podium.

"Easy. Hey, man, good to see ya."

"I heard about your new store. This place is gorgeous."

"Thanks, brother. You know I try."

"How much it cost you?"

"The building was twenty thousand and the work it needed was around ten."

"What's the mortgage?"

"I bought it for cash," Paris said, lowering his voice.

"Damn."

"Had a business deal turned out right."

"Business with Fearless Jones?"

Just hearing these words made him circumspect. He looked left and right and then even studied the children sitting across the way.

Paris was as much of a coward as Jackson Blue. Because they were the two most intelligent men I knew, I figured that their excellent brains picked out dangers that we mere mortals could not perceive.

"Let's go out back, Easy."

The short man jumped down from his stool and called out, "Myrna."

"Yeah, baby?" She came around the corner of one of the shelves. Myrna Salt was the color of rust-tarnished sand. She wore thick-framed glasses and a yellow-and-bronze-checkered pants suit. Short, she was still an inch taller than her boyfriend.

"Hi, Easy," she greeted.

"We goin' out back to talk," Paris said.

"Okay. I'll watch the cashbox."

"Hey, Myrn," I layered in.

"Easy," she said with pursed lips.

There was a small but lovely lawn at the back of Books and Things. Two round tables, yellow with green canopies, were set in opposite corners. We went to the far table and settled in.

Paris went right back into the conversation started at his desk. "Fearless met this rich old white lady named Toni Tricks, no lie. She had this nephew wanted to take her money and put her in a home. Fearless wanted to help her, but he needed a little research of the law first. That was my job. She was very generous."

"Looks like it," I said. "Fearless buy himself somethin'?"

"A good time for about three, four months."

"So he could use a few bucks," I suggested.

Rather than the laugh I expected, Paris gave me a serious gaze.

"What?" I asked.

"Fearless in jail, man."

"Jail? What for?"

"They stopped him for vagrancy. When the cop grabbed him and he pulled back, they added resisting arrest."

"How long?"

"Must be two months now. I been cash poor and he told me not to call you."

"Why not?"

"Pride."

Fearless had a couple of dozen wartime medals in his sock drawer — more than proof of that dignity.

"Can I do anything else for you, Ease?"

"Yeah. You got a copy of that book *Papillon*?"

11

John's unlicensed bar was still on Central Avenue, but it had moved location down to 103rd Street. It was now housed on the attic floor of a defunct furniture warehouse.

When I asked John why he moved, he told me that his new girlfriend, Millicent Roram, didn't want to sleep in the same bedroom that her predecessor had occupied.

John usually had an apartment attached to his business.

"Cuts down on the commute," he'd say.

Millicent was a Black woman from Wisconsin who felt oppressed by any temperature above eighty degrees. Because he loved her, John, for the first time, had air-conditioning installed in his bar. This made his place one of the most popular nightspots in the whole Watts community.

I got there not long before 2:00. The establishment was one very large room with twenty tables and a bar long enough to seat forty patrons.

The place had no more than a dozen customers at that time of day. Most of them were seated or standing at the bar. Millicent Roram was serving when I sidled up.

"Easy Rawlins," she said in greeting.

"Millie."

She was almost as tall as six-foot-two John, and her body was powerful. She was the color of a cantaloupe rind and seemed, somehow, like a stone statue that had achieved mobility.

"What's a workin' man like you doin' in a bar when the sun is still out?" she asked.

"Having a business meeting, of course."

She reached across the mahogany bar and pushed against my chest.

We liked each other because we both loved John.

"Easy Rawlins," said the oldest living voice in my mind.

"Ray," I replied while turning.

There he stood, flanked by two Asian women. To his right stood Lynne Hua. Hong Kong–born and more beautiful than almost any other American actress, Lynne had a smile that was a smirk, and her posture backed up this pride.

To Raymond's left stood Vu Von Lihn. A whole other kind of woman, Asian, and Lynn. She was from Vietnam, an undercover Vietcong when she was still there. Now she was in America, saying that she'd gotten tired of the war. Maybe that was true. But it was a certainty that she and Mouse were made for each other.

Vu, as I called her, had been in the vicinity of a bomb blast that wreaked a lightning-strike scar down the right side of her face. The eye on that side was white and blind. She was her own unique person. Just being in her presence brought out a feeling that was hard to explain. It was a mixture of fear and dignity, of history and the vanity of a doomed warrior.

"Wanna take the girls and get us a table, Ease?" Mouse requested. "I'll get the drinks."

*   *   *

I walked with the ladies to a table set against a far wall. I pulled out chairs and complimented them, truthfully.

By the time we'd gotten through the niceties, Raymond was with us, carrying a tray with our various preferences.

"How's the novel readin' goin', Ray?" I asked.

"I done read three novel fictions in the last six months, more or less."

"More or less months or books?"

Mouse grinned. He had a small black pearl embedded in an upper incisor. A vain man, he had style enough for two.

"Three books doesn't sound like much," Lynne Hua, the ex, commented.

Mouse turned toward her and smiled. Lynne was a big reader and she'd known Raymond since a time when no one would have been surprised if he'd never read even one single book.

"Jackson Blue told me that you can't read a book just one time, not no good book, not a book that means somethin'," Ray said, relishing the surprise on his old girlfriend's face.

"I know you read *Papillon*," I said. "What are the other two?"

"*I Know Why the Caged Bird Sings* and *The Godfather*."

For Raymond, three books meant three heists. In the early days of his high-level robbery career, he'd spend his downtime in public houses accompanied by b-girls who were drawn to his outlaw ways. In recent years he spent more time alone. But his kind of insanity didn't do well with self-reflection, so he started reading as a kind of balm for his turbulent mind.

Vu Von Lihn had been a mechanic in Saigon. She was plying that trade when I met her. Soon after that she met Mouse.

"You still workin' at the fancy car garage?" I asked the lady.

"No," she said with that raspy, jagged-edged voice of hers. "I started my own garage in Korea Town."

I asked her about the old job only to be polite, but I already knew about her business. She hired women mechanics who did the work almost at cost. Down below the regular garage there was a chop shop where the same lady mechanics toiled for profit.

"How about you, Lynne?" I asked.

"I have my own show," she said into my eyes.

"You do? What's it called?"

"China Girl."

"Why haven't I heard about that?"

"We shoot in Hong Kong. It airs over there and in Canada."

"Your own show. Damn. That's big," I said. "Damn. You gonna move to one of them places?"

"I don't know. You could get lost out there, thinking you found something."

"That's the truth," the other Lihn agreed.

"What about you, Easy?" Lynne Hua asked. "What are you up to?"

She was focused on me. For some reason this degree of attention made me want to open up.

"It's not what I'm doing, really. It's how I feel, how the world feels."

"What's that mean?"

I remember lowering my head to think for a minute and then looking up to meet her gaze.

"It's like every day is the same old war and all that changes is in me. I wake up on my mountaintop, water the plants, scratch the dogs behind their ears. I talk to my little girl, who is more of a woman than I am a man. Cops half my age stop me because they say I look suspicious. And all I do is rake leaves that keep fallin' and go to funerals in my mind."

If I didn't think about them, these words made sense to me.

"But you're making a world for your children and your people," Vu said.

"You know, Vu, I was in World War II back in the day." I found that it was easy looking her in the face if I concentrated on the scar. It was beautiful in its own way. Notched, blind, and indelible—the kind of mark that defined a life lived.

"Back then Black soldiers didn't have to fight," I went on. "The white side of our armies didn't wanna see us with guns blazin'. There was only a few of us signed up for battle."

The Vietcong didn't say anything, but her eyes asked a question.

"I don't know why I needed to fight. I wouldn't do it again for love or money. But...it's not me I'm talkin' about. Most of the young Black men that enlisted, maybe a hundred that I knew, all but four made it back home to the Fifth Ward. But two out of every three we knew back home was gone. Helpin' my people is like tryin' to sweep up sand at the seashore."

Even Mouse winced at that freehand statistic. "Damn, Easy," he proclaimed. "You never told me 'bout that."

Vu was nodding, contrasting, I believed, her war times with mine.

"Raymond said you wanted to talk to me, Easy," Lynne said.

"Yeah. I need to find somebody and I thought you might be able to help."

"Why don't you give me a ride home and we could talk on the way."

* * *

We four talked a while longer. Ray had some good stories about the old days between Houston and Pariah, Texas. People died in the wake of his bejeweled laughter. That was how people who lived in wartime entertained themselves and taught the true lessons of history.

"I better be goin', Ray, Vu," I said at last.

"Don't get lost out there, brother," Ray advised, and then he laughed.

Lynne's apartment was on Sixth Street, half the way between downtown and West Los Angeles. Hers was a turquoise structure with a wide stairway just inside the front doors. Her place was on the fifth floor, which was also the top stage of that prewar building.

The living room windows were floor to ceiling, allowing in the fading glow of daylight. I stood there at the glass, looking out over the smaller buildings and the streets. Cars outnumbered pedestrians at least seven to one. You wouldn't know by looking that we were a nation waging war on Vu Von Lihn's people. You wouldn't know the hatred and antipathy harbored between the races, religions, classes, and sexes.

They didn't know. Most people, at least most whites, thought that everything was fine. Children made more money than their parents did, peace had been retained by the war I'd fought in, and freedom was available to everybody who deserved it—as long as they spoke English while praising Jesus and the almighty dollar.

Lynne got into the space between me and the window. She

pulled my button-up sweater down past the shoulders and then started working on the shirt.

"What are you doing?" I chuckled nervously.

"Taking off your shirt."

"Ummmm?"

"I'm not going to fuck you with your shirt on."

Exhilaration and dread. That was the life I'd led. The two constants.

She reached down at the front of my trousers and hummed, "Mmmm. You want this. I could tell at John's you did."

My life had never been boring. Where most Americans were afraid of getting fired or their sports team losing to some rival, I was out there with my life on the line whether I wanted it to be or not.

After working the zipper, she whispered, "Look at it, Easy. How hard it is, how beautiful."

"Um . . . could we get outta the window?"

Grinning, she pushed me back until I fell on her deep red sofa.

I was a fifty-year-old fool, scared to death of this beautiful woman.

"What are you doing?" I asked her.

"You need someone to help you prove that you are alive," she philosophized as she climbed on top of me.

She was right. Most people came alive only at the moment their deaths were a certainty. Cancer or prison. Maybe careening off the side of a cliff.

I grabbed at the back of her dress, searching for the zipper.

"No, Easy," she murmured. "Pick me up. Carry me to the bed."

Smoke.

I awoke with a start. For a moment I thought there was a fire burning and Anger Lee in the bed next to me. Then I realized it was Lynne Hua, smoking a cigarette, watching.

"You got another one'a those?" I asked.

"I thought you stopped."

"On regular days I only have one in the morning."

"And what kinda day is this?"

I didn't have an answer so I inhaled deeply while staring into her dark eyes.

She smiled and handed me her cigarette.

Between shared inhalations she kissed me and wriggled around until she was installed on my lap.

"Would you come live with me in Hong Kong, Easy? They speak English there and you wouldn't have to work or anything."

"You don't even know me, girl."

Biting my ear she said, "I know everything I need to."

"Like what?"

"You command respect, you have good manners, and you look good in bed."

"That's all you need?"

"From you. I just want a man to be good-looking and on my side."

"What about smart and brave and true?"

"That stuff is overrated. You're a man and I'm a woman. That's all we'd need."

There was no place like LA. It was a town and a people with a future and no past. Lynne Hua couldn't have been a star in Hong Kong if she hadn't come through LA first.

"I got a daughter, Lynne. She needs me right where I am."

She got up off me and went out of the bedroom. Not long after she returned with a red lacquered platter bearing an iron pot of jasmine tea, two simple jade cups, and a few sugar cookies.

We toasted with the two impossibly thin nephrite cups.

"So, what is it you want from me, Easy?"

"I'm looking for a guy named Tommy Jester. I don't know if that's real or a stage name."

"It's both," she said.

"You know him?"

"It's a small town for TV bit actors. He was born Rayford Jennings but changed it legally when he started getting work in commercials."

"Do you know where I can find him?"

"I could find out easy enough. TJ has always wanted me to work for him."

"Doing what?"

"Things that a good girl doesn't talk about."

"So when can you get his information?"

"After we climb back under the covers."

"We were just there."

"That was for you. A warm, loving body through the night is for me."

12

The sun shone in through the bedroom window. Miss Hua was gone. I felt a mild wave of panic before remembering that I'd called home late in the night after Lynne was asleep. Benita promised to tell Feather that I was okay.

On the pillow next to my head was a tiny pink envelope upon which *Mr. Ezekiel Rawlins* was written. At the end of that line was a small drawing of a bulbous heart. The letter was scented and sealed. It read:

> Good morning sweetheart,
>
> I have an early meeting about my show. I hope you feel a little better. I sure do. Tommy Jester's address is below. I meant it about us in China. You could bring your daughter too.
>
> Love you
L

I got up, staggered to the toilet, then went to the window. No pedestrians at all, just cars, lots of cars. I must have stood there for quite a while. Realizing that I still needed sleep, I climbed back into the starlet's plush bed and drowsed for two hours more.

"Edgar," Anger Lee said to me while pressing a fresh bandage against my wound. "His name was Edgar and he wanted to own me like some kinda mothahfuckin' slave master. Shit, I mean, just 'cause you let a man share your bed don't mean he could do whatever he want."

She and I had just made love in her bed. I was seeping blood behind a pounding heart and understanding only too well what Edgar had felt.

"He daid?" I asked.

"Uh-huh."

"You scared?"

"Happy," she contested.

"Happy for what?"

Anger stroked my cheek with a warm hand. She smiled and said, "For a man like you, Easy Rawlins. A man stand up for his woman even though he know he bound to lose."

At that moment, even though he was dead, Edgar knocked down the door hollering and wielding that jagged black blade.

I jumped out of Lynne's bed, wide awake and scared for my life. Nearly half a minute passed before I realized that it was only a dream.

It was 11:00 and the room was chilly.

I dressed and drove to West Hollywood. Along the way I was thinking that Anger Lee had been my first client; thinking that and wondering where in the world she had gone.

* * *

The address Lynne gave me was for an apartment building on Lamar Street. It was a three-story box of a structure encased in sky-blue plaster and spattered with glitter. The entrance to the building, for some reason, was on the left rear side. There were signs prohibiting loitering, trespassing, and sales of any kind. But the back entrance was unlocked and unguarded.

I made my way to the third floor and sought out apartment 3G. The hall walls were painted a dingy gray and the carpet was soiled blue.

I knocked on 3G's scratched and dented rose-colored door and waited. There was no buzzer.

Having slept the morning away, I thought that maybe TJ was sleeping too, so I knocked a little more. I waited a full minute before knocking again.

Down the hall about twelve feet or so, a door came open. Two heads leaned out, one over the other. One was white and the other black. Both men. I looked at them and they at me. When no words were spoken I knocked again.

"Can we help you?" the white head asked.

"You know Tommy Jester?"

"What do you want with him?" asked the other head.

"Sorry, guys, but my business is with TJ."

"What kind of business?"

"That's what I want to talk to him about."

The heads regarded each other, then pulled back into the apartment, the door slamming shut behind them.

I heard a distant phone behind Tommy Jester's door. It rang twice.

A minute later TJ's door swung inward.

The white man before me was dressed in silken violets and pinks, mainly. He was three inches taller and forty pounds lighter than I.

"What the fuck you want?"

"Tommy Jester?"

"Who's askin'?"

"Mary Donovan."

His aggressive visage faltered. I might go so far as to say that he experienced a tremor of fear.

"Wh-who's that?"

"Look, man, Mary told me to tell you to call her."

"What's the number?"

I gave him the number Mary had given me. He didn't write it down.

TJ stalled around in his mind a minute or two, trying to somehow get the upper hand in a conversation that had already concluded.

"How'd you get this address? Mary don't know it."

"I asked around."

"What the fuck that mean?" he said, using the words as a kind of lift for the rage he felt he needed to oppose me.

He looked like he knew how to fight. The pastel colors and fear of answering a door didn't mean he couldn't throw a fist... or produce a weapon.

"I got a few actor friends," I said with a shrug. "I kept calling till one of them called me back."

The number of words and loose connections deflated TJ's rage a bit.

"What's Mary want?"

"She did not say."

"How'd she know you?"

A half smile made its way to my lips. "We did some work together a few years back."

Tommy Jester's eyes opened wide as if he were scanning the darkness for movement.

"All right. You did your little errand. Now get the fuck outta here."

He slammed the door.

I drove all the way down to Pico before going to a corner phone booth. Using a Franklin D. Roosevelt dime, I called my answering service.

Patty Deworth answered, "Stenman Service. How can we help you?"

"VIP51," I replied.

"Oh, hi, Mr. Rawlins," she said, dropping the professional tone.

"How's your mother, Patty?"

"Thanks for asking. She's down in Florida in the Keys with that no-good brother'a mine."

"Which one?"

"Ajax," she said on a nervous giggle.

Patty had six brothers, each one worse than the next. We usually spent two or three minutes chatting about our lives before getting down to business. It was good to keep the ladies of the service happy with me. Some of the calls that came in were emergencies.

"Any messages for me?"

"A woman, Giselle Fitzpatrick, called about half an hour ago. You want her number?"

* * *

"Hello?" was the feminine answer to my next call.

"Miss Fitzpatrick? Easy Rawlins here."

I could hear her quick inhalation, then she exhaled.

"Mr. Rawlins. Thank you for calling."

"What's up?"

"It's Curt. He called me. I told him that his parents were worried and that they sent you looking for him."

"What'd he say?"

"He told me that he wanted to meet you tonight." She hesitated and then said, "At a warehouse on Owens in Canoga Park." She gave me the address.

"Did he say he was going to call his parents?"

"Yes, um, but, but I think he wanted to talk to you first."

"Why? He doesn't know me."

"I don't know. He just said that he wanted to talk to you."

"What did he sound like?" I asked.

"I, I don't know what you mean," she pleaded.

"Was he nervous or scared?"

"I don't think so. I don't know. I, I have to go. My mother's at the door."

"Giselle."

"Yes?"

I waited a beat. In that silence I imagined her frightened heart fluttering. "Nothing. Thanks for the message."

13

I owned twelve apartment buildings at that time. A hundred and one units. Jewelle Blue's real estate company collected the rent for .08 percent of the gross and managed the properties. Her company was too large for this to make business sense except for the fact that we traded favors back and forth over the years.

My profit on each unit averaged out to about $21.33 a month. The rest went to the mortgages, upkeep, and Jewelle. That worked out to an income of roughly twenty-six thousand a year. At that time most white families made just under ten thousand annually, and brown families were quite a bit below that. I didn't pay rent for my mountaintop home, because the owner there used me now and then for my investigative skills. Again, favors.

I wasn't rich, but I sure didn't need to be going out among hammerhands and scalawags in the middle of the night at some desolate warehouse in Canoga Park.

No, I did not.

"Hello?" she said on the sixth ring.

"Vu?"

"Easy." I could hear the faraway smile in her voice.

"He there?"

"No." There was reticence now in the Vietcong's tone. "What's your number?"

I read it off the dial.

"That's your place?" she asked.

"A pay phone."

"I'll call you back."

It took twelve minutes for her to make that call. The feds must have been pressing hard on Raymond.

Finally, the phone rang.

"What's wrong, Easy?" Vu Von Lihn asked.

"I'm lookin' for a guy. His ex just told me that he wanted to meet at a warehouse in Canoga Park...at midnight."

"Are you gonna go?"

"Got to," I said, not able to keep the gravitas out of my voice.

"You have a gun?"

"Not on me."

"Meet me at the garage."

Vu Von Lihn's garage was on Eighth Street, in what they called the Mid-Wilshire area. Immigrant Koreans had been moving into that neighborhood for a few years by then. Lihn was Vietnamese but she knew how to fit in.

I parked on the street and walked to the customer door. Before I could knock, the portal opened, Lihn standing behind.

"Come on in, Easy."

She led me through a small office into a large area big enough to service six cars. From there we went to a side door that led down to the secret basement.

When she turned on the garish construction lights used down

there, I could see three cars in the work area—a late-model bright-red Cadillac, an emerald-green Lincoln Continental sedan, and a golden oldie: a Jaguar E-Type from 1961. Each car was in some state of being broken down. Doors, wheels, light fixtures. One car's engine had been excavated and set aside.

"Looks like a job undone," I said.

"I sent the ladies home so they wouldn't have to lie if someone asked about you."

In the far left corner of the basement garage sat a flat metal cabinet that was secured with an impressive padlock. Lihn went to the locked box and took out a key. Inside was a trove of weapons—everything from bayonets to hand grenades.

"What's your poison, Easy?" she asked.

"How you even know how to say that?"

"They used to sneak me into the officers' club in Saigon when they showed American films. Mostly westerns."

"And they didn't suspect you?"

"I was pretty before this," she said, touching her scar.

"You're beautiful now."

The love of Mouse's life looked down shyly, and I switched my attention to the munition trove.

Lihn was definitely loaded for bear, but I just needed a little insurance. I plucked out a comparatively innocuous pistol and said, "This thirty-eight'll do."

"Okay," she said. "I'll take the sniper rifle."

"What you need that for?"

"I'm going with you."

"The hell you are."

When she stood, the long-distance rifle in her left hand, I realized that there was no gainsaying her resolve.

"Do you think you're going into a trap?" she asked.

"I don't know."

"Mouse would skin me alive if I let you go out there alone."

"What would he do to me if I let you get killed?"

Lihn's leer was both encouraging and terrifying. Looking at that pale eye floating inside its scar, I knew that she was coming along and that she would survive any weak Western opposition.

We got there two hours early. There was no name on the block-wide building, and only one light over a featureless door near the center.

"If you go to the front door I'll be able to see you through the scope," Lihn said. "I could get up on the fire escape of the building across the street. All you have to do is stay outside."

There were drawbacks to her plan but, all in all, it was probably the best idea among the bad choices we had to choose from.

"You that good a shot?"

"Better than Raymond."

That was good enough for me.

She was dressed all in dark colors, looking up at the external latticework of the fire escapes across the street.

"I'll go up there now," she said, "and get settled in. We don't have to talk until after the meeting is over."

"How can I indicate to you if I'm in trouble?"

"Hit the ground if they come at you," she said. "I'll take care of the rest."

I found a late-night diner six blocks away. There I worked my way through a chili-size with a serving of canned asparagus dressed with mayonnaise, and a bottomless cup of black coffee.

The beginning of *Papillon* was quite wonderful. For the French, a novel could be fiction or nonfiction; this was both. I almost forgot about the dangerous rendezvous I was about to embark upon. Something about not being innocent and, at the same time, not deserving of punishment and then trying your best to escape — this was the Black American race's history rolled up into one Frenchman.

The time passed quickly and soon I made it back to the warehouse.

I tried to see Lihn somewhere on the fire escape across the street, but there was no sign of a sniper.

Then I approached the lighted door of the warehouse.

The building was so large that knocking seemed kind of pathetic.

He answered before I could knock a second time. A tall man in a powder-blue suit, dark-chocolate shirt, and raspberry-sherbet tie, his face had seen some punishment in its forty-something years. It was a face that looked as though it belonged to a hound whose only job was sniffing down blood.

"Rawlins?" the man asked.

"Yeah. Curt?"

The left side of the big man's upper lip, the scarred side, rose to form a sneer. "No. My name's Purlo, Ron Purlo."

"Giselle said that Curt called her."

"Why don't you come on in?" was his answer.

"I like the night air."

As he peered into my face I believe that he was wondering if he could press the invitation.

"Giselle called me," he said instead. With this assertion he stepped across the threshold into the pool of light I occupied.

"Why didn't she call Curt?"

"She don't know that number." His smile caused my muscles to tighten.

"His own girlfriend?"

"Curt's under a cone of silence right now, for the time being. The girl knew that and called me because she knew he needed to be left alone."

I had no response for this claim, so I stayed quiet, waiting for what else the powder-blue bad man had to say.

"She told me your name and I asked around about you," he continued. "People say that you're a man worthy of respect."

This was no surprise. A certain element of the city knew that I was connected to various individuals, from Mouse the killer to the gangster Charcoal Joe.

"So, we decided to talk instead of kickin' the shit outta you," Purlo concluded.

"Thank God for small blessings." There was no gratitude in my tone. "But I would still like to talk to Mr. Fields."

"I told you, he's what they call incommunicado."

"I appreciate that. But he's got straight-assed parents and they hired me to locate him."

"Tell 'em you couldn't find him."

"What if they go to the police?"

"Cops'll file him away under who gives a fuck."

"But they hired me."

Purlo's left eye squinted, and I was glad to have Vu Von Lihn out there in the darkness.

"Then you tell them you heard he's working for a big concern that needs to know that he can't sell their secrets."

"Yeah, okay, but how do I know you don't have the kid chained up in some basement—or worse?"

Purlo did not like being questioned. He was the man in charge, the one whom lesser men bowed to.

He glowered and then, suddenly, he smiled and said, "Like Mr. Epsilon says, 'He can see the ocean to the west and the mountains to the east.'"

I took a moment to digest his conscious, and unconscious, meanings and then replied, "I guess I'll have to take your word on that."

"I guess you will."

I got in my car and drove to the sidewalk across the street. Lihn appeared a few minutes later. The forever soldier threw the canvas bag that contained the rifle into the back seat, then jumped in beside me.

"That went smooth," I said as we drove away.

"I saw four men get there an hour ago," Vu said. "They were waiting behind that door, I bet. It was good you stayed outside."

"Good for stupid."

She leaned over and kissed my cheek. I don't think I've ever received a greater accolade.

14

I was up at six the next morning. Jesus had already made coffee on the second floor of Roundhouse. He never drank the bitter brew himself, but he'd made it for me almost every daybreak since he was five and I took him in as my son. He was a full-grown man since the age of twelve, but now, after returning from Alaska, he was something more than that.

"Beautiful up north?" I asked.

"Clear and mean," he replied.

"So how you gonna live down here in the smog again?"

"I miss my family."

I had once asked the well-informed, even academic, Jackson Blue who he thought the world's greatest poet was.

"Ain't no answer to that question," Blue told me.

"Why not?"

"The greatest poet," he opined, "is the man or woman who lives their poetry."

That man was my son.

The ladies all slept late that day. Jesus and I hung around the kitchen, him with his northern newspapers and me with *Papillon*. Now and then we shared a word or two.

I had three phones at that time. The house line that Feather and I used, the business phone among the roses upstairs, and then the closed-circuit line that connected all of the Brighthope houses to the Sicilian work and guard staff.

The ringer on the private phone was more like a low gong that sounded once every three seconds.

"Hello?" I answered.

"Mr. Rawlins?"

"Hey, Erculi." Erculi was the patriarch of the Longo clan.

"A man say his name is McCourt down here. He has a badge and wants to come up."

"Tell him I'll be right down."

I put on a burnt-orange T-shirt, straw-colored suit, and shoes the color of Meyer lemons, looked in the mirror, and decided to cap off the ensemble with a dark-brown Stetson woven from supple straw.

The senior cop was standing in the parking area next to his maroon Pontiac.

"Anatole," I said in greeting.

"Why wouldn't the wop let me up there?"

"Brighthope Valley rule: no police unless with a warrant or the say-so of the owner."

He looked as if he wanted to spit on my yellow shoes.

Instead, he asked, "Have you found Mary Donovan?"

"Not lookin' for her."

That answer squared the big man's shoulders.

The police captain was not only tall and good-looking. He was something more. Strong as Sonny Liston and violent someplace way down in his soul. Only a fool would have riled or disrespected him.

"I thought we had an understanding," he threatened.

"What is it with you and Suggs, man? He do somethin' to you?"

"Flew too close to the flame," Anatole opined. He took a beat and then said, "Tommy Jester was found in an alley near his West Hollywood apartment. He was facedown with a bullet through the back of his skull."

"Who's that?"

"You can't get away with that, Easy." It was the first time, ever, that he used my moniker. "His two neighbors said that a man look a lot like you was at his door yesterday."

"I wasn't there, but why would you even know that?"

"Jester was an associate of Mary in the old days."

"Must be a coincidence."

"I could take you in and put you in a lineup."

"Because someone said somebody looks like me knocked on somebody's door?"

"Are you saying that you never heard of Jester?"

"That's exactly what I'm sayin'."

"You can't help Melvin like this."

"Do a better job than you."

He was considering killing me with his fists, I was sure of that. I was ready for it. Sometimes a man has to put it out there. Has to.

Whatever violence Anatole felt, he also had admirable self-control. That's why I lived a little longer.

"You're gonna go down on this, Rawlins."

"We all do one day." I managed to put on a grin.

* * *

Watching the police captain's dark-red car drive away down the dirt road from my home, I had to make a decision.

The choice I made was to go back to Roundhouse, kiss my daughter, granddaughter, and daughter-in-law. Then I had breakfast with them and a really good conversation about almost nothing at all.

After the meal I went back up to my room, took off the glad rags, and donned worn blue jeans, a long-sleeved tan work shirt, and shoes that looked like a lifetime of hard knocks.

From there I went up to the roof, had my morning cigarette, and then I made a call.

"Hello?"

"Loretta?"

"Easy. How nice to hear your voice."

"You too, girl. He in?"

"Yes, he is."

The phone clicked twice and then . . .

"Mr. Rawlins," said a voice that sounded like a lion's cough.

"Our friend's in some trouble," I said, getting right to the point.

"Is he ever."

"How much for a spring?"

"Fifteen hunnert."

"I'll meet you out front at ten forty-five."

The criminal courts building is on Temple Street downtown. Concrete and steel, it's a monolith and an edifice, a symbol of the power of a justice system that has managed to hide the corruption fueling its machinations.

I got there on time, and Milo, as usual when it came to money, was early. Milo Sweet, the porcine blackberry of a disbarred lawyer turned bail bondsman. He was smoking a long cigar and unconsciously rubbing his hands together.

"Milo."

"Mr. Rawlins to the rescue," he replied.

I handed him a fat envelope.

"Eighteen hundred just in case something unexpected comes up," I said.

Taking the money, Milo proclaimed, "You know, Mr. Rawlins, no matter how hard we try, some souls are lost cases."

"That's true," I agreed. "But those are the people whose stories we can't wait to hear about."

Shaking his head and cracking a smile, he said, "Lemme get to work."

The walk from the courthouse to the 2120 Building on Wilshire Boulevard was just about thirty blocks. The 2120 was the second-tallest building in Los Angeles at that time. Thirty-nine stories, and reminiscent of the dark monolith in *2001: A Space Odyssey*. I tilted my head back to see the upper floors of the black-and-gray structure.

A cartoon figure came to mind: a white guy in tux and tails saying, "Remember what Mr. Epsilon says, 'From the 2120 Building to Bungalow Thirteen, property is the way to go for every man, woman and child.'"

I went through the dark glass front doors of 2120. About twelve steps from the entrance there was a reception area, a waist-high corral that contained three Caucasian security guards, all of them wearing similar grayish-blue uniforms. They watched me, ready to go into action if I tried to get any deeper into their preserve.

Despite expectations, I walked up to the kidney-shaped area and smiled.

"Hey. You guys got a employment office?"

The oldest among the guardians was around my age and balding. The uniform jacket couldn't hide the paunch he carried. Through golden-wire-frame glasses, he looked me up and down. Then, in order to meet my eye, the short man had to tilt his face upward.

"What kinda job you lookin' for?" he asked.

"What kind you got?"

The guard—his name tag read ELMER SIMON—didn't know how to answer that simple inquiry.

"The man asked you a question," said the guard named ROBERT CRESS. In his late twenties, Bob was my height with brown hair. Judging by his physique and demeanor I figured him to be an off-duty cop.

"Asked and answered," I said, looking the young man directly in the eye.

"You didn't say what job," Bob told me.

"I didn't ask for one neither. I asked for the employment office."

The third guard was between his comrades in position, height, and age. He watched the interaction like a broke bystander watching a hand of high-stakes poker.

"Mr. Simon," a man called from some distance away, near the elevator bank.

I turned my head in that direction and Elmer did too.

Coming toward us at a good clip was a tall man in a nice dark suit. His hair was black and shiny.

"Yes, Mr. Gentry," Elmer said. I could tell by the elder guard's tone that Gentry was boss on the ground floor.

"What's going on?" the suave boss asked as he came near.

"This one's messin' around," Bob answered.

"Did I ask you?" the man named Gentry said.

Bob didn't know how to respond. On the street he would've hit him with a billy club. But we weren't on the street.

"I wanted to know if you had a, you know, a employment office," I said to the boss. I was pretending and intending at the same time.

"And what did they tell you?" Gentry asked.

"They were just tellin' me where it's at."

This answer confused all four white men.

"Come on," Gentry said, "I'll take you there."

I managed not to make eye contact with the guards as I walked away with one of so many bosses whom I'd dissimulated before.

"What's your name?" the floor boss asked me as we waited for the elevator car.

"Ezekiel, Ezekiel Rawlins."

"We're not at full capacity, Mr. Rawlins. I'm trying to get the staff into shape."

I nodded, thinking that such a task would take decades.

"Where you from?" he asked.

"Houston. Before that, when I was a kid, I lived in southern Louisiana."

"Hot down there," he said showing his teeth.

"Yeah. In more ways than one."

A chime sounded and, three seconds later, one of the five elevator doors slid open. Gentry nodded for me to go in and I did.

"It'll be a good place to work," he said to me.

"Feels modern," I said in a tone of agreement.

"Have you ever done custodial work before?" Martine Shalimar asked.

Her dress was peacock blue and her necklace beaded with tiny red stones. In her thirties, she was both confident and friendly—traits that made her see me for what I presented.

"Oh yeah. For five years I did cleanup at P9 down on Wilshire."

"Why did you leave?"

"It's a good place to work at, so nobody hardly ever quits."

"Sounds like a good job."

Her hair had a golden sheen, almost as if it were metal. Her eyes were a mottled gray and her teeth just a little crooked, making her smile attractive in its humanity.

I think she saw me categorizing her features and was pleased by the attention.

"It was a good job," I agreed. "So good that nobody ever left."

"So, you had no room for growth."

"That's it exactly."

I never worked at P9, but the president, Jean-Paul Villard, had the head office make me a false history, for situations like the 2120. Trading favors was definitely a big part of my economy.

Miss Shalimar leaned forward on the blotter, indicating that the conversation was about to get serious.

"We're at only thirty percent capacity right now," she said. "The maintenance staff is working to put all the units and floors in order. There will, most certainly, be room for growth."

"That's why I'm here."

"Well," she said with a smile. "All you have to do is fill out an application for our files."

"I can do that," I said with real delight.

"Do you have any questions for me?"

"The man told me about the positions here was named Purlo, Ron Purlo, I think. You know him?"

The human resources professional shook her head and smiled with friendly apology spread across her face.

"No," she said. "But we have quite a few investors. Maybe he's one of them."

"Don't matter. I just wanted to thank the man."

"When can you start working, Mr. Rawlins?"

"Right now."

"Glad to see you want to get to it," she said with a smile that hinted at something else. "But I'll have to check your employment record and tell Mr. Henry first. He's the maintenance supervisor."

"So when should I come back?"

"Morning, day after tomorrow, should be fine. The custodial staff starts at seven thirty."

"Day after tomorrow," I said, pretending to do the calculations in my head. "That's Saturday, isn't it?"

"We have a six-day workweek here at the 2120," she said.

"Sounds good to me."

15

A little lost, I made my way back to the WRENS-L office.

The forty-three stairs to the third floor reminded me that I hadn't done my exercises in a few days.

"Hi, Mr. Rawlins," Niska Redman greeted.

She was sitting behind the big desk facing the door.

"Anybody else around?" I replied.

"No. Whisper's taking a meeting with a potential client and Mr. Lynx took his wife out for a late lunch."

"Oh, uh-huh. You know you can lock the door if you're alone up here."

She smiled.

"I mean," I said, "a woman alone has to protect herself."

"What's wrong, Mr. Rawlins?" she asked in answer.

"Nothing. Why?"

"You always bother about locked doors when you're worried about something else."

"I do?"

She nodded. "Uh-huh. Doors and windows. Unpaid bills and phone messages when the caller doesn't leave their name."

I had no desire to talk about my tells, so I asked, "You talk to Tinsford about becoming a detective?"

"He said that if you thought I had potential, that was good enough for him."

In my office I sat behind the grand desk, not thinking at all. No words or worries entered my mind, just sensations and light through the window falling upon the desk, floor, and my hands. Time passed but I didn't mark it. The sunlight shifted slightly in the window but I didn't care. Gravity kept me from floating away but my mind drifted.

When I finally got up, Niska was gone. The day was over.

I drove home to the mountain. Feather and Essie were playing some kind of card game near the indoor koi pond while the two dogs watched.

"Hi, Dad." Feather greeted.

"Hi, Grandpa," Essie added.

"My two favorite girls," I said out of reflex. "Where's Jesus and Benita?"

"They went down to the boat," Feather answered, "to clean it up and then get a fish fry. Juice told me that they might sleep on the boat unless we called and told them you weren't coming home."

"And we gonna have fwozen pizza," Essie cried joyously.

"Fwozen?"

"Yeah!"

On the rooftop rose garden the next morning, I was smoking my first and last cigarette of the day. Halfway through the Lucky Strike I decided to make a call.

"Hello?"

"It's me — Easy."

"Oh, hi, Mr. Rawlins."

"Easy."

"Easy. Why are you calling? Did you find Curt?"

"I want to see you." These weren't the words I meant to say.

"When and where?"

"Topanga Canyon. There's a little outside diner called Minnie's up in the village there. The people at the country store can point the way. Eleven thirty."

After a French toast breakfast, I took Feather to school and then drove Essie out to the pier at Redondo Beach where Jesus had docked his fishing boat. The little girl was overjoyed to see her parents.

On the way to meet Amethystine I began to obsess over the wording of my request of her. *I want to see you.* It was completely wrong and yet absolutely correct. I did want to see her, had wanted to since the last time we'd met.

There was an undeveloped knoll above Topanga Center. On the other side of that hillock was a house that Minnie Moore owned and lived in. That house also functioned as a daytime restaurant. No one knew how a poor Black woman from Mississippi could afford such an exclusive property, but who cared? The fare was soul food, and Minnie was a friendly face among an already happy populace. She had an outside seating area consisting of seven picnic tables set out for people liking her corn bread and fried chicken, pig tails and collard greens.

I was there early. Looking out over the hippie-populated canyon, I felt unusually at ease. The hippies were trying to do the impossible—make a world where everybody was happy as much as their individual natures would allow. They were young and, I knew, sooner or later they'd trade in these Utopian desires for good-paying jobs and the status quo. I knew it, but it was nice to be out there among them with their long hair and pot smoke, their perfect (if flawed) ideals and deep beliefs.

There was a bluesman sitting on a high powder-blue metal stool, playing an acoustic guitar that was connected to an electric speaker. Around my age, but looking older, he played good blues though I didn't understand most of the words.

After maybe twelve minutes I spied Minnie, a sixty-something tar-black woman, walking with Amethystine over toward my picnic bench.

"Here she is, Mr. Rawlins," the country-bred restaurateur hailed. "You be nice with her, now."

"Thank you, Mrs. Moore," Amethystine said through a sparkling laugh. "I think I can take care of myself."

"What you folks wanna eat?" Minnie asked.

"You have a menu?" Amethystine Stoller replied.

"In my head and on my tongue," she said, and then proceeded to tell us that day's offerings.

I ordered the vegetarian plate—black-eyed peas, mustard greens, white rice, and a small side salad. Amethystine asked for ultrathin fried pork chops, grits, and redeye gravy.

When Minnie left to fill our order, Amethystine took a moment to look around.

"It's lovely up here."

"Where you from, girl?" I asked.

"Not no girl, no matter who wants me to be, and I'm from the gulf of Mississippi, where music like this was borned."

I could have listened to that woman talk all day long. I think there was a smile on my lips and I was nodding.

"So, Mr. Rawlins?"

"Easy."

"So . . . Easy, why did you need to see me?"

"Harrison Fields."

"What about him?"

"He seems, um, bent."

"I don't know about that. He's a gambler . . . been a dealer, a floor manager in Vegas, you know, a man who loves what numbers can do. For the past fifty years he's been trying to figure out Russell's paradox."

"What's that?"

She thought about it for at least half a minute, finally saying, "Basically it's asking, in certain circumstances, how can you have a list of lists that doesn't include itself?"

I tried to make sense of what her question was asking for, realized that I could not, and so said, "Do you know a guy named Purlo?"

Something shifted in her eyes, but before that change could provide me an answer, Minnie Moore and her assistant, a strapping young Black man, shirtless in overalls, trundled up, him carrying our platters of food.

Minnie watched closely as he placed the orders before us.

"I hope you like it," she said before they walked back down to the house.

For a while we concentrated on eating.

Amethystine ate heartily and with real satisfaction.

"This is good," she said. "Real good."

I stayed quiet. That's probably why she looked up from the meal to me.

"What you lookin' at?" she asked, somehow making the question sound flirtatious.

"Just bein' country, enjoyin' how much you like the food."

Flirtation became deliberation in her golden eyes.

"Does Leonard have anything to do with Curt?" she asked.

"Who's Leonard?"

"Leonard R. Purlo. Some people call him Ron and others say Purlo. I just said Leonard to see how much you knew."

"You know him?"

"Before I went to work for Jackson, I was a cocktail waitress for a little speakeasy in Gardena. Ron was the floor manager. As a matter of fact, that's where I met Jackson. He used to study the logic of the different games. After he was finished with his studies he'd have three dirty martinis and watch the girls."

"You could use those last words for Blue's epitaph."

Amethystine showed off her broad grin.

"I watched him watching the games," she said. "When I figured out what he was doing I brought up Russell's paradox."

"You talked about it?"

"Yeah."

"You studied math at college?"

"Never went to college but I've always loved numbers. Numbers and words…"

It was, I think, at that moment, in the middle of her talking, that I fell in love with Amethystine Stoller.

"…I read and think in those two ways," she explained, "and after that, or maybe before, I take care of the twins."

"You and Curt got kids?" I asked, already knowing the answer.

"My younger brother and sister — Garnett and Pearl. They're teenagers now, but they still need lookin' after."

I had a thousand questions, but none had to do with Curt Fields.

"How you young folks doin'?" The bluesman was standing there next to our table. It was only then that I realized the music had stopped.

"Hi," Amethystine exclaimed.

"Ya'll mind if I join ya a li'l while?" he asked.

"Not at all," I said, not at all wanting him there.

Smiling, the musician showed that one of his lower teeth was missing.

"Amethystine Stoller," my business date said. She held out a hand.

"Easy Rawlins."

"My full name is Atwater Wise," our guest offered. "But e'rybody call me Soupspoon."

"That 'cause you always hungry?" I asked.

"Uh-uh. When I was a boy I couldn't afford no instrument so I played the spoons up and down my legs an' chest."

"Your playing and singing were wonderful," said Amethystine. "Made me think'a home."

"Thank ya kindly, ma'am, I likes playin' for the hippies in these hills but it's always good to have Black folk out there too."

Our conversation went on like that for a few minutes. Then Atwater Wise got up and went to another table, and another one after that. It struck me that part of his job was to socialize with the clientele between sets.

"So?" I asked Amethystine when we were alone again.

"One night Harrison came to pick me up when Curt had to work late. Harry and Ron hit it off, and before Harry left, Purlo offered him a job."

"And Curt met Purlo after that?"

"I guess. I mean, I'm really not sure."

"Purlo told me that Curt was fine, that he was doing some kind of hush-hush job for him. You know what that could be?"

"So you met Ron?"

"Yeah."

"How?"

"You engaged me to find Curt, right?"

"Yeah. Wow. No, I don't know what Curt could be doing with Ron. I mean, I guess everybody in business needs an accounting now and then."

After a long while I said, "I think I might know where Curt's holed up."

"Where?"

"I want to check it out before tellin' anybody. You know, till I'm sure."

"How long will that be?"

"Soon," I said. "Very soon."

She studied me then, her left eye almost closing.

"What?" I asked.

"You could'a got all this on the phone from me. We didn't need to come up here."

"No, we didn't." I wasn't going to say any more and she didn't press me.

16

The next morning, I got up early and dressed for an honest day's labor, donning rumpled and stained tan canvas work pants and a threadbare white T-shirt that had splotches and flecks of drab green paint here and there. For my feet I chose dark brown and hardy boat shoes that Jesus used to wear when he was working on his first boat, years before. Then I put on a pair of glasses that had clear panes for lenses. I got that trick from Jackson Blue, who believed that white people were less suspicious of Black men who wore glasses.

I was down on the kitchen floor by 5:30, but Jesus was already there, coffee made.

I got to the 2120 Building by seven. Elmer was the only guard I recognized. He took me to a room on the fifth floor. The sign on the door read CUSTODIAL STAFF.

"Mr. Warren," Elmer said to the only man in the room, seated at a fifteen-foot-long folding table.

"Yes, Mr. Simon?"

"This here is Ezekiel Rawlins. He's been okayed by the personnel office to work for you."

The head janitor looked up at me, biting the inner flesh of his left cheek. He was a pale white man with gray hair and a gray uniform too.

"Welcome, Mr. Rawlins. You can call me Doc."

"You a doctor?" I asked while pulling out a chair.

"My parents named me Docherty."

"Never heard that name before."

"Mother liked it. Said that if I ever had a nickname, it would be Doc."

I liked the guy.

"You're half an hour early, Mr. Rawlins. Staff gets in at seven thirty. Want some coffee?"

On a diaphragm-high shelf across the back wall I saw a Pyrex jug on a hot plate.

"I'll get it," I said.

Once I was seated and drinking, the boss man asked, "You know how to strip wax buildup off a floor, Mr. Rawlins?"

"You got a buffer, or do I have to get down on my hands and knees?"

"You got the job," Docherty said.

A few minutes later the staff started trickling in. Including me there were twelve janitors working under the white-on-gray man. Mostly Black men, most of them under thirty. It was interesting how the plantation model had survived a century after its *demise*. I heard all their names and shook most of their hands, but I only remember Morty Mattan and Dorothea Lamprey.

Morty was very dark-skinned, mid-twenties, good-looking, and strong. A recent transplant from Alabama, he was full of himself, arrogant, ambitious, and willing to bully his way past anyone, white or Black, in order to succeed.

When we were all seated at the long table, a work-world version of the Last Coffee Break, Morty sat across from me.

"What's your name again, brother?" he asked me.

"Rawlins."

"And how old are you?"

"Old enough to remember the war in Europe and Africa." I stared right at him.

"You cleaned out toilets in North Africa?"

"I killed Germans whenever and wherever I fount one." That claim turned a few young men's heads.

"And all they let you do now is pick up after them," Mattan said with the flair of a poet signing his name at the bottom of some sonnet.

"I don't see you up at the penthouse in no Brooks Brothers suit," I said, trying to sound like who I was pretending to be.

"Shit, man, I'm at LACC at night, learnin' how to be a photographer."

"Oh, come on, now, Mortimer," Dorothea Lamprey decried. "You only got that camera to get girls to take off their clothes for you to look at."

A few of the young men laughed at that.

"My name is Morty."

"I give you ten to one that ain't what yo mama named you," Dorothea claimed.

The three women custodians were all past thirty. Dorothea was a few years beyond forty. Well-built and powerful, she was the kind of woman that attracted me.

"All right, everybody," Docherty Warren announced. "Enough of this nonsense. Time to get to work."

He told almost everyone where they should begin and what they needed to get done.

At the end of his orders he said, "Rawlins, you're with me."

There was a hopper room at the back of the big office. The door's lock was Sargent and that made me happy. Doc pulled out a chrome buffer with an extra-long extension cord and four round steel-wool scrubbers.

"You get the bucket and the scrubber detergent," he told me.

I found what he asked for, filled the rolling bucket with hot water and cleaning fluid. Then we took the maintenance elevator to the thirty-second floor.

We went to a very large office space that had been used by the builders when they were finishing the inside of the 2120. The floors had been waxed, rewaxed, waxed again, and scarred by many work boots and the movement of heavy machinery. I slathered water on the linoleum and Doc wielded the buffer left and right, stripping off the old waxes and the new scars.

"This was the main office?" I asked the boss man on a cigarette break.

"Yeah. This is where the magic happened."

"Why didn't they take the penthouse?"

"The owners put some folks up in there."

"Oh? Who was that?"

"I didn't ask, and they didn't say."

A while later I told Doc that I needed to make a call to my kid's school.

"Can I use the office phone downstairs?" I asked.

"Sure. Go ahead."

* * *

Saul Lynx had collected master keys from every major lock-maker in America. I always carried a ring of them on a job like the 2120. Down in the custodians' office I used my Sargent master on the hopper room door. The key cabinet was against the back wall. It was no trouble picking that lock. In there I had my choice of the more exotic keys.

I took what I thought I could use and then hurried out of the hopper room, closing the door behind me.

"Hey, Easy." It was Dorothea. She was sitting at the long table.

Caught, I said, "Ms. Lamprey," giving a slight nod.

"Come have a seat with me."

"Doc expects me back upstairs."

"Tell him you was helpin' me."

I went to sit across from her.

As I said, Dorothea was a handsome woman. Her eyes were speaking to me in a language known around the world and down past all the epochs of humankind.

"You called me Easy," I said to open negotiations.

"That's what EttaMae Harris calls you, ain't it? Her an' Raymond Alexander."

"I had no idea I was so, uh . . . well-known."

"You ain't no Superman hidin' behind a pair'a glasses," she said with a smile. "But I guess one outta a dozen or so ain't too bad."

"Bad enough. One sour note and I'm on the street."

"Why you here anyway?"

"This and that."

"You lookin' for sumpin'?"

"I'm not here to steal."

"For a girlfriend?" she asked, her eye honed on mine.

"If you asked me two days ago I'd'a said yeah."

"That's too bad."

"How 'bout a hundred dollars instead?"

I went back upstairs after giving Dorothea her money. I always carried two or three hundred when going on a job like the 2120. Most often people who recognized me didn't say anything. Back then silence was second nature to Black people. But if someone, like Dorothea, wanted something, it was good to have that something in my pocket.

Years earlier I had been a custodian for the Los Angeles Unified School District. I had been trying to live the straight life but that was easier said than done. I did learn the job, though.

By the end of the day Docherty was impressed with my work. I liked repetitive jobs and empty conversation, so we got along just fine. He told me that he needed an assistant supervisor and I might be just the right one after serving three months' probation.

After work, I got two chili burgers and cheese fries at Tommy's on Beverly and ate in my car. After that I drove down to the central branch of the LA library. The doors were locked by the time I got there, but there was a white guard standing behind them.

"Closed," he said through the wire-reinforced glass.

"Herbert Mellon," I responded.

"What about Mr. Mellon?"

"He asked me to drop by."

"I don't think he's here."

"Extension thirty-six forty-three," I suggested.

Ten minutes later Assistant Head Librarian Herbert Mellon appeared at the locked door.

"Mr. Rawlins," he said, a furtive look of fear on his face.

"Don't worry, Herb. I just need to look up something in the architecture section."

Mellon was a small white guy with an oval-shaped head. He had a problem with another man over a woman. Because the conflict crossed racial lines I was suggested as an intermediary.

Ever since then he let me in when I needed information.

There was a room on the top floor of the main library that contained blueprints, construction plans, and floor layouts for every building built in LA County since the forties. When I'd perused the information for the 2120 to my satisfaction, I took an elevator to the basement to make a call on a pay phone down there.

"Creek Answering Service," a woman answered.

"Mary Donovan, please."

"Your number?"

I gave her the pay phone's digits.

"I'll try to find her," she said.

The basement floor of the central library would have been like *The Prince and the Pauper* for me when I was a boy—me being the pauper. I was a successful man, but my life was defined by the barbed wires of deep poverty. Sitting there, looking out over the vast marble hall, I felt, once again, like a refugee. In some way, I was sure that this was why I felt such a draw to Amethystine. She knew the same things I did, saw the same worlds.

In the middle of that reverie the phone rang.

"Mary?"

She got right down to business. "TJ called me, but I haven't heard back from him yet."

"And you won't either."

"Why?"

"Somebody shot him in the head."

She had to take a moment to absorb this information, gleaning the possible ramifications.

"Tell me what you know," she said at last.

"We need to meet, lady. There's too much here for us to solve it on the phone."

"Where?"

"I'll leave that up to you."

"Okay. Good. Tomorrow, eleven thirty, top floor of the art museum."

"See ya then."

My next call was home.

"Hello?" she said, sleep in her voice.

"Hi, honey."

"Daddy."

"You okay?"

"Uh-huh. We made chili dogs and French fries with home-made catsup."

"Sounds delicious."

"Essie liked it, but Benita got a little sick. You comin' home?"

"Not tonight, I don't think. I'm downtown and I have some things to take care of in the morning. So I'll probably sleep at the office."

"Okay. But call me in the morning, all right?"

"Aye, aye, Sergeant."

17

I made my way down a small dead-end alley on the west side of the 2120 Building. It was 12:13 a.m. and I was hyperaware of the surroundings. I knew where the side entrance of the building was located, but there was no way of knowing if someone had seen me going back there or if there was nighttime security roaming the halls.

The side door was metal and unusually small. None of the keys I'd taken from the cabinet in the hopper room worked on it.

But I wasn't through. Where Saul had given me master keys, Whisper had provided us both with snap guns.

Highly illegal for people like me, the snap gun worked on almost all cylinder locks by searching out the tumbler sequence. One shot and I was in.

I searched out the stairwell and made it to the fifth floor. The maintenance elevator was there, waiting for Docherty's crew. The car was locked but I had keys.

Indirectly, Purlo had told me that Curt was here. When he quoted Mr. Epsilon talking about seeing from the ocean to the west to the mountains out east, he was parroting a cartoon that I'd seen with Jewelle at a real estate conference we'd attended. Mr. Epsilon was the cartoon mascot of the company that managed the 2120. Purlo didn't think that I'd understand the reference because you never saw Black faces at conferences like that—almost never.

I took the elevator to the thirty-seventh floor so the motor sounds wouldn't alarm anyone on the thirty-ninth and final floor.

The first person I encountered was on the landing of floor thirty-eight. He was lying in a heap formed by his own body. I shined a flashlight on him. The cigarette he'd been smoking had fallen on his burgundy sports jacket and burned through to the skin. I doubted if he felt it, though. His dark eyes were open wide but seeing nothing, feeling nothing, due to the gunshot wound behind his right ear.

The driver's license from the wallet in his breast pocket told me that his name was Aaron Oliver, that he was born on July 9, 1949, and that he was a resident of Nevada.

I sat on the stairs above the slain man for a few minutes, wondering if I should continue the climb. Going over the facts as I knew them, the only sensible answer was for me to make my way back down to the ground floor, go back to the roof of my mountain home, and thank my lucky stars. Maybe I would stop at a phone booth along the way and notify the police.

Having the right answer, I climbed up to the thirty-ninth floor anyway.

It was mostly dark and completely silent. There was no fixture or furniture except for a cubicle erected in a far corner next to a window wall. From this collapsible compartment a weak light shone.

I was armed with the pistol Lihn had provided, and I was scared.

"Anybody here?"

I took my finger off the trigger, not trusting the clench in my hand.

"Anybody here?" I called again. It was almost a plea.

Half a minute passed, and I started the long trek from the floor entrance to the far corner.

The office booth contained an empty desk, a swivel chair set back away from it, and a dead body slumped on the floor between the two useless furnishings.

The body was still warm. It was a youngish white man wearing dark trousers and a short-sleeved white shirt with ample blood on the back collar. The wallet had the young man's California license with his photograph and name—Curt Reginald Fields. Under the body was a sealed envelope, spattered with his blood. Scrawled on the letter, in pencil, was the name Amethystine.

I slumped down on the floor next to the recently murdered man. The wail of Atwater Soupspoon Wise, the Topanga bluesman, came back to me then. I was dressed like a sharecropper and those words sang to me. The twelve-bar blues washed over blood spilt, blood coming from wounds of work and war, wear and tear, and senseless, drunken brawls. And it wasn't only blood. There was pigs' fat being rendered into candles, the stench of chitlins stewing all day on a woodstove, sewing needles made from the stripped tin of bean cans. I remembered foraging for berries in the deep woods and fighting a man over a few pennies. I cut him bad.

It was just after 1:00 when I came back to myself.

The rotary phone had a lock on the finger loop of the number 3. I used my pocketknife to snap it off.

"Yes, who is it?" a young woman answered.

"May I speak to Anatole, ma'am?"

I heard the receiver knock against wood and then a few whispers.

"Who is this?" the police captain demanded.

"It's me, Anatole."

"What do you want?"

"Thirty-ninth floor of the 2120 Building."

"What's there?"

"A dead man. Actually, two dead men."

"Who?"

"Curt Fields on the thirty-ninth and Aaron Oliver in the stairwell outside the thirty-eighth," I said. Then I hung up.

Within fifteen minutes there were one and a half dozen cops on the thirty-ninth floor. When there's a dead man on the top floor of the second-tallest building in Los Angeles, they send eighteen cops. Down where most of my people live they never send more than two, unless there's target practice to be had.

The first three officers to arrive put their hands on me.

Pushing away, I said, "Hey, man, what's happenin' here? I'm the one called you guys."

They got hold of me then.

"Calm down," one of them said. "We're going to put you in cuffs."

There were more police arriving and I could see the futility of resistance.

"What's your name?" a plainclothes officer asked.

"I'll wait for Anatole."

"You'll tell me your name," the tall and thin detective threatened.

"Yeah," I said. "You keep thinkin' that."

"I know who you are," he said, "and who you think you are. But it's a new day. Commander Suggs is in the wind, and your ass is ours."

I actually felt a moment of concern, not for me but for my friend Mel.

After that confrontation two uniforms were tasked to stand by me while the rest studied the crime scene. I didn't like being cuffed in that room filled with white men with guns.

Anatole arrived about a quarter hour later. It felt longer than that.

"What's this man doing in cuffs?" the captain asked the detective who'd staked a claim to my ass.

"We didn't know why he was here, Captain," the man answered, using a much softer tone than he had with me.

"I left a clear message that Ezekiel Rawlins was the one called me."

"I, uh, I didn't get that message."

"You're saying that dispatch didn't tell you?"

"Um, I don't know. I mean when I heard a murder maybe, um..."

"Get out of my face," McCourt told him. Then he turned to my personal guard and said, "Release him."

Before the cuffs were off, Anatole had moved to the second dead man. He studied Curt and his environs over a five-minute span that would have been hours for any normal investigator. Then he came over to me, near a far window.

"You touch him?" was his first question.

"Yeah. He felt warm and so I tried to see if he was maybe alive."

"Man's got a bullet in his head," Anatole doubted.

"I saw men in the war live with that kinda injury, others died from a scratch on the butt that got infected."

I liked mentioning my war experience when talking to cops. That way they knew they had to take me seriously.

"You find anything?" Anatole asked.

"No."

"Nothing?"

My hands said, *What don't you get about no?*

"Nordell," the captain said, summoning one of the uniforms.

"Yes, Captain." Nordell was older than the other cops. At about five nine, his face was formed from loose flesh and hard living.

"You search him?" Anatole asked, indicating me with a gesture.

"Yes, sir."

"What you find?"

"Wallet, ID, some change, a pistol, and this." He held up the snap gun. "You want me to have the pistol checked out?"

Taking the snap gun from Nordell, Anatole said, "No. Give him his stuff, the pistol too."

"You sure, Cap?"

"Oh yeah." The big man was looking into my eyes. "I'm sure." He didn't like me, but over the years of our proximity he had begun to harbor a grudging respect.

I wasn't worried about being found out, because Amethystine's letter was nestled in my boxer shorts.

When Nordell left, Anatole held up the illegal lockpick and said, "Give me a reason not to charge you with suspicion of murder."

Taking the burglar tool from his hand I replied, "If you don't arrest me, I'll find Melvin for you."

That slowed him for a moment or two.

Then he asked, "What were you doing up here?"

"Looking for Curt."

"Why here?"

"That man I told you about, Purlo? He let it slip."

"What's that mean? He was holding him here?"

"I don't think so."

"Where's Mel?"

"I'm workin' on that one."

"What you got now?"

"Tomorrow I have a meeting with someone knows him."

"Mary?"

"No. Not Mary."

"Who?"

"Look, man, I'm tryin' here. Right now, I got to go to this man's wife, mother, and father and tell 'em that he's dead. So, don't push me."

"I'm not pushing, just asking some questions."

"Yeah. Me too."

McCourt heard something in my voice, something that I might not have been aware of.

"Look," he said. "I want to help. Where can I find this Purlo guy?"

"I honestly don't know. I heard his name, asked around about him, and then he calls me outta nowhere. Tells me to meet him at a parking lot in Canoga Park and mentions a cartoon character that I only know from this building."

"That's not enough."

"No? A name like Purlo, obviously bent, and you can't get some kinda lead on 'im?"

Anatole stared at my forehead. I had enough time to count to thirty-seven.

"All right," he said. "Okay. You can go. But I expect you to be in reach if I need you."

18

I slept on the sofa in my office from about 2:45 till six the next morning. After splashing water on my face, I walked down to Pico and Robertson to the twenty-four-hour supermarket, Toluca Mart. They made fresh nugget-like and glazed buttermilk doughnuts every morning. Two of those with twelve ounces of black coffee and I was ready for the day.

I made it to the six-story brick building on Temple. The front door was unlocked because the people I was going to see all got to work by 6:45.

Taking the stairs to the top floor, I knocked upon the huge oaken door festooned with bronze signage that proclaimed MOFASS ENTERPRISES. The 2120 might have been open six days a week, but Jewelle's real estate business worked seven.

A minute passed before a young Black woman pulled the heavy door inward. She had the features of a dark-skinned Mongolian princess—almond-shaped eyes, straightened hair, and all.

"Yes?" she asked, holding the partly open door almost like a shield.

I was still dressed for custodial labor, and they didn't deal with janitors at that office.

"Jewelle in?" I asked civilly.

"No, she's not. What do you want with her?"

"How about Amethystine?"

She received this question as if it were a surprise wake-up slap.

"And who are you?" she asked, looking me up and down.

"My name is Rawlins and I have an appointment with either my friend Jewelle Blue or her associate . . . Amethystine Stoller."

The doorwoman studied me, and my unexpected language, longer than was polite.

Finally, she said, "Wait, wait here."

She closed the door, after which I made out the clacking sound of a bolt being thrown.

One of the things about the TV age is that people around the nation were slowly being brainwashed. This is what I believed then and now. They turn against their own and themselves because of impossible renditions of goodness, beauty, intelligence, and, worst of all, humanity.

That young woman — I never knew her name — couldn't find it in her heart to forgive my poverty-scented invasion of her perfect soap-opera world.

Jewelle Blue, whose office it was, had only well-dressed women working for her. Mostly Black women, with a few Latinas, Asians, and sometimes a native woman. They were of all ages but the same in their professionalism and, usually, their good manners.

When the door opened again Amethystine stood behind it. Her smile bore the deep satisfaction of a real woman, truly happy to see the face of a child who had survived one more day.

"You scared our receptionist," she said.

"Was it my clothes?"

Amethystine's grin widened and she stood aside, making way for the pauper prince.

The entrance area of the office was a broad room where five women sat clacking away at IBM typewriters, putting the final touches on leases, contracts, letters of complaint, and making and answering calls.

On the floor below, Jewelle had the teenage daughters of some of the women looking after the younger children of others.

Everybody got paid and fed, trained, and, most often, promoted.

Jewelle would have never called herself a feminist; she liked the broad shoulders and sharp stench of men too much for that. She simply knew how she was raised to work, to serve, and to receive what her work, and others', deserved.

Amethystine guided me down a long hall of private offices where more office workers plied the real estate trade. Three doors down we came to her workplace.

"Go on in," she said. "Take a seat."

Her manner was down-home/formal.

I did as she said, feeling a double tremor in my chest. One quaver was for the feeling that seeing her gave me. The second came from the news in my pocket.

Amethystine closed the office door and went to sit behind her oak desk.

I looked around the room in the time it took her to settle. It wasn't a big office, more like a cubbyhole inhabited by an underpaid clerk in a Dickens novel. There was a window, but it looked out on the dirty-white plaster wall of another office building less than six feet away.

My perusal of these environs ended at her. She was wearing a violet pants suit accented by a large-collared pink button-up blouse.

Her not-quite-smiling visage brought to mind some kind of philosophical farmer standing amid an infinite field of patience. This equanimity called up a feeling of guilt in me. Not that I was culpable or insincere, but more like I bore a sin as old as Adam's and now I was about to blame Eve.

"So?" she asked, smiling.

"Your husband is dead."

The look on her face was like the crumbling wall of an already overflowing dam. She did not speak.

"What, what happened?"

"You know the 2120 Building on Wilshire?"

"Yes, yes."

"He was working on the top floor. Somebody shot him, killed him. I found this."

I took the sealed bloody letter from my pocket and held it out across the expanse of her desk. For long moments she stared at the death note. Her eyes flicked up at me, sharing a pain that all warm-blooded creatures know.

Taking the bloodstained envelope, she studied it for a moment, then took a letter opener from the green blotter. After unfolding the handwritten one-page letter, she read it many times over before setting it down. Then she got up from the desk and went to the window.

Looking out at the plaster wall across the way she said, "You didn't read it?"

"No."

She turned and asked, "Why not?"

"Because. Because it felt, I don't know, private."

Walking back to the desk, she picked up the dispatch and held it out to me.

Dear Amy,

It'll be difficult sending this letter to you, but Aaron leaves me alone sometimes when he goes out for a smoke and there's a mail-chute in a far corner. They don't block up the slot. I know that because one time one of the guys who stays with me had me write a letter to his mom and then dropped it in the chute. Now all I need is a stamp.

They're holding me incommunicado so they can be certain that no one outside of Purlo sees the numbers I'm generating. I'm going through the books of the Exeter Casino in Vegas, on the strip. He hasn't told me, but it must be that he's representing a syndicate that wants to get a foothold there. Everything's going okay. Tell mom and dad that I'm fine. I really am. I'm going to get a lot of money for this. Maybe you and me could take that trip to Paris I always promised.

I love you, I love you, I love you

CrF
P.S.
Sturdyman tried to get in on it
but didn't make the cut.

* * *

The letter was written in pencil. I read it twice, shoved it back into the envelope, and tucked it away.

"I need to hold on to this in case I have to prove a point at some time."

"You're sure he's dead?"

"Yes, I am."

She pulled out the chair from the desk and sat down heavily.

"I called the police," I told her.

"What can they do?"

"Nothing, but we have to start making a story for ourselves."

"Why? We haven't committed any crime."

"Innocence don't make you innocent in the eyes of the law."

She looked up at me and winced. "Do you trust me, Easy?"

I pondered the question a second or two and then asked, "Who's Sturdyman and what does he have to do with all this?"

"I never heard the name before." She hesitated and then said, "I have to tell Curt's parents."

"Okay," I said. "Let's go."

She opened the bottom drawer and pulled out her purse.

19

We were quiet the first few minutes of the drive. She was downcast and I had nothing to offer. When we made the freeway, she turned her attention to the radio.

I was somewhat surprised at her choice: 93 KHJ, the bubblegum station filled with loud a.m. DJs, their impossible giveaway offers, and lots of ads. I didn't listen to the radio much because my time driving was, most often, used to work out problems. Problems that came with consequences. Even when the radio was on, I didn't really listen.

But that morning was different. Amethystine's ex had already suffered the most serious consequence. There was nothing to work out.

The first cut was Diana Ross and the Supremes singing "Someday We'll Be Together." After that a guy named B. J. Thomas sang "Raindrops Keep Fallin' on My Head." And then the Real Don Steele, pop DJ extraordinaire, came on identifying KHJ Boss Radio. After a commercial, called the Top 30 Giveaway for the record store Wallach's Music City, they played "Take a Letter Maria," by R. B. Greaves. It stunned me that radio had become so deeply integrated. My entire life the radio kept Blacks and whites separated. And here Greaves even had mariachi-style horns backing him up.

"You didn't answer my question," my passenger chided amid this minor revelation.

"What question?"

"If you trusted me."

The song "Aquarius," by the Fifth Dimension, started. I liked that song. After a few seconds I said, "I learned a long time ago that when somebody you barely know asks for trust, there's a problem somewhere."

Amethystine smiled at that, smiled and remained silent.

By midmorning we'd come to the tiny-house ridge overlooking the small park and, beyond that, the Pacific Ocean. We disembarked and walked to the shabby porch. I knocked and before long the door opened.

Winsome Barker-Fields stood there, looking worried.

"What?" she said.

"We came to talk to you about Curt, Winnie," Amethystine answered softly.

Skinny Alastair emerged from shadow. He placed a hand on his wife's shoulder.

"Talk about what?" he said.

"Can we come in?" Amethystine asked.

They turned to each other for an answer to this question. Taking the couple in was almost like reading a book. To begin with, Curt wasn't with us. This alone was bad news. Why invite trouble into your house? That's what they were wondering.

"What do you want?" Winsome asked, putting off the inevitable.

"Excuse me." The unapologetic voice came from somewhere behind us.

Turning around, I wasn't surprised to see the police. The two young white men were uniform in uniforms. Both hatless and brunette, clean-shaven and a whisper under six feet, armed, of course. The guy on my right rested his palm on the butt of his gun, where his partner was the one speaking.

"Can I help you?" he asked me.

"No."

That was not the answer he expected. His brown eyes tilted at me, and a stony demeanor recast his face.

"What the hell?" the other cop uttered.

"Can I help you guys?" I asked.

"What are you doing here?" the cop on my right demanded.

"Talking to the Fieldses."

"Do you know these people?" the cop on the left asked the elderly couple.

After a brief, worried silence Winsome said, "Yes, Officer. This is Amy, my son's ex-wife."

"And what about you?" the other cop asked me.

"What about me?"

"What are you doing here?"

"This is Mr. Rawlins," Winsome said. "He's doing some work for us."

"What kind of work?"

"Installing hummingbird feeders," I said on a lark. "You know, everybody loves hummingbirds."

Those cops didn't love us. Like old-fashioned radio, Amethystine and I were supposed to be played on a completely different bandwidth from nice white people.

"Come on in, Amy, Mr. Rawlins."

We did as she asked, leaving the cops on the dowdy porch.

She closed the door on them.

The lady and her husband put us on one couch, and they took the other. We sat for a brief, uncomfortable moment. The parents didn't want the bad news that Amethystine was better suited to tell them.

"I'm so sorry," she said, "but Curt is dead."

The cry that Winsome let out tore at my heart. She bent over her knees and spoke words that weren't language, blubbering and chittering at the same time.

Alastair looked as if he'd just been struck.

"What do you mean?" he asked me.

"Where's Harrison?" was my reply.

"What does he have to do with this?"

Amethystine moved to sit next to Winsome. She sat her up and put her arms around her.

"When Harrison walked me to my car the other day, he mentioned that your son knew a man named Purlo," I said to Alastair. "You ever hear that name?"

"No," Al said. "Who is he?"

"He's a gambler, and it looks like he had hired your son to do some forensic accounting for him."

I might as well have been speaking Greek.

Winsome was still gibbering, still raging. Amethystine struggled to physically contain her elder's grief and fury.

"What does any of that have to do with Curt?" Alastair asked me.

"I don't know," I said honestly.

"How do you know that Curt is dead?"

"I found his body, called the cops."

That sat the little man back.

"Why was he dead?" Winsome managed to utter through animal-like panting. "Why?"

"Somebody killed him, but I don't know who or the reason why."

Winsome pulled away from her ex-daughter-in-law and wrapped her arms around her husband's neck. She hollered so loud I worried about the old man's eardrums.

Amethystine put a hand on Winsome's shoulder. "I'm sorry," she said.

"Get your hand off of me!" this universal mother yelled, pulling away. "It's your fault. You destroyed my beautiful son."

After that she fell back into tears.

"Mr. Fields," I said.

"What?"

"Where is your brother?"

"What do you want with Harrison?"

"Do you know the man called Purlo?"

"No."

"I think your brother does. It would be good information to share with the police."

"I never knew any of Curt's clients. And, and, and Harry told us that he was going down to San Diego to visit Chita, the sister of his dead wife."

"What's Chita's last name?"

"Moyer. Chita Moyer."

"When did Harrison leave?"

"Not long after you did. He called her and she asked him to come help her with something."

"Did you talk to her?"

"No, no."

At that moment Mrs. Barker-Fields jumped up shrieking. She took a water glass from the coffee table and hurled it at the picture window. The drinking glass shattered, leaving the windowpane whole. Then she grabbed a cushion from the sofa. Amethystine tried to stop her but the elder lady slapped at her with the flat bolster.

That's when I got up and wrapped my arms around the distraught mother. She struggled and fought, even scratched at my arms. But I didn't let go, and finally she held on to me, crying softly.

We stood there in the middle of the small living room.

"He's dead," she said. "Dead."

We held on to each other. I understood what she was feeling. I had children. I thought about the cut on Jesus's face, about the attack on the native man he fought to protect. I thought about Amethystine's husband's impotent promise to take his ex to Paris.

Winsome's heaving cries softened. When I let her go, her husband took my place.

"Have either of you ever heard of someone named Sturdyman?" I asked.

They were beyond my questions by then.

"I'll stay with them," my actual client said. "I'll call the police and maybe go with them if they have to . . . identify . . ."

"You sure?"

"Yes."

"I'd go with you, but I've got another appointment."

"You go on."

20

Soon after leaving the Fieldses' house, I noticed a police cruiser in my rearview mirror. It kept back pretty far, at least a block away. This meant that they were still wondering about my intentions. A passive investigation of this nature was no surprise. *I* was the perpetual surprise, always showing up at places I wasn't expected or wanted. It was the job of every policeman in America to make sure that people like me were not up to some mischief. It had been their job since before the Civil War.

I made my way over to Olympic and then took the on-ramp to Highway 10, the Santa Monica Freeway. The police broke off pursuit there. Whatever threat I represented, it was no longer their concern.

After a long life of being hounded, followed, and stalked by men and women of all colors, I had learned to let it go, to move around carelessly and unconcerned, like a very small fish in a tank full of sharks.

The Egg and the Eye, a supposedly omelet-only restaurant, was across the street from the art museum. They sold low-cost art and craft pieces, served eggs of every stripe, and even had a little theater in back where they screened independent films and unusual documentaries. I ordered their prime rib eggs Benny and took out *Papillon*.

I read and ate until about eleven and then I struck out for the museum.

Back in those days the LA art museum was just a four-story atrium with different eras of art displayed on each level. The basement, for the longest time, had a collection of down-at-heel sarcophagi that reminded me of discarded bathtubs. There was usually only one new exhibit at a time in the collection.

This season the new work was on the third floor. Mary said to meet her on the top level, but that wasn't for another quarter of an hour. So I decided to wander around. Maybe Feather would like to come with me to see the new exhibit.

It was a modest offering, four paintings by Paul Klee. They were simple landscapes of different subtle and abstract places, all of which were under a red sun that seemed to me somewhat cold. It was as if these were the drawings of some Inuit child, using colors derived from berries and clay, describing various wintry landscapes on clear days.

"Easy." She'd come up behind me like I'd imagined Fearless Jones had done a hundred times to unsuspecting German sentries—behind enemy lines.

"Hey," I said. "I thought we were meeting on the top floor."

"I was early. Thought I'd check out the new pieces. You?"

"Mediocre minds think alike, Ms. Donovan."

"It's Mrs. Suggs."

"You guys got married?"

"Three months ago. In Reno."

She was turned out in a tight floral minidress that might well have been silk. It was a sexy ensemble dominated by various shades of red. I knew from this choice of attire that she was intent on influencing me. A force unto herself, Mary was criminal in the eyes of the law. But the only judges she recognized were Instinct and Power. She was the living personification of Melvin's vocation. That was why he couldn't resist her.

"I need to find your husband."

Her nostrils flared mere millimeters, but that was enough. If I were a male spider and she the female, I would have had to worry about being slaughtered no matter what happened next.

"Melvin said that you're one of the most dangerous men in LA," she offered.

"You don't need Mel to tell you how the world works."

Her wariness formed into a sneer.

"No. I don't."

"Just like I don't need to be told about how dangerous you can be."

"I'm just a defenseless girl, Mr. Rawlins."

"Tell Tommy Jester that."

She turned away to regard one of the childlike masterpieces.

I was pretty sure that Mary's appreciation of that painting was in no way like my own. I might have gotten distracted by that thought if she hadn't turned back to me.

"Tommy Jester was a pimp," she declared.

"He ran men?" I was really surprised.

"Women."

"How did he keep 'em in line?"

She smiled. "When I asked him that one time he said, 'Kindness—kindness and razor blades.'"

"He's dead."

"That's what you said." Her expression was like the powerful lens of a seventy-millimeter camera, now and then altering ever so slightly. It was all in the muscles around her lovely, deadly eyes. "How?"

"Shot in an alley down from his apartment," I said. "Before that you talked with him?"

"Yes."

"You wanna go out to the park?"

Grassy and passive Hancock Park surrounded the museum and also the fenced-in tar pits where many an ancient mastodon and saber-toothed cat had met their end. Mary and I commandeered an empty bench next to the sulfurous, oil-stained waters.

"TJ had a guy did work for him named Bernard," Mary said after looking around, making sure that we would not be overheard. "He did odd jobs."

"Like what?"

The new bride gazed into my eyes with an intelligence that was daunting.

"Bernard took secret films of TJ's powerful and rich clients. Tommy told me one time that he had done one on Terrence Laks."

"The underchief?"

She shrugged.

"And you offered to buy the film from TJ?"

"He wanted ten thousand."

"Wow."

"Yeah...but what good's money if you don't have love?"

I didn't understand those words coming out of her mouth but, then again, I didn't need to.

"You reached out to TJ, he called back and asked for the cash, then he called Underchief Laks..."

"Looking for a better deal," Mary finished my sentence.

"So, Laks might be after you."

"People been after me since the first grade."

Talking to Mary was like looking out on an impossibly ever-growing vista. It was both vast and frightening.

"Tell me about Bernard."

"His last name's Kirby. That's all I know."

"Tall Black guy? Receding hairline?" I pointed at my head with two fingers representing back-slanting horns.

"Yeah, you know him?"

"I know who he is."

"Then maybe I can give you the money."

"I don't think that'll be necessary."

"But you'll talk to him?"

"I'll look for him. But I need to talk to Mel."

"I honestly don't know where he is."

I chuckled hearing this invocation of truthfulness. I mean, she probably didn't know where Mel was, but her conniving mind could never have been wholly straightforward or true.

"You drive here?" I asked.

"Taxied."

"Good. We can take my car."

"Tell me everything that happened and everything Mel said the last time you saw him."

We were in a rented room on Figueroa near Sixth Street. The motel was called François's Lantern and I was well acquainted with the proprietor. We were seated, facing each other, I, perched on an unfinished pine chair and she at the edge of the high queen bed.

"He came home on Tuesday last, just a little bit after three," she replied. "That was strange all on its own because he usually had a four-thirty meeting with the shift captains on Tuesdays. That's when he told me about the blackmail—"

"For the first time?"

"Yeah."

"He didn't tell ya when it first happened?"

"You think I'm'a lie about that?"

"Go on."

"He said that Laks wanted to know why he let the prisoner go and so he was going to have to disappear for a while."

"And he told you it was because of what you did?"

"Yeah."

"Okay. You need to tell me about that, then."

"Why?"

"The more I know, the better I can help."

She took a minute to think through all the possible outcomes of sharing her truth with me.

"My father used to say, what you don't know won't hurt you," she ventured.

"Down where I come from, ignorance is death."

Her smile was both radiant and, somehow, grateful.

"I killed a man..."

Usually when I hear those words I put my palms up against my ears and hum loudly. But not that day.

"I have a goddaughter," she continued. "When she was eleven a man named Roman Zell, vice principal of her school...he raped her. The cops said that there was no hard proof. No proof."

There was nothing I could ask about that. A criminal court might have found her guilty, but no red-blooded human being would. No conscientious objector, off-duty Supreme Court

justice, pope, mother, or child would have blamed Mary Donovan for that act. Instead, they would have offered her a chair and
a drink, sad soft eyes, and, probably, no questions.

"How'd you do it?"

"Shot him in the head"—she paused—"multiple times."

"Who's the blackmailer?"

"I don't know."

"Mel didn't tell you or he didn't know himself?"

"I don't even know that, Easy. All I can say is that he's aware
of what I'm capable of. He didn't give me any details, not even
who he let go from jail."

"So, you're saying that somebody got Mel on the phone, told
him that he knew you killed Zell, somehow he could prove it,
and so Mel let somebody outta jail? That don't make no sense.
Wouldn't Mel ask you before doing anything?"

"He knew what I'd done." Mary looked away from me, probably thinking about how knowledge causes pain. "Before we got
married, he wanted me to tell him about the worst of me. I
told him."

Her sorrow reminded me of Feather when she was seven. The
mother of a school friend had died. Feather cared about her friend,
so tried in her own way to share Lida's grief.

"Daddy," she asked me one night at bedtime, "am I gonna die?"

Life is filled with unanswerable questions.

"Okay," I said. "Let's come at this from another way."

Mary smiled. She needed someone she could trust to scruti-
nize the predicament. Usually that person was Mel.

"Did anybody see you?"

"No," she said. "I broke in the house when he was at school. I was dressed like a schoolkid, wore a wig and glasses."

"Whose gun did you use?"

"I bought one on the street, but after I searched his place, I found one'a his."

"You shot him with his own gun?"

"Yeah."

"Multiple times?"

"I was gonna shoot him just once and then put the pistol in his hand. But I was mad and the first shot just creased his head. He came at me and I shot five more times."

"All in the head?"

"Yeah."

"Did you tell anybody about it?"

"No."

"Not even the girl's mother?"

"Course not. She had an alibi, but I wanted the news to hit her fresh."

"Did anybody see you leave?"

"I doubt it. But even if they did, they could'a never identified me."

"You left the gun there?"

Looking up in disgust she said, "Yes, I did. Stupid, stupid, stupid."

"So maybe there's some piece of a fingerprint on it," I said aloud.

"And they wanna hang my Mel over that."

"What caliber?"

"It was a twenty-two. That's probably why nobody heard it."

After another spate of silence I said, "Mary."

"What?" It was a whisper in the dark.

"You didn't tell anybody about Zell? No one?"

"That's the first thing you learn," she said with conviction. "Never tell."

"Could somebody have figured it out?"

"There was the detective. I forget his name. But he just asked some questions. And that was only one time. But it couldn't be him."

"Why not?"

"He believed my goddaughter's story. Told me that the prosecutor couldn't make the case. But that was just one meeting. At my apartment. Nobody ever came again."

"Okay. I think I could work with that. What kind of clothes did Mel bring with him when he left?"

The question caught her off guard. If the stakes we played for weren't so high, and the dangers so clear, I might have felt I had scored a point in a lifelong competition.

"Nothing," she murmured in a way that made you know there was more. "But..."

"What?"

"I was looking through his closet the morning after he left. You know, thinking about him. And something...was off. It wasn't till you just asked that I realized it was his overcoat gone, missing from the hook on the back of the closet door. It was one of those heavy woolen East Coast coats made for deep winter. Does that mean anything to you?"

"No," I said, but that was a lie. That overcoat sparked a memory that I would not share with Mel's Lilith. "Was anything else missing?"

"Not that I remember." She was eyeing me.

"Anyplace he was talkin' about? Friends in other cities? He told me that you guys were going to Europe. Did he have a passport?" I didn't care about any of that. I was pretty sure where Mel was, and I didn't want to share that knowledge with Mary.

"He got a passport for Paris, but it's still in the bureau."

Leaning forward, my friend's wife put a hand on my knee. "You're going to look for him?"

"I'm gonna find him."

Her hand stayed on my leg. Her eyes were in mine.

"What can I do for you?" she asked.

There are times when the straightforward approach is best. She was going to do anything she could to save her man. And, maybe, if I were a dozen years younger, I might have fooled myself into believing that she needed some loving in these hard times. But I was fifty and she didn't need anything but for me to do what I promised.

"Well," I said, and paused as if it was a hard question. "I know you know how to take care of yourself, but I'd feel a whole lot better if you let me put you someplace where I could be sure that you were safe."

Mary retracted the hand and smiled. "Whatever you say, Mr. Rawlins."

When she went into the bathroom to freshen up, I went outside into the parking lot. There was a pay phone next to the office door.

"Mofass Properties," a young woman, Maybelline Carson, said over the line.

"Jewelle come in, Maybe?" Her nickname always made me smile.

"Oh, oh, Mr. Rawlins. She here all right."

After a few clicks she answered, "Easy? How are you, darlin'?"

I explained about Mel's bride and how she needed to be pro-tected. I also said that she should keep Jackson completely in the dark about her.

"Why?" she asked. "You think Jackson gonna get his nose open behind her?"

"Mary is what they call an apex predator. She would eat that poor boy alive."

"You are such a sweet man, Easy. Takin' care of everybody. There should be a statue of you in some park square. Sure, drop her by."

21

Manheim's gym was older than the Olympic Auditorium. The business was owned and run by Frieda Alouette Manheim. She was the widow of Vicario Manheim (aka Turk Stone), a middleweight who would bang a full fifteen rounds with anybody masochistic enough to climb into the ring with him. Turk ended the careers of some boxers even when he lost the bout.

The drafty space was the size of a high school gymnasium. It had a skylight but still felt dark and heavy. It smelled of liniment, sweat, and tanned leather. There were two full rings, with sparring partners in each one, and a few dozen stripped-down men torturing themselves in order to experience the potential ecstasy of coming out victorious in one-on-one combat.

A cacophony of gladiatorial sounds greeted me there. The slapping sounds of dancing feet and leather jump ropes tapping the floor, the impacts of gloved fists on flesh and on punching bags, and a chorus of grunts and exhortations accompanied by the lesser sounds of laughter, approval, and pugilistic instruction. Black, white, and a whole range of brown skins made up the men there. There wasn't much room for racial hate. These men stored up their rage for any opponent of any color or creed. They were doing push-ups, running the circumference of the vast room, fighting with their own shadows, and hitting, hitting, hitting.

There was no apparent organization to this mob of violence. I had to wander around until happening upon a familiar face.

Pinky Richards was standing at the far side of one of the raised rings. He was watching a skinny white guy dance around a much larger Black opponent. The larger boxer kept missing with potentially devastating punches. The little guy regularly landed blows that had no effect.

"Come on, Oswald," a flush-faced Pinky yelled. "Try and touch 'im, you don't need to kill 'im."

Pinky was nicknamed after the baby finger. He was thin, white if you thought of a perpetual flush as white, and short enough to pass as a middle-school kid. He'd been a flyweight in his twenties and was probably still around the 112-pound limit.

A towheaded boy holding a stopwatch in one hand and a hammer in the other suddenly struck the bell that sat before him.

Pinky shook his head at the big boxer as he went to his corner.

"Hey, Pink," I said then.

Turning his wily face in my direction, the trainer squinted with his right eye.

"What you want, Rawlins? Frieda's out back."

"The big guy a prospect?" I asked.

"If you lookin' for somebody to swing a sledgehammer at a stake in the ground."

That was when the big Black bruiser climbed down to pay obeisance to Pinky.

"I'll do better the next time, boss," he said.

"This ain't no street fight, Oswald," Pinky cried holding both hands up. "You can't hurt him if you can't touch him. You have more control over your mitts if you reach out and tap him — anywhere."

"Okay, boss. Okay."

"Go throw three-punch combos at the wall. At least it won't fight back."

Oswald trotted off, happy that someone at least cared enough to give him instruction.

"So, Mr. Easy," the life-tired trainer said, "what you need?"

"How about a hundred dollars in your pocket?"

"Who I got to kill?"

"I don't think it'll come to all that. Bernard Kirby."

"Benny don't hang around nowadays. When the only offers he got anymore was back-alley prizefights, he went into sales."

"Selling what?"

"Boxes with bruises on 'em."

"Where do I find him?"

"Where's my hundred?"

The trail Pinky laid out didn't lead right to Kirby. First I had to go out to Bellflower to Kirby's ex-wife, Mona. She was a white woman, around forty, with bags under her eyes that were reminiscent of bruises. She didn't know where her ex was and didn't care. But she took twenty dollars to get groceries, she said. For that she suggested Uncle Uno. Uno, while not being related to Bernard, had been a good friend of his father's.

I was aware of the numbers runner. Uno might have been the only man in generally hatless LA who wore a top hat. It was what they called a low top, with a crown no more than six inches high. It marked him so that no one could fail to identify Uno Pasquale.

I found him on the southern outskirts of downtown LA. He was sitting on a backless wooden stool in front of a barbershop called Leo's. I saw him from down the block and watched for a while. He was smoking a slender cheroot, looking very satisfied with himself. Now and then, someone would walk up to him, they'd exchange a few words, and then the visitor would wander off.

Uno's talent was remembering everything he ever heard—word for word. This made him nearly invulnerable as a numbers man.

After maybe seven customers had been serviced, I walked up to the streetside bookie and asked, "How you doin', Uno?"

He was older than I, early sixties by white-man standards. That is to say, he would have looked even older than that down in my old neighborhood.

After a few moments he found my entry in his large file of names and faces.

"You're that friend of Blue's," he said. "Easy."

"No flies on you, Uno."

"Not till they walk across my dead eyes." He exhaled a cloud of cigar smoke.

"I need some information," I told him.

Uno was a businessman. He didn't need me to waste time shooting the shit. Time was money.

"What kind of information?"

"You have a godson name of Bernard Kirby."

"That's a fact, not a question."

"I need to talk to Bernard. He's got something a friend of mine wants to buy."

The dandy studied me, and then he asked, "You got a problem with Benny?"

"No, sir."

"Because he's the kinda kid gets into trouble at the drop of a hat."

"That may very well be." Language adjusted itself in my mouth depending on who it was on the other side of the conversation. "But I'm looking for a transaction, not an altercation."

"How much?"

"I got a hundred dollars burnin' a hole in my pocket."

The teeth in Uno's smile clenched down hard on that cigar.

"There's a Ping-Pong palace down next to Chinatown on the westward side. They call it King Pong. In the back room they do poker. A man calls himself Francis Drake runs the game. Benny plays bodyguard there."

I saluted him by tipping a nonexistent hat. Then I reached for my pocket.

"Not out here, boyo," he cautioned. "Go inside and give it to the barber in the last chair."

I went into the small three-chair men's salon. Everyone at Leo's was white and so I got a few stares. The first two barbers were clipping away. There were four men and one boy waiting for service. The last barber, a lanky-looking long-haired youth, was lounging on his mechanical chair. When I walked over to him, he looked up and I handed him a fold of five twenty-dollar bills.

That done, I left the shop at a good pace.

"Hey, Easy," Uno called.

"Yeah?"

"Be careful with Benny. That boy's got a hair trigger."

There was good reason for the warning—I knew. Bernard hit a guy in the ring so hard one time that his left eyeball popped out and hung down on his cheek. If they still had bare-knuckle boxing, BK would have had a shot at being champion of the world.

I was always a little nervous standing around in a white neighborhood. That fear was composed of four hundred years of experience crushed down into fifty short years of life.

But in spite of my fear, I stopped at a phone booth and made a call.

I had to go through a switchboard and a receptionist before Anatole McCourt got on the line.

"Captain."

"Mr. Rawlins. I've been trying to get in touch with you."

"Here I am."

"I'm gonna have to ask you to come in and answer a few questions."

"Sure. But first I need you to do something for me."

We met in front of the county jailhouse in the midafternoon. The big man had on a three-button suit the color of high-desert sand. His shirt was cobalt blue, with a necktie of light- and dark-blue squares.

"Captain. You're lookin' stylish."

"What you got on Mel?" he replied.

"You mean other than you were the one who warned him that they were building an airtight case against him?"

The heir of Viking blood went speechless for a good eight seconds. And even after that he could only utter, "I don't know what you're talking about."

"Okay. I'll accept that for now. But we got other business."

In another life Anatole and I would have probably been friends, riding side by side running from or chasing down some enemy, or friend. Our temperaments were first and foremost familial and, after that, political as far as politics represented human rights. Everybody, in our estimation, deserved a plot of land where they could sleep and, later on, be put to rest. Any other legislation from officials elected by hard cash, we believed, was a tier or more below human consideration.

We should have been brothers but instead we were stationed on opposite sides of a demilitarized zone that had existed as long as there'd been a New World.

"Come on," the juggernaut cop ordered.

We strolled up to the heavily armored and guarded front door of hell. Passing that threshold was worse than standing on the street in a white neighborhood. The dampness of the jailhouse atmosphere felt as if it arose from human sweat. The uniforms had an occupying-military feel to them.

I didn't say a word.

Anatole followed a man he spoke with, and I followed him.

We were brought to a room made from stone, like a basement chamber in a castle-cum-dungeon.

There were a few dozen denizens in that ultra-secure ante-room. Mostly women and their children, there for men who were only possibilities for them right then. Also there were brothers and mothers, a father or two. It wasn't the first time I was made aware that incarceration was an enterprise and a social gathering that was open for business twenty-four hours a day.

This was the waiting room that led to prisoners with blood on their hands and wounds on their bodies, forgery artists and

combat sportsmen, sex therapists and madmen, professional out-
casts and those who were so angry that it was eating them up
from the inside out.

And it wasn't only my people, so-called Black people. There
were whites and Mexicans, Chinese and Koreans, Hasidic Jews
and devout Catholics. The only one missing was God. That
celestial being had abandoned this particular multicultural tribe.

I sat down at the end of a long bench and stared at the concrete
floor, practicing minding my own business.

"Are you my daddy's friend?" a voice asked.

It was a girl-child, seven or possibly eight years old. Not yet
five feet tall, she had dark skin and maybe eleven pigtails that
were tied back. Her face was sleek, like some very cute predator's—a child of Man, one might have said.

"Who is your father?" I asked.

"Clarence D. Simpson the third."

Over her tentacled head I could see what was probably her
mother—watching.

"I don't think I know him," I said. "What they call you?"

"Marla."

"Marla Simpson?"

Her grin showed one missing tooth. She had on jeans and a red-
and-blue lumberjack shirt that looked like it was made for a doll.

"Uh-huh," she told me. "They arrested him, um, because they
said that he was in this big place and some things got stoled. But
nobody saw him take nuttin' an' nobody could prove it."

There were angry tears in the little girl's eyes.

"Is that your mother over there?" I asked, pointing at the
woman who was watching me.

"Uh-huh."

I brought out my wallet, from which I retrieved a five-dollar bill and a gold-embossed business card.

"Give these to your mama and tell her I said she should call the woman on the card."

Marla grabbed the strange treasure and went running back to her little brood.

I was, once again, looking down at the stained concrete floor when a shadow came over the scene.

It was Marla's mom. She had on a blue blouse with pearlescent buttons done up along the shirt-edges and a pink skirt that went down to her shins. She was a small woman but gave the impression of uncommon strength.

"What is this?" she asked me, holding out the card I'd given Marla.

"Pinca Novalis."

"And what's a Pinca Novalis?"

"She's a lawyer I know. Her preferred clients are women and children and the men they care for."

"We cain't afford no lawyer."

"There's not a soul in this room could afford to be in here without a lawyer."

Marla's mother was so filled with emotion that she actually started to shiver.

I stood up and offered her my hand.

"Ezekiel Rawlins. My friends call me Easy."

After a moment's hesitation she took my hand and said, "Martha. Martha Simpson."

"Well, Martha, Pinca needs money too. That's a fact. But she got all kinds of ways for workin' people to afford justice. If all your husband can get is a public defender, then call Ms. Novalis. Don't hurt to talk."

"How do you know if my husband's guilty or not?"

"I don't. But the one thing I'm sure of is that it's maybe one person out of a hundred that's truly innocent: white, Black, brown, ordained minister, or beat cop."

"Easy Rawlins!"

I turned away and never saw Martha Simpson again. Coming through the iron door was Fearless Jones in the custody of three jailhouse guards and followed by Anatole McCourt.

Fearless was clad in gray shirt and pants, light-brown shoes, and visor cap, also gray. I might have thought that he came out in a prison uniform if I didn't know that this was what he wore whenever he did physical work. This told me that Mr. Jones had been arrested while doing honest labor somewhere.

"How you doin', Fearless?"

"Okay. Got to show this one and that what the rules is. After that jail is just fine."

It was a secret pleasure to see the two physically toughest men I know standing side by side. Anatole was taller and at least fifty pounds heavier, but I was pretty sure that Fearless had a sharper left hook.

Anatole handed Fearless a folder with his release papers inside.

"The officer that blamed you for assault dropped the charges."

"Thank you, Captain," I said. "I'll have what you asked for in as few days as possible."

That got me a nod.

22

In a parking lot two blocks away from the county jail, Fearless and I reached my car. I got in behind the wheel, while he lowered into the seat next to me.

After a block or two he said, "You know, Easy, I didn't want you comin' here to throw my bail or bringin' that cop to make 'em let me go. A man got to take care his own business in this world. I ain't nobody's child nor bitch."

"Only reason I'm here, Fearless, is 'cause I need your help, and gettin' that help conflicted with your situation."

"I did not assault that cop. He just pushed with less strength than it takes to move a man like me."

"I know that. If Fearless Jones assaults you, you have to consult with either the doctor or the undertaker."

"Paris send you?"

"I went to Paris lookin' for you. He told me that you forbade him lookin' me up. But he didn't look me up. I went to him. Lookin' for you."

Fearless absorbed my words, adjusted his newly free heart, and, finally, nodded.

"Thank you," he said.

"Nuthin' to it."

"So, what you need?"

"Lotta things. But first, how's your Ping-Pong?"

"I played every day in jail. You know they got niggahs in there could beat the Olympics."

I laughed. Almost everyone that knew him thought that Fearless had the limited intelligence of a child. They didn't understand the natural genius of a natural man.

"Um," Fearless hummed. "You know, Easy, I'll help you any way you want, but first I'd like to take a room at the N&T Hotel on Grand, take a shower, and then have two cherry juice and bourbon cocktails like they make."

"We could pick up the fixins and I could take you home."

"Ain't got a home right now, brother. I was livin' with Bonita Williams, but she told me that the next time I get in trouble I'm out."

"Maybe she changed her mind."

"I used four collect calls to ask her that. She refused every one."

The N&T Hotel was a pencil-thin six-story pink building down among warehouses, furniture builders, a sewing machine factory, and an illegal clinic that pretended to produce rubber gloves.

Inside, the N&T was very plain and businesslike, with the exception of a smaller square room made from blue-tinted glass that sat in the middle of the entranceway. Seated in this office within an office was a white man, also pencil thin, who wore a tan suit, sporting an ultrathin mustache.

"Mr. Cargill," Fearless greeted the crystal-encased concierge.

"Mr. Jones. You need the usual?"

"And two cherryB cocktails."

"Two thirty-two," said Cargill. He put the flat of his hand against the blue pane before him and slid it to the side.

I didn't understand the mechanism involved. No glass extended past the limits of the cage. Nothing seemed to move at all, but an empty space appeared before Cargill.

"You know I ain't got the money, Easy. But I figure you plan to pay me anyway."

I counted out the requisite bills and handed them over.

"Room six-A," the hotel clerk told Fearless.

We walked down a hall behind the glass office, turned left, and came to a small elevator door.

"He didn't give you a key," I said.

"Naw," Fearless grunted, "NT don't have no keys. Elevator don't have no buttons except down to the first floor. Other than that it's all automatic."

The door slid open and we went inside.

The walls, floor, and ceiling of the lift were painted a festive yellow in a chamber that might accommodate four men. The moment we were in, the door closed and the chamber began its ascent.

"What you mean no keys, no floor buttons? Somebody got to run this shit."

"This here is the most private roomin' house in LA," my friend replied. "Back in the day Khrushchev and Kennedy could'a met here and wouldn't anybody ever know."

Our elevator reached the sixth floor and I was surprised that there were two exits, on opposite sides. One had the letter A on it and the other had B. Door A slid open.

We stepped right into a well-appointed and surprisingly large room. The furniture was modern and the window the kind that could look out while no one else could look in. Two dark-red cocktails sat on the table next to a sky-blue sofa. Fearless sat next to the libations.

"You want me to send down for a drink for you, Ease?"

"Naw, man. I just need to make a call."

"Go through that do' right there," he said pointing. "There's a phone on the night table."

"How you ever find this place, Fearless?"

"They needed protection once or twice and one'a their regulars suggested me."

The bedroom was done all in white, with mirrors on three walls. The phone was next to the bed.

"Stenman Service," said a woman whose voice I didn't recognize.

"Rawlins, VIP51."

"Hello, Mr. Rawlins, my name is Pixie, Pixie Lowman. I just started today."

"Welcome to the telephonic universe, Pixie," I said. "You got any news for me?"

She answered on the third ring.

"Hello?"

"It's Easy, Mary."

"I been waitin'."

"I been working."

"You find Mel?"

"Not quite yet."

"But you know where he is?"

"I think I do."

"Where?"

"Mel didn't tell you who was blackmailing him or who it was he let out of jail. That means he wants you out of it."

"You are not my man, Easy Rawlins."

"No. But I'm Mel's friend, and I don't want him mad at me for sending you out gettin' inta all kindsa trouble."

There was silence on the line for a few seconds.

"You got Mouse with you?" she asked.

"He's outta town, so I drafted Fearless."

"That's probably better. Mel doesn't really like Raymond."

"Where's Jewelle got you?"

"Studio City. In a garden apartment."

"That sounds nice."

She gave me the phone number and told me to call every day.

When I got back to the sitting room, the cherry cocktails were down to the dregs and Sarah Vaughan was singing "Can't Get Out of This Mood." Fearless was leaning back on the sofa, his eyes closed and his lips approaching a smile.

I sat quietly down on a sky-blue chair and waited for the full bloom of his grin. I liked Sarah too.

Maybe twenty minutes later, with his eyes still closed, Fearless said, "Gimme ten minutes for a shower and I'm ret to go."

"Sounds like a plan."

I drove us a little bit north to Chinatown and then a few blocks beyond. On a dowdy street above the Asian neighborhood was a storefront that had the sign KING PONG above it.

We parked across the street and surveyed the environs for maybe a quarter hour. This was eye work. There was nothing to say about what we intuited, but there was no reason for silence either.

"I was thinkin', Fearless."

" 'Bout what?"

"That NT place."

"What about it?"

"Seems like such a fancy and discreet place would cost more than two hundred thirty-two dollars."

"I aksed that very question of the guy runs it, man name'a Charles Charles. Charlie told me that room rates were based on availability and other things."

"What other things?"

"Well...Like, for instance, Charlie said that one time Kennedy really was there, meetin' a man that he shouldn't'a. Now, that there's a whole different rate."

After another five minutes I said, "I guess we got the basics."

As we crossed the street Fearless told me, "I played Ping-Pong a whole lot durin' the war."

"Which war?"

"Korean."

By then we were at the glass door of King Pong. We could see a very healthy young Asian gentleman sitting upon a high metal stool on the other side. Beyond him there were maybe eight Ping-Pong tables with at least six pairs of adversaries whacking away.

When the doorman climbed down from his throne I could see how lithe and light-footed he was. He pushed the door open, glanced at me cursorily, then took in Fearless from head to foot; he knew where the danger would come from.

"Hi," I said.

"Private," he replied, his eyes still on Fearless.

"I'm Easy Rawlins and this is Mr. Fearless Jones, here to pay our respects to Sir Francis Drake."

The ocher-skinned Asian was no more than five six, but his movements were superior, like those of a feral cat on the hunt. He turned only his head toward me. I saw then that his eyes were pale blue, like the dim light of morning before the sun has broken the horizon. I wondered if this genetic anomaly was why this specimen had so much violence bundled in his shoulders and hands. Maybe he was treated as an outcast among the dark-eyed people of his clan.

"Not here," the blue-eyed warrior informed me.

"Maybe he came in late," I suggested as mildly as I could. "I make that mistake all the time."

There was another man standing maybe eight feet away from us on the inside of the parlor. He was the doorman's size, race, and nature, watching to make sure that if trouble happened it would go their way and not ours. Fearless had already sussed out the sentry's threat. He was ready. I was hoping that my words would carry the day, and the gatekeeper was trying to disentangle his dignity from his job.

"Wait here," he barked.

I nodded as obsequiously as possible.

He went away and the man backing him up came to the door. This man had dark eyes, lighter skin, and a scowl designed to wage war.

Again, Fearless and I were silent.

It was twilight and now and then a car trundled past, scenting the air with the fumes of burnt fuel.

My friend smiled at the second doorman. When the guard bristled, Fearless's grin grew.

He was my friend and whenever we worked together it was him working for me. But Fearless was his own man. The first guard was trying hard to do his job, but his number two simply wanted to intimidate. And Fearless didn't do well with bullies.

Luckily the first guy returned.

He pushed open the door and said, "You come with me."

He led us down the aisle between Ping-Pong tables. When we got to an empty one Fearless stopped.

"Hey, Ease," he said. "There's a guy here look like he wants a partner. You don't need me to talk to Francis, do ya?"

Fearless gestured to a chubby Chinese kid and I followed my usher through a wood door that had been slathered with green paint.

The back room was about the same size as the front. It was mostly empty, with some boxes, cleaning materials, folding furniture, and Ping-Pong paraphernalia along the sides. In the center was a green-felt-inlaid octangular table with seven poker players and a buxom brunette card dealer. Other than these eight seated inhabitants there stood Bernard Kirby, a beefy and darkish Black man maybe six two and carrying two hundred pounds.

Kirby eyed me and the doorman and then uttered something I couldn't make out.

A dandy sitting next to the dealer looked up and slowly focused his eyes on me.

"Easy Rawlins," the middle-aged rake hailed.

Francis was wearing a cream-colored suit jacket with a few bright-purple irises in its lapel. He was one of the rare male individuals of that era who sported an earring. It was a stunning blue gem embedded in his left earlobe. The light-brown mustache was reminiscent of a centipede and his nose looked to be whittled down from a greater edifice.

"Sir Francis," I hailed.

"You wish to speak with me?"

"I do indeed."

The turn of words pleased the gambler.

"Deal me out for a couple of hands, Inga," he told the woman.

When he stood up, I could see that his trousers were midnight blue while his shoes were black with white spats.

We walked back out to the Ping-Pong room, followed at a respectful distance by Bernard Kirby.

Fearless and his rotund nemesis were going at it.

Francis noticed the fervor of the two players and said something to an older man standing near at hand. The man spoke in some dialect of Chinese and Francis nodded.

"That your friend?" Francis then asked me.

"Yeah," I said. "People call him Fearless. They say he's pretty good."

"Is your business urgent?"

"We can watch if you want."

"A hundred dollars on Min to win, giving you five points," Francis said to me.

"What did your friend say?" I asked, exhibiting false hesitation.

"That the score was five to one, your friend having the one."

"You're on."

The game got hotter after that.

"You know Raymond Alexander, right?" I asked Drake.

He was concentrated on the game but said, "Of course."

"Mouse got his hands on a truckload of IBM Selectric typewriters. He busy with other shit and gave 'em to me to sell."

"Why come to me? I'm a gambling man."

"Oh," I feigned. "I see. I must'a been misinformed when they told me that you facilitated deals like this now and then."

That list of words earned me a centipede smile.

"Why don't you come back round midnight, Mr. Rawlins. Maybe Kirby can do something for you after I leave."

We shook hands and then turned our attention back to the game.

Fearless was a natural-born athlete. He was balanced and strong with lightning-quick reflexes, an uncanny sense of the next movement, and, of course, no fears whatsoever. Min, his opponent, had probably played table tennis for twenty-eight of his thirty years. He'd seen it all and despite his size he was no slouch.

Many of the other players stopped to watch. They cheered both men when they made an extraordinary effort, either defensively or in attack. After maybe twenty-five minutes the score was 11–10, Min in the lead. Eleven was the winning score except for the fact that victory had to be by at least two points.

Half an hour later the score was 20–20, even.

Both men were sweating, but Min seemed to lose the tiniest bit of focus. Fearless, on the other hand, was a veteran of at least three wars. Focus was a life-and-death thing for him.

Over the next volley Min went up by a point. Then it was Fearless's serve, but instead he put the ball on the table and laid the paddle on top of it.

"I give," he said, raising his hands in surrender.

Min exhaled deeply and voices around the table called *no* in a variety of dialects — including English.

"I suppose that makes you the winner," Francis Drake said to me. He reached for a pants pocket.

"Naw," I told the fop sportsman. "Fearless resigning means he's the loser. If anybody should pay, it's me."

Francis smiled and nodded ever so slightly.

"Come back around midnight, Easy. I'll be gone but Kirby will be here still."

"Until that time."

23

We went to Tommy's on Beverly and ordered four chili burgers, two chili-cheese fries, and a few cans of Cel-Ray soda. I sat eating at one of the picnic benches the twenty-four-hour burger stand provided for customers. Fearless borrowed a few coins and went to a pay phone to make him a call.

He returned after fifteen minutes or so.

"Long call," I commented.

"Bonita."

"Your girl?"

"Oh yeah. You know, Easy, if I had come to her house she would'a cursed me out and th'owed my clothes in the mud. She might'a even tried to stab me."

"Because you was in jail?"

"Not exactly."

"What exactly?"

"She missed me," he said on a shrug. "You know when you in love and your friend is gone, some people get all crazy."

I thought then that Fearless, in spite of his less-than-stellar intelligence, would make a great psychotherapist. He understood feelings the way a boxer knew when a blow was coming from behind.

"You a good man, Fearless Jones."

"That and a dime, Easy, that and a dime."

For the next hour or so I let him regale me about his adventures in World War II.

"...I come on this one house outside Munich where this group'a Allied soldiers had trapped six or so women," he was saying. "They had 'em in rooms and was usin' 'em—you know."

I did know.

Fearless tightened up and glowered at his food.

"I had to kill two of 'em before they give up their crime. I would'a killed 'em all if I had to."

That was the way it was among Black people back then. We killed and were killed, fought and lost a thousand battles before a life was done. I didn't ask Fearless the race of those soldiers. That didn't matter. It wasn't about race. In his perfect heart there was only right and wrong.

"Fearless!" a woman from somewhere screamed. "Where are you!"

"Uh-oh," Mr. Jones uttered. Then he called out, "Ovah here, B."

She appeared out of the darkness like some ancient Scandinavian goddess with black skin come down to count the dead. Her dress was silver. Her handbag, red as blood, and her hair was dyed blond. Bonita Williams was twenty-eight going on a century, fine as any woman could want to be, and filled with a passion that wanted either to make or take a life that night.

She strutted up to our picnic table with her fists clenched and her eyes at odds with each other.

"Excuse me, Easy," she commanded.

I would have moved away if Fearless hadn't spoken up.

"Uh-uh, no," he said. "I'm sittin' here talkin' wit' my friend and you got no right to send him away."

"I need to talk to you," Bonita told Fearless.

"Oh yeah? For the last three months I needed some talk. I needed a woman to bring me chocolate or make my bail. I needed a friend when all I could count was enemies."

"I couldn't," she said and stalled. "I couldn't bear to see my beautiful man in that place."

"Lucky for me there was another woman could."

"What woman?"

"Missy," he said in as blasé a tone as I ever heard from him.

"My...my mother?"

"You better believe it. She told you to come see me, and then, when you said no, she come herself. Now, take your red bag and your silver ass home and I might call ya when me an' Easy finish our business."

Bonita didn't know what to do. She wanted him to pay for her pain but now saw that he was willing to let her go. She stared at him with killer eyes, and then, all at once, she turned and stormed off.

Fearless and I sat quietly a moment, two.

"I suppose we should be gettin' back to King Pong," I suggested.

By the time we got back, the indoor sports parlor was closed. I knocked and Fearless peered through the tinted window into the shadow-shrouded room.

"Easy Rawlins," a man called from the corner of the building.

Down the dark block, thirty yards or so away, stood "Hard

Hand" Bernard Kirby. Jawbreaker, Skull-Buster, Bone-Bruiser Kirby.

He walked up to us with all the pride and confidence of a world champion. We were nothing to him, little people sitting in the nosebleed seats.

"BK," I said when he got to us.

"You're Fearless Jones, right?" he asked my friend.

Fearless nodded demurely.

Kirby turned to me then. "What you want, Easy Rawlins? Drake said that it was sumpin' 'bout some typewriters and Mouse. But I know Mouse don't sell hardware and you work for the cops."

"I work for myself and my clients."

Hands clenched, Kirby took an aggressive step in my direction.

"An' those clients got a truckload of typewriters?" He could have broken my jaw with either fist.

I gave a weak shrug and said, "I wanted to keep my real question a secret, so that's what I told Drake."

"Tell me why the fuck I don't kick the shit outta you and your boyfriend right here and now."

"Thousand dollars."

The boxer's shoulders did something that made him seem much less aggressive. I gleaned for only a moment the kind of topography that boxers must witness in the ring. Just that one movement told a complex tale.

"For what?" Kirby asked, almost politely.

"You have a movie clip concerning Terrence Laks..." I began.

Those docile shoulders turned into a pair of Sherman tanks within the span of a fruit fly's heartbeat. But, faster than that,

Fearless hit the boxer three times: in the head, in the head, and in the head. This wasn't as straightforward as it sounds, because Kirby's head was moving at a downward arc from the first blow.

Once he was on the ground and unconscious, Fearless turned to me and asked, "You saw that, right?"

"I saw it but that was just about all."

"You should go get the car, Ease."

I did as he asked.

"We both gettin' old, Easy," Fearless said from the back seat as we drove out toward the woods beyond Griffith Park.

He was sitting next to the slumped-over form of Bernard Kirby and I was driving with a purpose but no particular destination in mind. I wasn't worried about getting in trouble over Kirby. Even if the cops stopped us, he would never turn us over. At that time almost all Black men, and women, over a certain age knew that anything having to do with the law ended badly for everyone involved. So, when a cop asked a man of my hue, "What happened?" he was, most often, met with glacial silence.

"What you mean *old*, Mr. Jones?"

"You should'a at least pulled back from Benny, and in my younger days I should'a put him down with one punch."

"There's a turnoff up ahead, man. Looks like some trees beyond that."

I parked and got out to make sure that we weren't in somebody's front yard. Once I was certain that we were alone, Fearless pulled the groggy BK out and leaned him up against the hood of the car. The fresh air along with a few hard slaps brought him to awareness.

What he saw was Fearless Jones and me.

I had the gun Lihn had lent me and was ready to use it on one of his extremities. Bernard was a boxer by trade, and he would, more likely than not, feel that he could fight his way out of any predicament. That conviction was usually negated by bullets.

"What the fuck you niggahs want?" he challenged.

"We want to give you some money and in the process save your life," I said with as much equanimity as an armed man can muster.

"Save my life how?"

I had his attention out there in the darkness, among the crickets and the cooling air.

"Tommy Jester reach out to you lately?" I asked.

"What if he did?"

"Tommy's dead. Shot down in the alley around the corner from his apartment."

The boxer glanced down at my gun hand.

"We didn't do it, brother," I said. "I asked him the same question I'm gonna ask you. But instead of lookin' after himself, he called the man in question."

"The what?"

"He called Terry Laks."

Kirby was no genius, but he was pretty good at one plus one.

"So, so you think he was tryin' to get a better deal from the cop?"

"Nobody else in the game."

"And they know about me?"

"I doubt it."

"Why?"

"Because you're still breathing."

That took a few mental steps, but he made it there.

"What if I did the same thing that Tommy did?" Kirby conjectured.

"First of all," I opined, "you'd end up in the same street. Second, you won't do it."

"Why not?"

"Because you are going to give the film to us."

"Or what?"

"Or I put you in the ground and plant bamboo on your ass," Fearless Jones replied.

I had to forgive my friend his anger. He'd just spent three months in the Los Angeles County Jail—a place worse than war.

Kirby could fight when he thought he had the chance to win. Fearless Jones fought when there was no chance whatsoever. He was a Black soldier who went behind Nazi lines when Germany was still winning the war. He was a killer.

"Well then," Kirby said with a pleading tone, "why don't you cut me in on it?"

"This is not some kinda blackmail thing," I said. "The thousand dollars comin' outta my own pocket."

"How'm I gonna believe that?"

I raised the muzzle of my pistol to his knee level with every intention of shooting. But outpacing that fruit fly's heart once more, Kirby said, "All right, all right."

24

Bernard lived in a small rented house on the 5000 block of McKinley Avenue down in South Central LA. Set back from the street, the front of the house was also behind a screen of bushes and two trees. He led us into the front room and turned on the overhead light from a wall switch.

"Anybody here with you?" I asked.

"My girl's up in Sacramento with her sister."

"Anybody comin'?" Fearless wondered.

"Not that I know of."

"Okay then," I said. "Let's get to it."

The only bedroom was small but had an unusually wide and deep double-doored closet. Inside that closet most of the clothes were piled on the floor, emanating a strong musty odor. Benny rummaged around for and found a small flat sixteen-millimeter-film container box with the words *Sex Film* scrawled upon it.

"Here you go," our temporary prisoner said, handing me the little package. "Now, where my money at?"

"This ain't over yet, brothah," I said.

"Why not? You got what you asked for."

"I need to see it."

"Hold it up to a light," he said, trying to dismiss my request.

"No, man, no. You gonna show us this shit or you'll spend the rest'a your life wishin' you had."

The concern and contradictory craftiness on Kirby's face caused me to raise the pistol and pull back the hammer.

"Hey, hey, hey, hey," the boxer complained while holding up his hands. "That's the tape you aksed for right there."

I wanted to kill him. I did.

"If you don't have a film projector somewhere in that mess, I'm gonna shoot you right here on this bed," I said.

"It's, it's, it's in the checkered box ovah on the right side, in the corner."

Fearless pulled out the projector and started setting it up on the long bench placed at the foot of the bed.

"Is this the right tape?" I asked our prisoner.

"Naw. That was another one Tommy had me do. I figured it would'a looked good if you didn't have no projection."

"You better have the real one."

"In the night table draw."

We projected the real film on the pink door of Kirby's moldering closet. Six minutes in length, it depicted Laks standing between two young women, one white and the other Black—both on their knees.

The white one had her face buried in his butt while the Black one was playing flute along his stubby erection. I wondered if whoever saw this tableau would hate the Black girl for being Black or the white one for the tattoos on her side and ass. In those days tattoos were the domain of merchant marines,

Japanese gangsters, and convicts who hated everything, even their own skins.

"You got my money?" Kirby demanded.

I eased the hammer back into place and then hit Kirby upside his head, harder than I remember ever hitting any man, or beast. He was out before landing on the mattress. After that I sprinkled the money on his chest.

"Let's go," I said to my friend.

"What's wrong with you, Easy?" Fearless asked as we drove west down posh Sunset Boulevard.

"What you mean? I'm all right."

"Naw, naw, don't be fuckin' around. You know what I mean. You don't go round beatin' on some niggah just 'cause he got a bad attitude. Shit. We the ones put him in that mood."

The road was nearly void of traffic. We passed huge mansions, UCLA, and vast, parklike lawns. It would have been a lovely journey except for the fact that we were two Black men in a part of town that wasn't particularly welcoming. The white residents were wary of men like Fearless and me, and the police were given more or less free rein to make sure we felt unwelcome. But that was business as usual and I was acquainted with most of the patrolmen who haunted Sunset.

I wasn't looking over my shoulder for official threats. I was looking for an answer to Fearless's question, but there was no clear explanation.

After a long internal search, I only managed to come up with a tale from my youth.

"When I was a young man," I said, "maybe nineteen, I was

down in Fifth Ward Houston raisin' hell and believin' I was grown."

"I remember them days," Fearless said. "Shit. Back then even the cops kept away after the sun went down."

"Yeah." Slowly, the thoughts that bound me were becoming not so much clear but...present.

"One night back then I got a message from EttaMae Harris," I said. "She sent Little Liam over to the place where I stayed. He told me that Etta said that Raymond was at the Blacksmiths' Bar and that I should get over there quick. I asked him should I talk to her first and he said that she said I could talk to her after.

"I loved Etta. Mouse was my best friend, still is, but I loved Etta. She was the kinda Black woman stand right by you, no matter what."

"Yes, she is," Fearless said. "She used to bring her son down to Paris's old bookstore in the day. Just the way she looked at you made you feel like bein' a man was all right by her."

"Yeah," I agreed. "Anyway. I found Raymond at Blacksmiths' Bar maybe two in the mornin'. I knew there was trouble because the other bargoers were more quiet than usual. Raymond was sittin' at a table by hisself and the tables on either side of him were empty."

"Uh-oh," my passenger said.

"Yeah. I walked up to where he was sittin' and said his name. He looked up, squinted, waited for almost a full minute or more before sayin', 'Ease.'

"I sat, drank from his bottle, and waited till he started talkin' all on his own.

"He told me that he was at a woman's house the night before. Her name was Bertha Bee. And after a drink or two they started fuckin' like wolves out on the plain—his words. They just couldn't stop. Mouse had been with a lotta women but he said that he nevah felt that strong before. And then her boyfriend, Nate Grimly, came home. He grabbed for his pistol but Mouse switched it up, he threw a chair at his ass. When he went down, Raymond jumped up an' started beatin' him like he was his daddy. He told me that he had every intention of killin' that niggah. But Bertha put her arms around his shoulders and pulled him away to the bed. She started kissin' an' tellin' him that she needed it bad...'"

"Damn," Fearless uttered. He could feel the conflicting passions in Raymond's secondhand memories. "What happened?"

"That's what I asked him. He told me that Bertha dragged him to the bed and fucked him till he couldn't no mo'. Then she fed him whiskey till he passed out."

"What happent to Nate?"

"Bertha drug him to a hospital and sat ovah him for three days till he opened his eyes. Mouse tried to get in touch with her, but she let him know that she wouldn't be with him ever again."

"Whoa," said Fearless Jones. "She realized how much she loved her man while Raymond was just about killin' 'im."

"Yeah. He been lookin for that kinda love ever since."

"He didn't feel it with Etta?"

"I guess not."

"Okay, okay. All right. But that was a long time ago and you ain't Mouse. What any'a that got to do with you hittin' Benny like that?"

"I don't know," I lied.

25

We had come to a stop on the moonlit dirt path, deep in the Santa Monica Mountains.

"Where the fuck you got me, Easy Rawlins?"

We climbed out of my nondescript automobile and approached the tiny cabin.

As we moved toward the little domicile, a light snapped on and the rough-hewn sentry emerged. That night he was wearing clothes made from thick wool and hard canvas.

"Cosmo," I said.

"Mr. Easy," he replied.

"This is my friend — Fearless."

The Sicilian looked Fearless up and down, nodded slightly, and then said, "With a name like that you must have to prove yourself every day."

Nodding modestly, Fearless replied, "That's a Black man's load on these shores."

Cosmo grinned, showing us a smile missing at least four teeth.

"Gaetano up on the hill?" I asked the gatekeeper.

"Matteo. He went up after bringing Feather home."

I touched Fearless on the shoulder and pointed at a hillside down the way from my mountain.

"One man to guard the gate and one to open fire if he need it."

"What is this place?" my friend asked again.

"Paradise," I said as Cosmo Longo opened the double-deep chain-link gate.

He walked us the fifteen steps to the funicular.

Before Cosmo pulled shut the sliding door I asked, "Who's up there?"

"Jesus, Benita, Feather, the baby, and dogs."

"Full house, huh?"

Cosmo grinned and locked us in.

"What is this, Easy?" Fearless asked again.

"My home."

The car began its grinding ascent up the mountain. Fearless grabbed on to the door and I felt a little spark of pride that I made the much-decorated war hero a wee bit nervous.

We walked past the circular concrete landing of Brighthope Canyon and then down the long blue-brick path past the other five mansions there.

We made it maybe halfway across the broad single-room first floor with its high walls and the natural stream flowing through. At that point my friend stopped and gaped.

"This is your house?"

"Yeah."

"How much it cost?"

"I got it free from the woman owns the mountain."

"She just give it to you?"

"Ninety-nine year lease."

"For real?"

"I signed the contract almost two years ago. Paid her with a two-dollar bill. One dollar for me and the other for Feather."

"And what that cost?"

"Every now and then she ask me for a favor, but most the time she just likes to watch Feather practice in the pool."

Shaking his head my friend said, "You the luckiest niggah I ever met in my life."

"Mouse once said that to me," I chortled. "I told him that I had plenty of bad things in my day. He said, 'I didn't say you had good luck, just luck, and a whole lot of it.'"

Fearless laughed heartily.

"Dad," came a voice from the curved stairway that spiraled its way up the round-walled four-story house.

"Juice," I said to the son of my heart.

He bounded down the stairs wearing white overalls with long sleeves and about a dozen pockets.

"Hi, Mr. Jones," the young man greeted before hugging me.

"Jesus," Fearless greeted. "What you doin' up this time'a night?"

"Going over plans to start a fishin' business."

"Easy, don't you have no lazy kids? You know, that sit around all day wonderin' when they was gonna be football stars."

His joke brought up a question in my mind.

"How many kids you got, Fearless?"

He grimaced and rubbed the fingers of his left hand across his brow.

"Ohhhh, maybe fifteen if nobody lied. But, for that matter, maybe twenty if they did."

Many women wanted Fearless to be the father of their kids,

but few of these wanted him as a husband. He was not a man open to domestication. If he met a mendicant with a problem, he'd bring that soul home. If he lost his temper, war wouldn't be far behind. He might lose his house, his car, his bank account, at a moment's notice, and that was not marriage material.

"You guys want some coffee?" Jesus offered.

"Tea for me," Fearless said.

Upstairs, on the second-floor kitchen level, the three of us sat at the high table-ledge surrounding the cooking area of the kitchen. Below our stools sat the yellow and brown dogs that belonged to my sleeping daughter.

"You know sumpin', Easy?" Fearless said. "I'm'a get you a real dog, a guard dog."

"I already got two."

"These here are nice toys for chirren," he said, "but a man like you, a man your age, needs a serious mutt. I'll take care of it."

"Whatever you say, Fearless. Juice?"

"Yeah, Dad. Get our guest some blankets and show him the sleeping couch downstairs."

"Okay."

The scent of coffee aroused me, along with the sun through my upper-floor window.

I stumbled down the stairs to the third floor, where the children stayed. But they weren't there. Jesus had made his and Benita's bed. Even Feather's blankets were tucked in.

They were gathered on the kitchen level, sitting around the raised table-bar. Fearless had made his specialty, buckwheat cakes and bacon. The kids and dogs were all excited. Fearless was the kind of family friend that everybody loved.

"Mr. Rawlins," my friend of many years greeted. "I don't think I ever remember you sleepin' this late."

"Like you said, Fearless, gettin' old."

Fearless regaled the assembly with PG-rated tales of his adventures in various wars and military actions. There were bridges blown off their moorings and ammunition stores ignited by fire. He told these tales because, as a listener, you were far enough away not to have to think about blown-apart and burnt bodies.

"Do you ever want to go back to war?" my adolescent daughter asked, her eyes aglimmer.

Fearless looked into Feather's eager face and a shadow seemed to come between them.

"Naw, baby girl, naw. I mean if your daddy or maybe Paris had trouble, I might motivate myself to do this or that, but war don't give a damn about the butcher or the baker. If you just a ordinary citizen in war today, they more likely to kill you than they are a real soldier."

That was a fitting end to an otherwise joyous morning.

"So, guys," I called while Benita and Jesus washed the dishes and Feather played patty-cake with Essie on one of the high chairs.

"What, Dad?" Jesus asked.

"What if we had Fearless stay up here a while?"

Feather and Juice got serious looks on their young faces.

"Something that bad?" they asked in unison.

"Not if he's here," I said with equal gravity.

Essie started crying.

"But, but Erculi and his sons already guard the mountain," Feather said.

"Yes," I agreed, "but they're here for everybody and they work for Sadie. Fearless is our friend."

The mood lightened again. Essie laughed again. In that pleasant space Fearless and I made our way back down the mountainside and into my car.

Our first stop was a gentlemen's clothing store on Flower downtown. Fearless's clothes were at Bonita's house, but neither of us wanted to encounter her brooding anger. That would have taken too much time.

On top of that, where we were going, Fearless needed some winter clothes, and so did I.

Etienne's Compleat Man had everything. Men from around Los Angeles went there to cover their nakedness in style.

Fearless got two pairs of trousers, three shirts, one sports jacket, and a pair of leather shoes. We both got overcoats, winter hats, and heavy gloves in preparation for an expedition.

The tailor had to adjust Fearless's buys and so we didn't get to Police Central until midafternoon.

Following our usual route, we made it to the front desk and asked the officer sitting there if we might be announced to Melvin Suggs's office.

"Commander Suggs is not in today," the blocky and pale senior sergeant informed us. He had a huge, bright-pink discoloration over his left eye and another one on his right cheek.

"We're here to meet with his assistant, Myra Lawless," I countered.

"Meet with her about what?"

"That is a private matter."

"How am I to know that?" he challenged softly.

"By calling her and saying that Mr. Rawlins and Mr. Jones are here for our meeting."

It's always pleasing when logic trumps simple tribal hatred.

We negotiated a mostly unused hallway to its far end, scaled six flights of stairs, and then came to a door, which opened onto another door, upon which we knocked.

A short but not small gray-haired woman answered. She gave me a pleasant enough glance, but when she got a load of Fearless she broke out into a grin.

"Mr. Jones," she exclaimed, "and Mr. Rawlins," she added for the sake of civility. "Come in. Come in."

Myra poured us coffee from a pot she kept on a pine file cabinet behind the desk.

"Coffee-Mate?" she offered.

"I like the stuff from the real cow," Fearless said, "not no powder come from a test tube."

I think Myra would have laughed if my friend had recited the ABCs.

"I'll take some," I said, knowing the bitterness of the ancient percolator's urn.

She poured our coffee. I took the creamer cylinder and shook yellowy-white powder into my cup.

We made small talk for a while. Fearless knew Myra's pets by name, species, and disposition. That little powwow went on for maybe five minutes.

"How you doin', Myra?" I asked, getting down to business.

"It's been hard, Mr. Rawlins. Melvin is gone and I have no idea when he's gonna be back. I don't even know where he is or why he left. Just that all his messages have to be sent to Captain McCourt."

The coffee was hot. It singed the tip of my tongue.

"But you must have some idea," I suggested. "I mean, nobody in the world knows Mel better than you."

"No, not really." She looked down at the desktop feeling a sadness that only friendship can conjure. "But I don't have any idea of where he might have gone."

"Well," I said, "then will you let me ask a couple of questions?"

"Questions about what?"

"Mel. He's my friend and his girl, Mary, is worried."

"Mary," Myra spat. "That bitch is the cause of all his problems. You can bet on that."

"Be that as it may. He loves her and she him, in her own way."

Myra settled a bit and then looked into my eyes.

"What do you have to ask?"

"Mary says that there was an overcoat missing from Mel's closet. When I heard that I remembered, before he ever knew her, he used to go to a cabin somewhere up in the snow."

At first Myra looked at me with suspicion that might have turned to violence in some.

Then she turned to Fearless and asked, "Can I trust you to protect him?"

"Yes, ma'am."

I was taught from an early age that you had to respect people and be straightforward in your dealings with them. This was true even for white people—as far as you could trust them not to lynch you from a poplar tree.

"All human beings have souls and so deserve respect." That's what my old-man mentor Sorry told me when I was no more than eleven and scratching for my daily crumb. Because of my deep respect for that ancient elder, I tried in my dealings to be good and fair without, as much as possible, manipulating folks.

I have tried, over the many years during and since my hard-scrabble orphanhood, to be honest, truthful, and fair. But, living these long hard years of American freedom, I have had to learn that most people exist in a complex maze of manipulation.

Fearless, for instance.

He was a child of nature who knew things that he was not aware of. Women, children, creatures large and small, were drawn to him. For many he was a touchstone, an almost magical being who transcended the mortal flaws and foibles that limited most members of the human race.

He didn't know all that. Fearless thought that he was an every-day sort of guy. He foraged, fucked, fought, and freely shared whatever he had, and expected these qualities in others. Anyone who strayed from these *norms* Fearless saw as a deviant, though I doubt if he would have ever used that word. Because he was, probably still is, so guileless, people like Myra Lawless could see that he was a kind of human shelter, someone, even something, that could be relied on as constant in the everyday chaos of human relations.

That sounds beautiful. Mother Nature's son and a woman who could see him for what he is.

It would have been the perfect honest relationship...if not for me. Myra could trust Fearless but not me. My job was to find Melvin, help him if I could, but also use him to untangle a woman whom I didn't know at all from a crime that might be the end of me.

So, Fearless promised Myra that she could trust him. He believed this. She believed in him and so said, "It's a cabin up outside of Big Bear City. Maybe five miles up into the mountains from there, on a road called Myer's Peak."

26

We'd made it through Pomona, past Ontario, and were half the way to Fontana when Fearless started his line of inquiry again.

Seemingly out of nowhere he said, "I get it that Raymond Alexander is crazy. And I know what it's like when you with a woman and somebody try and get in the way. I could even understand it why a man might get mad that a woman lay down with him to save another man that she truly love."

"That's a lotta understandin', Fearless. But what are you tryin' to say?"

"Same thing. Wonderin' why you hit Benny in the head when you didn't have to."

"Why that matter so much to you?"

"Because I'd bet dollars to doughnuts that that's the same reason we drivin' up to the country."

"Why you say that?"

"Com'on, Ease, you ain't got to be no genius to see trouble starin' you in the face. You ain't nevah even took me up to your house before and now I'm a invited guest. Don't get me wrong, I appreciate the invite, but I can tell you gettin' ready for some kinda war and I just like to know the sides."

Again, I was using Fearless. This time it wasn't even a

conscious plan. I knew that he saw and felt things that I did not. I knew that he was more than just a strong arm and a man I could trust. What I didn't know was that he was about to reveal my heart to me.

"I met a girl," I said, "a woman."

"She got sumpin' to do with the cop?"

"Not a goddamn thing. At least not on the face of it."

"Then what?"

I told Fearless about Amethystine Stoller, her missing (now dead) ex-husband, and how I wanted, more than anything, to set her free.

"So, you knew from the beginnin' that you needed the cop—Suggs?"

"Naw. I was just tryin' to take a shortcut with him and then I found out that he was in trouble too. I could see that if I got him through whatever problem he was havin', he might could help Amethystine if she needed it."

"Hm," the war hero grunted.

I let that pass.

Myra had given us pretty good directions and so we made our way past the snow line, up into the San Bernardino National Forest. It wasn't yet evening, but the sun had gone down by the time we passed the ski resort. After that we drove along the shore of Big Bear Lake until reaching the village they call Big Bear City.

A few people stared at us as we drove down the main street, past isolated restaurants, souvenir shops, and stands.

After that we were making our way up a barely paved road, onto a mountain that seemed to hunch over the lake. The cabin we were looking for was certainly isolated.

Every hundred feet or so there was a light pole giving some notion of the dividing line between the forest and the road. Even though it had been plowed, the zigzagging path was slippery. Once or twice, it felt as if I was going to lose control.

Then Fearless called out, "Over there, Easy."

I don't know how he saw the weak electric light and the slanting flash of synthetic blue wall through clumps of dark-green pine needles. There was no car parked there and no other sign of life. But we pulled to the side and made our way up a long and uneven trail of disintegrating wooden steps.

Fearless and I had a slippery time negotiating that climb. Our shoes weren't made for walking on snow and ice. Our socks didn't do much to keep our feet warm either.

There were thirty-nine steps up the steep incline and I couldn't help but think of the movie, the book, and Alfred Hitchcock. The porch, which was just a jagged line of four-by-four pine timbers, tilted this way and that, emulating a drunkard's attempt to toe the line.

By the time we got to the front door we were both out of breath. I knocked, wondering if maybe I was on some hopeless campaign that would end in failure. Then the door came open, framing the pathetic figure of the fifth-most-important cop in the LAPD.

His hair was askew, and the buttons of his red-and-black woolen lumberjack shirt were fastened out of sequence. His facial hair had been growing but had not filled in, and would not soon do so. The whites of his eyes were red and their violet centers unfocused. Rye whiskey scented the atmosphere around him.

There were other, bodily, fragrances too.

"Easy?" His voice was hoarse, as if it hadn't been used for some time. "What the fuck you doin' here?"

At that moment Fearless began to shiver.

"What do you think, Mel?"

He stared at me, leaned forward, almost toppled, but then righted himself using the doorjamb. He looked up and it was as if he was now seeing me for the first time, again.

"Easy?"

"Hey, man," Fearless said. "Can we get in outta this here cold?"

"Oh," the muddled cop said. "What you doin' here?"

I walked past him into the rude but spacious one-room cabin. Fearless was no more than a step behind me. The walls, floor, and roof were rough-hewn and unpainted. There was a large loft above the cooking area that had its inner wall open to the room. The huge fireplace was dead and cold, so Fearless began to work with the logs scattered before it.

"Fireplace don't work," Mel managed to say. "Smoke comes right back down."

Fearless grabbed an adze that was leaning against the side of the hearth and started poking at the inner walls of the chimney.

"Come on, Mel," I said, taking him by the arm.

"Where?"

"Shit, shower, and shave. Hot coffee, clean clothes, and hard talk."

Sometimes men need each other's help. In an ideal world we want to be strong and independent. We'd rather die than ask for a handout, rather go hungry than go on the dole. On top of all that, fighting was second nature to the men of my generation. And the best fights were the ones we knew we couldn't win.

What you say to me? Pee Wee demands of the behemoth.

But after the fracas, when the colossus has laid Pee Wee low, his buddies take the defeated hero home and patch him up. That's what Fearless and I were there for. Melvin Suggs had put his entire demesne on the line to protect the woman he loved. Heroism like that takes it all out of a man. Women go through pain like that every month—more often, sometimes. In many ways that has been women's lot in history. But... that said, they need us to be heroes now and then too. They need us to at least try to get it right. And when we try, usually failing, we need our brothers to be there.

I led Mel to his toilet, sat outside on a three-legged stool through his toil, threw him into an ice-cold shower, and shaved him myself. While I did these things Fearless literally disappeared up the chimney, picking and chipping the black and brown creosote from the smokestack walls.

"How you doin' up there, Fearless?" I called into the funnel at one point.

"Least my blood is runnin'."

While Fearless was clearing a passage in the flue, Mel and I swept the debris away from the area surrounding the hearth. Before we were done Fearless had reduced eight squat logs to kindling.

While the war hero worked on starting a fire, I heated canned chili over a butane grill. This I poured over Fritos and grated cheese while I made coffee and Fearless washed off the soot. Mel watched us, unable to do much more.

When the hearth was filled with flame, Mel roused himself to clean off the dining table by pushing all the papers, tin dishes, and other detritus to the floor. I served the food on paper plates, took Mel's bottle of rye from his hand, and seated myself between my friends.

We ate and grunted, talked about the fight that Emile Griffith had waged against José Nápoles, and how beautiful the mountain was.

We'd made it all the way through a third cup of coffee when Mel asked, "How the fuck you two find me?"

I explained in detail each of the steps and missteps that had brought me and Fearless to Commander Suggs's decomposing front porch.

After that he told us pretty much the same story Mary had reported.

"I thought it was gonna be easy," Melvin said.

"You're kidding."

"No. I let the guy think I was setting him free when really I got my sergeant to temporarily misplace the evidence. That way I could pull him in anytime I wanted to."

"So, what happened?"

"Laks."

"Yeah, I heard he put out a warrant on you."

"Where you hear that?"

"From Mary."

"You talked to her?"

"Anything wrong with that?"

"She told me she was leaving town."

"I'on't know what to tell ya, man. I called her tryin' to find out what happened to you. She came out to see me on the mountain, asking me to get in touch with this dude Tommy Jester."

"Where is she now?" he asked, cutting me off. It was obvious that Mel was more worried about her than himself.

"I got one'a my people to put her in a place nobody could find."

I don't think anyone had ever stared at me harder than Mel did right then. He studied me like a hunted man looking for the flaws in his pursuers.

Finally, he said, "She's safe?"

"The queen of England in her royal bed."

He gazed at me a moment more and then let his head fall, no longer able to find the strength.

"There's no warrant out on me," he said to the tabletop.

"That's not good," Fearless Jones intoned. "If a cop is after you, then you're safer with a warrant."

Mel raised his head to regard me.

"Anybody follow you?"

"I sincerely doubt it. Most of the road we traveled was empty, ahead and behind."

"You tell anybody where you were going?"

"Myra gave us directions. I don't think she'd tell."

"Where'd you meet?" he asked.

That question turned my head toward the front door.

"My office, huh?" Mel added.

"You really think he'd bug you? You?"

The only electrical outlet in the cabin was a double plug connected to a space heater set down next to Mel's reading chair. Apart from one standing electric light, the rest of the lamps were kerosene.

Fearless went around turning them all down low.

For some reason the darkness increased the feeling of silence. We hunkered down in that quietude, listening for the trouble that Mel's semi-sobriety had just brought to light.

"I should go out there," Fearless hissed after a few minutes.

"We all should," Mel added.

"No." My heart was beating fast. And there was a feeling in my chest that I hadn't experienced since 1944. "When he wanna be, Fearless is the shadow that a shadow casts."

At that moment, maybe even before I finished saying those words, I saw something like an afterimage in the window over the table where we'd eaten. By the time I'd registered the wraith-like passing it was gone and I was shooting, not at the window but at the thin pine wall just below. I had six bullets and shot five.

Fearless belly-crawled to the front door and then said, "When I say 'now,' throw somethin' through the glass."

Mel picked up a coffee mug and nodded, looking somewhat like a bulldog.

"NOW!"

The pane shattered, Fearless lunged through the front door, and two more shots were fired. Then, once again, there was silence.

I was back in the final days of World War II. My buddy, my comrade, had just risked and maybe lost his life doing his duty, as so many of us had done in that great conflagration. My heart was a young man's heart. My fear went all the way back to a time before machines or even written language.

There were a few rustling sounds and then, "It's okay," Fearless called out. "He dead."

Mel shone a flashlight on the body. Then he turned the corpse over.

"Bradley Mirth," he said.

It was a big white man in military-like fatigues. His face was broad, with one eye open. He'd received at least six wounds.

"Who is he?" I asked.

"Used to be LAPD back in the days of Parker and his Night Riders. The ones who enforced laws that were never written down."

"He was with my people in the war," Fearless said. "They say he was as good as me but that he took a few more chances."

"Then why didn't you recognize him?" I pointed out.

"Just knew the name. The major run the unit made sure we never crossed paths. You know, what they call philosophical differences."

"You think anybody gonna come up here and check out the shots?" I asked Mel.

"Hard to say. There're shots at night out here pretty often."

"All we got to do is pull out that ratty old couch to cover the bullet holes and the blood," Fearless opined. "If anybody aks, you tell 'em you saw a bear out the window and shot at it 'cause you were drunk. You guys do that, and I'll get rid'a Mr. Mirth here."

"No." That was me.

"No what?" Fearless challenged.

"Help me wrap him up in a carpet or somethin'. I'll get rid'a the body while you make the place look decent."

We argued some.

Mel was unused to witnessing a crime and not reporting it. He certainly didn't want to cover it up. He felt that innocence was its own reward. But I was able to persuade him that a body, one of an ex-cop, would lose him his influence and probably make Mary into a fugitive.

Fearless was of the opinion that he was best qualified to

dismember and discard a corpse. All things being equal, he was probably right. But all things weren't.

"Help me load him in the trunk," I told my friends, "and I'll take him down the hill. After cleaning up here, Fearless, you go with Mel in his car and put him up in that hotel you showed me."

"What if any'a his friends are out there?" Mel asked, quite reasonably.

"Mirth was a loner," Fearless said. "I've heard it that even his mama couldn't stand him."

Melvin had no carpeting in his rustic pied-à-terre. He did have four woolen blankets and about twenty-five feet of thick hemp rope. Fearless and I wrapped and trussed up the bloody corpse. Carrying two hundred pounds' worth of deadweight was a lot, even for three men. By the time we got him into the trunk of my car, my hands and feet were numb, and I was shivering.

"Where's your car, Mel?"

"Up the path a little."

"Okay. If I'm lucky I'll see you in the morning."

27

Later that night, on the way back to LA, I stopped at a twenty-four-hour filling station to make a long-distance call.

"Shep," a man answered on the ninth ring.

"Tell her it's a starry night," I said, and then I hung up.

There I was, a Black man in 1970, driving through the countryside with a corpse in the trunk. I had a trick or two up my sleeve and a loaded .38 in my pocket.

One of the good things about having lived half a century under the weight of second- and third-class citizenship—bad luck was never a surprise.

If they wanted me they would get me. That was all there was to it.

It was just shy of 3:00 a.m. by the time I got to the edge of one of the last wooded areas in Compton. When I drove up, she emerged from the bamboo thicket.

Tall, Black, wearing a long dress that would have been in style somewhere in the world in any of the last five centuries, Mama Jo gestured for me to drive into a cleared-out spot in the cane. After I drove in she pulled a bamboo scrim to hide the dark car.

Jo was twenty years my senior, but she was still vital and strong. She kissed me on the lips and I opened the trunk.

"Any metal on him?" were her first words to me.

"Naw," I said, shaking my head. "Fearless and I both checked him."

"Okay then, I got a wheelbarrow right ovah here."

We dumped the corpse, blankets and all, into the pushcart and wheeled Brad Mirth to a place behind a rude cabin.

The backyard of Jo's medieval cottage was carpeted with thick grasses and surrounded by heavy oaks. It was lit by a high-powered soda-vapor lamp that topped a ten-foot concrete pole. There were two deep-set wooden chairs and a table that was also a trunk. I never knew what she kept in that trunk, but there was an eight-foot-high double-walled oak barrel that was nestled in a three-foot depression under the oldest tree. It was a barrel I knew quite well.

"You look kinda peaked, Easy," Jo said when we were both seated.

Not knowing what to say, I hunched my shoulders and swung my head a few inches to the left. I had no idea what these gestures might mean, but I was pretty sure that my host did.

"There's a jug down on your left," she said. "Take two good chugs."

I reached for the heavy ceramic jar, lifted it to my lips, and took the first draft.

"We didn't even talk, Jo," I said. "How'd you know I'd need just this blend?"

"You a sensitive soul, baby," she said in an up tempo. "If you was gonna ask for a starry Night, I knew you'd need a swig of Tranquility. But now I see your eye, I figure you need at least two."

I took the second dose. The flavor was like a whole lemon that had been blended in an Osterizer, seasoned with strong vinegar and fresh loam.

The effect was immediate, though I find it a little hard to explain. I was aware of my breath and also the space that my body occupied. The strong light of the soda lamp felt as if it had weight, and this pressure seemed to buoy rather than oppress me.

Mama Jo was a witch in the oldest understanding of that term. She had knowledge of a great history of natural medicines, drugs, and ways to enhance and even elongate life. She also knew poisons. She had mastered elixirs, vapors, powders, and even stones that, when they came in contact with the skin, could cause anything from temporary suffering to permanent psychosis to death.

She was the Black woman who lived on the outskirts of town that no one messed with. There's one in every southern hamlet and village. A woman who had apprentices who would avenge her death should any harm come to her.

When I was a teenager and she was nearly forty, Jo took me as her lover for a night, or maybe it was two. While making love she whispered to me, telling me things that I will never forget. She pampered and pounded me, fell in love with me in a way that she'd never abandon.

"What's up with you, Easy?"

Fearless had asked me that question and I'd answered him after a fashion, but Jo's inquiry, along with those swigs of Tranquility, had a whole other effect.

"I'on't know, Jo. I mean, I met a woman who is all the way serious, know what I mean? Smart, pretty, Black, and not worried one whit about what somebody think."

"Sounds like a woman made for you. A woman drawn to the kinda world you live in."

"She asked me to find her ex-husband and I did...but he was dead. Murdered."

"That sound even more like you."

"Uh-huh. It does. And you know, usually I know how to keep my distance. Like a, like a, like a junkie know where the junk's at and still stay away."

I took a third swig of Tranquility.

"You know, baby," Jo said with the gentlest smile on her generous lips. "A man can run his entire life, but that don't mean he gonna get away. You know what I'm talkin' 'bout."

I did. I did, and I also knew that there was no more to say about Amethystine Stoller right then.

"His name was Bradley Mirth," I said, tilting my head toward the wheelbarrow. "He was gettin' ready to kill me and two friends."

"You the one kill him?"

"Yes. Up in the pinewood forest near Big Bear."

"Why not leave him for the forest to eat?"

"He tied in tight with LA cops."

Jo had huge nostrils. When she took in a deep breath it was like an event.

"Okay," she said, standing up from the heavy chair.

I pushed the barrow to the barrel and peeked over the side. The vat was three-quarters filled with an oily liquid that seemed to contain a night sky full of stars. There was depth to the lustrous liquor that suggested an even greater depth than the huge barrel encompassed.

"Come on, Easy, let's get him up. Remember, we got to let him down slow, 'cause even one drop on yo skin will make a mark for life."

This was only the third corpse I'd brought to Jo's funerary barrel, but I was very aware of its bite.

We raised Mirth's blanketed head up to the edge of the barrel and then slowly lifted until his body was leaning over the side. Even though his head was now enveloped in the bitter brew, it took us another ten minutes or so until releasing his feet.

We took a good six steps back, in order to avoid the noxious fumes. Then Jo said, "Why don't you say the words this time, baby?"

This was a surprise because Jo was usually the one in charge of her domain. She loved men; loved them. But her sense of rightness in the world was most definitely matriarchal. And so her request that I deliver the eulogy over the man I'd killed was, in its own way, a blessing.

"Bradley Mirth was a serious man, a man who was deeply committed to a way of life that did not forgive error. He was no coward and in his own way, probably, pious. I don't believe he would hold his death against the ones that killed him, and I regret that his people will never know what happened. But that was the life he lived, and I am sure that his soul will be at peace with this final tribute."

"Amen," said Mama Jo.

"Amen."

28

Jo walked me back to my car, parked behind the false screen of bamboo. There she kissed me again and said, "Can you gimme a ride?"

"How long before?" I asked as if in answer.

"His bones'll be soup before we get where we goin'. And even if somebody come in now and turn the whole thing over, his remains would dissolve in the grass."

We drove mainly on side streets from Compton, talking little and listening to a UCLA radio station whose nighttime jazz DJ was playing nothing but Ella. It was when she started in on Cole Porter's "Begin the Beguine" that Jo started talking again.

"You cain't get away from death, Easy. I mean, not no more than you can hide from the sun. You cain't control it. You cain't ignore it. You cain't say it ain't true."

"The sun?" I asked, truly confused.

"Even if you dug you a hole a mile deep and stayed down there the rest'a your days, the sun would still kill you by its, uh, its, what you call it? Its deprivation."

We were coming up to the Bel-Air arch on Sunset. Three cars in front of us were waiting to turn in.

"So," I said to continue our talk, "you're sayin' that Mr. Mirth lived under the same sun we do and that he lived by the same rules."

A pink El Dorado at the front of the line made its turn.

"I'm sayin' that when you meet a woman like this girl you talkin' 'bout, there's not a hole deep enough for you to hide in."

Mama Jo was a part of my life. She didn't mince words, would one day face death without a qualm, and had a heart that beat for everyone and everything she ever encountered.

It was now our time to turn. I executed the rotation well enough, but still an official-looking security automobile flashed its lights and blocked our entrance into the wealthiest part of the city.

"I guess that it was white people in those other three cars," I said to my elder.

"Here you go, baby," Jo said, handing me a shiny red business card.

I couldn't read the name in the dim light, but that didn't matter.

I rolled down my window as the two private security guards walked up to my side and Jo's. They had their hands on the butts of their pistols and so my passenger and I weren't making any fast moves.

The pudgy, pasty, and pimpled guard on my side was, at most, half my age.

"Driver's license."

I handed him the red business card. He used his flashlight to study it. Then he held up the card for his partner to see. That guard left Jo's window and went back to their brown-and-gold vehicle.

"What's your name?" I asked the glorified doorman standing at my car door.

"Jerry," he murmured with a hint of deference. "Jerry Fram."

The other guard, who was taller and better built, gestured at Jerry.

"You two can go on," Jerry said.

"Why'd you stop us in the first place?" I just had to ask.

"We check out everyone who comes in this late."

"There were three cars in front of us. You didn't stop any of them."

"We knew them."

"You knew 'em? One of those motherfuckers was a taxi…"

"Easy," Jo said. "Let's go."

I realized that the three swigs of Tranquility had loosened my tongue beyond the confines of common sense. So, I slowly depressed the gas pedal and moved us along.

The route up into the hills of Bel-Air was circuitous and, at times, steep. But Jo knew where we were going.

"What that card have to say?" I asked after half a dozen turns.

Ignoring the question, she said, "It's that driveway up ahead. Turn in and go to the top."

The mansion was big and broad, with four floors at its highest point. The front doors were ivory white and brightly lit by spot-lights that I was sure had been turned on for Jo's benefit.

She cracked her door and then said, "You comin'?"

Before we reached the front doors, they swung inward.

I don't know what I was expecting, but it wasn't a white waif of a woman who looked sixteen but was more probably forty-six.

"Isabelle," Jo said.

The woman-child ran into Jo's arms and held on as if for life.

After the embrace had run its course Jo said, "Izzy, this is one of my oldest friends, Easy Rawlins."

To my surprise Izzy gave me a hug with the same heartfelt passion she showed for Jo.

She was wearing an emerald-colored slip and fabric house shoes that looked as if they had seen many leagues of pacing.

"Come on in, you guys," Izzy said. "You hungry?"

"Naw, honey." Jo sighed. "Easy and me both tired, but I wanted to sleep up here and he give me a ride."

The living room was nearly half the size of my whole four-story house. The ceiling was twenty-five feet high, and the rectangular floor was a good two thousand square feet. The center of the room was dominated by a squat table, six by six feet in dimension, most likely cut from a single stone of nephrite jade. It was gray and green with veins of tawny yellow here and there. This table was surrounded by couches of very different and unique styles. One was made from Chinese rosewood and upholstered with golden fabric. Another was made from rough-hewn timbers and had a seat much higher than its Asian cousin. I could explain the other two but that would only be repetitive in its rarity.

We each chose a divan and talked about many things, most of which I no longer remember.

The only thing that stayed with me was a conversation I had with our hostess.

"How'd you and Jo meet, Isabelle?"

"Call me Izzy." Her smile was somehow both innocent and feral.

"How'd you and Jo meet?"

She paused, appreciating, I think, the fact that I managed not using her name again. Then she shot a glance at Jo, who nodded ever so slightly.

"My parents died when I was seven," Izzy said in a voice that was both clear and rough. "It was in a plane crash in Venezuela. My dad owned oil wells down there. After that my aunt Gala and her husband, Bob, moved in. They were nice but I got so sad about Mama that I was sick a lot. Bob knew Jo because she helped him one time when he had this infection..."

Jo knew many people in the alternative medical community. If you had enough money, or tenacity, you might find a way to her door.

"...she moved into my room with me and stayed there for a long time," Izzy continued. "After that I was better."

"What did she do?" I asked even though Jo was sitting right there.

"She just sat there. Every time I woke up she was sitting in the chair next to my bed, not smiling or anything. Just sitting there."

There's a lot to learn from the creatures of the earth, Jo had whispered to me sometime during our two-day love affair. *They know how to heal themselves without anything but their warm bodies and steady eyes.*

29

The three swigs of Tranquility knocked me out. I awoke on the Chinese couch around seven the next morning, washed my face in the downstairs bathroom, and made my way to the car. I got it to the N&T Hotel at a few minutes past eight that morning. The woman at the kiosk was strawberry blond and fair to the point of almost being real white. My aunt, Hannah Leroy, would have said that God meant her to be round and smiling.

"Oh, yes, Mr. Rawlins," she said after I introduced myself. "Tristan and Mr. Suggs are in their rooms. I could call them if you want."

Very few people knew that Fearless's given name was Tristan.

"What's your name?" I asked the desk clerk.

"Aura."

"Well, Aura, I'd like a room and a bed. Whenever Melvin or Tristan want me, I'll be ready."

I closed my eyes but they might as well have been open. My thoughts jumped from Mary to Mel, from Fearless to Mama Jo's ward—Izzy. There were gangsters and dead men, pimps and boxers. There was the corpse of Curt Fields.

When my mind's eye settled on Curt, my head's eyes opened. I sat up and made a call to a number that I had memorized without effort.

"Hello?" she said on the second ring.

"Hey."

"Where are you?"

Amethystine Stoller was at my door twenty-seven minutes later. She came in and took a long look at me, after which she embraced me much like Izzy had done. But there was a difference. I felt Amethystine's embrace—way down deep. When she let go I understood how Jo cured Isabelle, why Mel loved Mary, and also the passion that most women had for Fearless.

"Is this because of Curt?" she asked me.

"Is what because of him?"

"I can see you're hurting, Easy. I can see it. And if it's this job I got you on, you can just walk away. There's no saving Curt anymore anyway."

"Listen," I said. "You asked me a question and I didn't really answer it."

"Yeah?"

"Yeah. You asked me if I trusted you and the answer is—I don't know."

Amethystine's posture improved on the sky-blue Naugahyde chair.

"Go on," she whispered.

"It's all too easy. I mean, Curt's parents comin' to you—okay. Maybe even Jewelle tellin' you about me. That makes sense. But then you workin' for the man who hired Curt and somethin' about Curt gettin' you out of a jam. By itself that's a lot, but when you add in Harrison knowin' about Purlo *and* Shadrach and then him gone from the house as soon as I show up...That takes more than trust. That there's askin' for faith."

I don't think she wanted to, but Amethystine smiled.

"What else was I supposed to do?" she asked.

"Nuthin'. What's done is done. The only question is what can you do to make me have faith in you?"

She looked at some spot on my face that wasn't my eyes.

It was my turn to smile.

"What?" she asked.

"The way you're looking at me."

"What about it?"

"It's like that laser beam Theodore Maiman invented. A coherent ray of light. When Jackson talked to me about it, he called it single-focused."

Her eyebrows rose in appreciation, wordlessly saying that I knew who I was talking to even if I couldn't trust her.

"I just wanted you to find Curt," she said. "I wanted him to be safe. There was no other agenda, as far as you were concerned."

"Yeah, I know, find Curt. But then there's Purlo and Shadrach, a casino probably worth millions, and a girl who somehow managed to get out of a jam."

"A woman," she corrected. "A woman with responsibilities."

"I got kids too," I countered. "Adopted, but mine. One of them is married with a kid of his own. We all got responsibilities."

We were gazing freely into each other's eyes by then, like bear-Jo and cub-Izzy.

"Men like me," Amethystine uttered. "They see something they think they need, they want. And no matter what else happens, they end up wanting to use me..."

"Shadrach or Purlo?"

"My little brother had an infection that required an operation. That much is fact. Shadrach loaned me the money, but after that I would have had to work for him for almost nothing until it was paid off. Then Shad sold my debt to Purlo."

"And what did Ron want from you?" I asked, feeling the anger rise in my chest.

"At first, he wanted me to entertain his high rollers. I told Curt about it and he went to talk to Purlo. He told me that they'd made a deal."

"To investigate the books of the casino Purlo wanted to control," I stated.

"I guess."

"He didn't tell you?"

"I thought that he'd taken on the debt and was paying it off. That's what he said."

"And what about Harrison? How did he fit into all this?"

"He got me the loan from Shadrach."

"What was his angle?"

"I really don't know. I mean, I thought he was just being nice."

Faith trumps belief every time. I thought about the gangsters, the murder, and this woman who did all she could for the people she loved.

"I had Jewelle put a woman away in a property she manages. Do you know where that is?"

"Mrs. Blue owns places that nobody knows about but her. If you asked her to keep it secret, she wouldn't tell a soul."

"Do you have Jewelle's number?"

"Sure I do."

"Call it."

She did as I said and I got on the line.

"Hey, J, how you doin'?"

"Fine, Easy. What you doin' with my employee?"

"I want you to put her with Mary Donovan."

"Why?"

"Puttin' all my eggs in one basket."

"What kinda sense that make?"

"A fool's sense."

After a long sigh, she said, "Whatever you say, Easy."

Once I had worked out the details, I told Amethystine to go to her office and let Jewelle take her where she needed to stay.

"You think I'm in danger?" she asked.

"Could be."

"I'll need to get my brother and sister, then."

"Work that out with Jewelle."

She snorted daintily and then asked, "Why'd you call me?"

"Because I wanted to see you."

"But you don't trust me."

"Not yet."

Amethystine considered me and then said, "Take off your clothes."

I must have looked a little confused because she added, "Don't worry. It's not about sex."

She undressed me and then took off most of her clothes. We got down on the bed and she hooked her right arm under the back of my neck.

"This is not about sex?" Even at fifty, my erection was straining as it had that one night with Anger Lee.

"No."

For some reason this answer got me even more excited.

"It's about you," she uttered. It almost felt as if I was nineteen again, in bed with Mama Jo, or maybe fifteen, bleeding from my shoulder and kissing Anger Lee.

"This does not feel like resting."

That's when she pulled her trick. She placed her left hand over my eyes and said, "Let it go."

I was going to say that I wasn't holding on to anything, but I was asleep before the words could make their way to my tongue.

Amethystine was sitting across from me at a small round-top glass table. She wore a lovely golden hat and white gloves.

"I don't remember a thing," I was saying, and then the phone rang, waking me from the dream.

"Hello?"

"Ease," the caller intoned.

"Fearless."

"We on the roof."

Sitting up, I experienced a series of revelations. The first and deepest feeling was Amethystine's absence. The second was that I was completely rested. Part of this rejuvenation was probably Jo's elixir, but my client played a part in it too.

"You in there?" I called into the bathroom.

There was no answer, of course.

The certainty of my solitude brought to mind a simple fact: if only for that one morning, Amethystine Stoller brought to me succor without asking for a thing. This was a rare event in my half century of life. In those long decades, which seemed to span centuries, I had been brutalized, ripped off, lied to, pursued, and kissed in kind, but as rarely as an orchid blooming in winter was I given what I needed without asking.

* * *

The roof of the N&T Hotel was covered by maybe three-quarters of a foot of soil. Planted in this loam was a lawn of Californian blue-eyed grass. It was an extravagance that felt almost preternatural. At the western corner of this urban meadow was a whitewood table that would have seated eight comfortably. There sat Fearless and Melvin, drinking coffee and sharing words.

I walked up to the unlikely duo, said, "Gentlemen," and sat a chair away from either one.

"Where'd you go last night, Easy?" Fearless asked.

"A long way from here."

"You took care'a business?"

I nodded.

"No one came up to the cottage," Mel said. "We cleaned up pretty good."

"Good."

Fearless poured me a cup of coffee and I left it black.

After four sips I asked Mel, "Who did you get out of jail?"

He winced and then stared, shook his head maybe a quarter inch, and said, "Peter Barth."

Fearless leaned back and I merely waited.

"He'd been arrested," the cop continued, "for the distribution of stolen property — boating equipment."

I chuckled. "You mean captain's wheels and like that?"

"Mostly mechanical stuff. From engines to fishing sonar. I got a guy in evidence to mislabel the inventory, like I told you. That way I knew I could bust him again just as soon as I figured out how to get at the guy threatening Mary."

"Who's that?"

"I don't know."

"How's that work?"

"It was a note with a Polaroid picture of a weapon."

"The gun she used?"

"From what she told me, it looks like it."

"How did Laks tumble to it?"

"That's the question. It feels like a setup. First he uses Barth as an excuse to bring me up on charges, and then he has one'a his people threaten to send Mary to prison."

Fearless's grunt sounded like a depth charge targeting some unseen submarine.

"Why would Laks wanna do you in?" I asked.

"There's been some stories about him," Mel ventured.

"What kinda stories?"

"I don't like runnin' a guy down without proof," the lifelong cop said with some finality.

"He the one runnin' you down, Commander. He put your name out there and then sent that man Mirth after us."

"There's no proof he did that."

"Mary sent me to a man named Tommy Jester. When Jester got killed—"

"Killed?" Mel erupted. "Who killed him?"

"Jester called Mary. She asked a question and the next thing anybody knew he had a bullet in his head."

"What question?"

"I wasn't on the call, but I think it was if Bernard Kirby had possession of a film clip showin' Laks in the company of prostitutes. The way I figure it, Jester called Laks and then met his maker. We came damn near that very same end."

Mel's stare was long and deep—a man looking for some barely knowable thing.

When he found what he was searching for he said, "Everything you say makes sense, Rawlins. Everything but why you're sitting here sayin' it. I mean, none of this is your business."

"I came to you for help and found that you were missing."

"So what?"

"Com'on, Mel. We ain't no nine-to-five kinda guys. No punch clocks. No ranch-style house out in Pacoima. No boss we owe our souls to. You know how I do things. I need help and you do too. Put that together and you have why I'm here."

"What kinda help you need?"

I told him about Curt Fields, his family, and the gangsters that employed and probably murdered him. I even mentioned Amethystine, without using her name.

"Okay, but what can I do?" Mel said with a shrug. "I'm damn near a fugitive myself."

"Yeah," I agreed. "That boy Laks got you by the nuts. You on the run, but Anatole ain't."

"He works for Laks."

"Bullshit. He the one warned you about Laks."

Mel actually grinned at that evaluation.

"Damn, man," I continued. "The way they sayin' it, you jumped ship like an hour before they came lookin' for you."

"Yeah," the cop agreed, "and they the ones let Anatole know...so they could get me on the run."

"The only question is," Fearless added, "why does Laks want you dead?"

That simple declaration sat Suggs back in his chair.

It's important to say here that the LAPD, at that time, was a cult.

Maybe all police departments everywhere in the world are bound up by toxic orthodoxy, I don't know, but back then the LAPD didn't believe in anything but the righteousness of their struggle to survive on streets at least partly of their own making. If a criminal needed killing sometime, he could be found dead, clutching a pistol that had no pedigree attached to him. Gangs were set one against the other and these deaths were seen simply as collateral damage.

I'm not saying that every cop felt like that. But the greatest sin among them was turning a brother in blue over to the justice system. In order for this system to work, the members had to believe in the righteousness of their clan.

Suggs believed. At least he did until Fearless honestly assessed his situation.

"That's right, right?" Fearless pressed Mel.

Mel gave my friend an eighth of a nod in answer.

That was all he could manage before turning to me and saying, "And you, Rawlins, you got a dead man and a grieving family. Why not just let it go? Let it all go."

"There's gangsters around this that know the client. They're standing at the doorstep of something big. I'd like it if no more bodies dropped, most especially mine and my client's."

"I can't be seen anywhere near Anatole."

"Right. And I'm known by the men killed my client's ex-husband. You got a badge and there's only an unofficial APB on your ass. We could help each other here."

"You trust this client of yours?" Mel asked, staring me in the face.

"I don't know. Maybe."

Mel sat back in his whitewood chair, waited a beat, and then nodded.

"Then it's settled," I said. "Fearless?"

"Yeah, Ease?"

"Go get the car and Mel'll be down in a few minutes. After that you can take him out to John's. Once he's there, I'd appreciate you goin' up to stay at my place."

"Sound like a plan."

30

When Fearless was gone, Melvin said, "So, Easy, what is it that I can do for you, exactly?"

I told him all that I could about Amethystine looking for her ex, him winding up murdered, and then how Shadrach and Purlo might have played parts in that.

"I need to figure out how the gamblers were involved with the dead man," I said.

"The girl your client?"

"Woman, and yeah, she put me on it."

"The ex is dead. What else is there for her in this?"

"These guys are dangerous. She's not all that worried, but I'm dotting our i's."

"You know I can't do anything directly."

"You could talk to Anatole."

The clouds above us were the size of atolls, moving fast in the upper atmosphere.

"Okay," he admitted. "What else can the LAPD do?"

"Curt had an uncle named Harrison Fields. He's the only one in the family who seemed to know anything. I talked to him the first time I went to the parents' house, but by the time I went there again they told me that he was with a girlfriend down in

San Diego. Her name is Chita Moyer. She ain't listed. It would be good to find her."

"Anything else?"

"No, nothing," I said. "Get me as much as you can on them and I'll play whatever hand I got."

"Anatole's good for strength and straight-ahead investigation, but he colors inside the lines. And I can't be seen. Two out of every three cops would report it if they saw me."

"Fifteen years on the force and those the best odds you got?"

The cop commander gritted his teeth against the heartbreak of a truth spoken out loud.

"But you can trust Anatole," I said. "Right?"

"Not to break any laws."

"Okay. Maybe a bone or two, but no laws."

"Which one you think Annie's best to go after?"

"Annie?"

"Your people ain't the only ones who make up nicknames. Who do you need him to look into? And how do you expect to work with him?"

That final question was a good one. Even though I had my own detective agency, I rarely worked jointly or in unison with anyone.

"Tell him, uh, tell him to look into the gangsters. If he gets something on 'em, then bust 'em. If not, then he could pass anything he finds on to me, or else to you if he feels it's too, um, sensitive."

Melvin nodded, enjoying his sobriety, I think.

"And what you gonna do for me up ahead?" he asked.

"When you talk to Anatole, ask him to give you all he's got on the man doin' the legwork for Laks."

"Okay." I could tell by his tone that Mel was impressed with me.

Simultaneously we took deep breaths and then rose to our feet. The time for talking was over. We were foot soldiers with marching orders. Mel headed down to meet Fearless, and I called the front desk to stop the elevator at my floor.

The phone jangled me awake at a few minutes past three that afternoon.

"Yeah?"

"It's Captain McCourt." He was definitely perturbed at having to call me. Maybe he was also bothered by the afternoon sleep in my voice.

"Mel asked me to get you information as it came in, so—"

"Where you callin' from?" I asked, cutting him off.

"A phone booth down the street from my office." He didn't like being interrupted or questioned, but these were extraordinary times. "That okay with you?"

"Go on."

"Shadrach Tellman lives in Hawthorne." He gave me the address.

"Thank you, Captain. You got my answering service number?"

His reply was hanging up the phone in my ear.

The silence of the confidential hotel bade me to sleep a bit longer. My eyes were drowsing when the phone rang again.

"Yeah?"

"Sleepin' on the job, Brother Rawlins?" Melvin Suggs asked.

It was strange hearing his voice because the sleep didn't register much time between now and when I last saw him.

"S'up, Mel?"

"I got Chita Moyer's numbers in San Diego."

I jotted down the address under the one Anatole had given me. For some reason it felt as if I were penning a last will and testament.

"Why didn't Anatole gimme this?" I asked. "I just talked to him."

"I got it from a guy I know in the intelligence unit. I took a chance that no one told him about the trouble I'm in. Those guys are great for questions like that. They got files on everybody."

"Okay," I said. "Great."

"Talk later," Mel said.

I was asleep in less than a minute after cradling the receiver.

In the dream I walked up to the bare door of an unpainted shotgun shack on Concord Street in Third Ward Houston.

I knocked.

"Hold on," a sweet feminine voice called. "I'm comin'."

A few moments later Angel Lee opened the door. Black-skinned and barefoot, the thirty-something woman wore a bright-yellow dress.

"Mrs. Lee?"

"Yes, young man, can I help you?"

"My name's Ezekiel Rawlins, but e'rybody calls me Easy, ma'am. I'm here lookin' for Anger."

The smile on her face dimmed but did not disappear.

"I haven't seen her in a few days," Angel said. "She come by to pick up some'a her church clothes and then lefted. Are you bleedin'?"

I looked down at my left shoulder and saw, under my undershirt strap, that blood was seeping from my wound.

"It happent more than a week ago," I told her. "It's okay."

"Nonsense," she said, her smile strengthening. "Come on in here."

She sat me on a plastic-encased sofa and changed Anger's dressing from five days before.

"What happened?" she asked while moving her feather touch around the wound in my shoulder.

"A man," I said, "a man tried to take Anger away and when I went to stop him, he stuck me."

Angel leaned back, still working on the bandage.

"That was a man named Edgar that stabbed you?"

"Yes'm."

"Are you an' my daughter close friends, Easy?"

"Yes'm."

"You care for her?"

"She saved my life."

"Then you'll understand it when I tell you that she done left Houston for good."

"Why?" I whined.

"That man Edgar has a lotta friends that don't feel too kindly toward my girl."

When I awoke, it was to a pain in my chest. Thinking or dreaming about Anger Lee often left me feeling wounded.

I tried to remember if I had really gone to her mother's house in Third Ward and she, Angel, actually ministered to my wound. It felt real but I think Angel left Houston around the same time Anger did.

It didn't matter anyway. All that was a long time before, and I had a job to do.

31

I was still in a sour mood when climbing the stairs to Mr. Shadrach Tellman's second-floor apartment.

Standing at his door, I could feel the wrong that Fearless had seen in me.

A roll of quarters clenched in my right fist; I pressed apartment 2L's button with the point finger of my left hand. There was a faint buzzing sound beyond the heavy oak door. After a few seconds more I knocked—again with my left. Then suddenly the door swung inward. On the other side of the threshold stood a muscular and clean-shaven white man wearing a darkish dull-green bathrobe. He was holding the doorknob in one hand, with the other clutching a black-bodied semiautomatic pistol down at his side.

For some reason this deadly confrontation made me smile.

"What?" he barked.

"Shadrach Tellman?"

"What the fuck you want?"

"Sturdyman wants his money."

"Sturdyman? I don't owe him a goddamned dime."

"That's not what he told me."

"Oh?" That word, in his mouth, had blood all over it.

"Yeah. He told me to tell you that the casino deal is going through and you need to pay him over that."

Shadrach's gaze was heavy upon me. He was trying to figure out the puzzle of my words.

I had no idea what the implied threat was. I mean, there was a casino on the auction block, a man named Sturdyman who'd been cut out of that transaction, and also there was Curt working on the sale before he was murdered. But whatever challenge I presented was wholly in Shadrach's mind.

I remember thinking that the smartest thing for me was not to be there.

"What's your name?" Shadrach asked.

"Morell. Pete Morell."

"How'd you get my address, Pete?"

"Curt Fields."

"He don't know where I live. Hell, he don't even know my real last name."

"He knows people that know you."

This last made-up claim caused Tellman to open his eyes just a bit wider. A sly look stole across his face, and he said, "Maybe you should come in, Pete."

I had the urge to drop to the floor but then remembered that Vu Von Lihn was no longer backing me up.

"Sure," I agreed jauntily.

What happened next might have been a second-tier last-ditch plan in Mouse's playbook of desperate acts.

I walked past Shadrach and, for maybe a second, he turned his attention to pushing the door closed. With my left I grabbed the wrist of his gun hand. Then, with a good deal of torque, I swung the clenched thumb and forefinger of my right fist, hitting him directly on the temple with the roll of quarters.

I hit him three more times before taking the pistol and shutting the door.

Shadrach was a beefy guy, but I managed to drag his deadweight into a dining room that was just beyond the foyer of the stylish apartment. The dining room table was surrounded by four strong maple chairs—replete with heavy armrests.

That's when I took the second-greatest risk of my ill-advised incursion. I looked around for the kitchen and went through drawers until I found what I needed—a roll of electrical tape, a purple pad of paper, and a yellow No. 2 pencil.

When I got back to the dining room Shadrach was moaning but not yet conscious. I hit him one more time and then pulled him up into one of the chairs. Once he was there, I lashed his wrists and ankles to the armrests and legs of the throne-like seat.

He was out but I couldn't rely on that lasting for long, so I found the bathroom, located a washcloth in a hamper, and brought it back to the dining room.

(Only when I was in the bathroom did I realize my greatest mistake: I hadn't searched the apartment for any other inhabitants. Luckily, we were alone in there.)

I shoved the washcloth into Shad's mouth and wrapped black electrical tape around his head to hold the gag in place. Then I went to the front door and affixed the chain.

After maybe a quarter hour my prisoner started regaining consciousness. When he realized what was happening, a frightened look came into his expressive eyes. He tried screaming but that was muffled by the washcloth. Then he began wrestling with the tape. This was also hopeless. He was bound and muzzled like a mad dog.

I pulled up a chair to face him and he calmed down enough to glower at me.

"I don't want to hurt you, Mr. Tellman," I said. "But I will if I have to."

Glare turned to stare in his eyes.

"I need you to answer some questions," I continued. "So, I'm gonna free your right hand, put a pencil in it, and some paper from the kitchen that you can write on. That way we can have a conversation without me having to stab you for screamin'. You understand me?"

His nod came across like a plea.

I used a kitchen knife to cut the tape around his right wrist. Then I put down the purple pad of paper and put the yellow pencil between his fingers.

Immediately he started scribbling.

Cant breathe. My nose is stuffed up.

"You answer my questions quick enough and you might not suffocate."

He looked as if he was about to cry. I'm ashamed to remember how good his suffering made me feel.

"What was Curt Fields doing for Ron Purlo?"

Research, forensic stuff on the Exeter Casino.

"What was the money trouble Curt got Amethystine out of?"

I can't breathe!!!

"Then stop wasting time and answer my questions."

She borrowed money for to get her brother a operation.

"What kind of operation?"

I don't know. Appendix or gut or something.

"Why'd you sell her debt to Purlo?

Purlo had asked Curt to work on the casino thing and he said no. When Ron bought Amy's bill, she talked him into doing it.

His breathing was becoming labored.

"Was Harrison Fields involved in any of the Curt, Amethystine, or casino transactions?"

Didn't he already tell you that?

"No. Why would you say that?"

Because Sturdyman is Harrison. That's what Purlo called him.

"Answer my question."

Shadrach hesitated a moment and then wrote, *Harrison put some money in and was going to be a stockholder. He helped Purlo get to Curt. Please. I can't breathe!*

"Who killed Curt Fields?"

That put a temporary damper on my prisoner's moaning. He looked into my eyes for a very long moment, then wrote, *He's dead?*

I knew when to be quiet.

I don't know. I swear. I didn't even know he was dead. There wasn't any reason to kill him unless he was fool enough to talk about Purlo's syndicate's bid. And he couldn't have done that anyway because he was locked up in the 2120 Tower.

I went over all the possible questions I could ask but decided against each one because Shadrach was probably going to survive the interrogation and I didn't want him knowing too much through any intelligence he might glean from those questions.

I grabbed his wrist and taped the hand back to the armrest. Then I dragged his chair into a bedroom where there was a closet just big enough to hold him.

The whole time he was trying to holler and struggle. I slapped him pretty hard once he was ensconced within the closet.

"Shut up and be quiet," I said sternly. "I'm going to make a call. After that I'm'a come back and take the washrag outta your mouth. If you stay quiet I won't have to slit your throat."

In the kitchen I dialed a number that was becoming a part of my memory.

"Captain McCourt," he answered.

"You remember that guy lives in Hawthorne?"

"I do."

"I heard that somebody hog-tied him and left him in the bed-room closet."

"I see."

"I'm sure he'd be grateful if somebody pulled him outta there."

After that I went back to my temporary prisoner and removed the tape and gag from his mouth. Gasping for air, he seemed a little out of it.

I left him like that, proud of myself for not having killed him.

32

I felt like I needed to do something, but it was late. So I drove back to my mountain home and spent the night cooking for my daughter. In the morning, I took her to a training swim-race down at the beach. There were six races, and she placed in each one, even came in first for one of them. After that, I drove her to Jackson and Jewelle's house, and, finally, I started working again.

The drive down to San Diego was peaceful. Not much traffic, with small white and yellow blossoms from flowering weeds on either side of the highway. The ocean was on the right. In its northern quadrant the sun was sinking down over the Pacific. I liked driving alone. No radio or idle chatter and the only thing to be vigilant about was the traffic.

I wondered about Anger Lee for a twenty-mile stretch of lonely road.

I searched for Anger six or seven years after she left Houston, until I was finally drafted into World War II. She had four uncles and three aunts, all in and around the Fifth Ward. Most of them didn't have time for a lovesick youth who didn't have two nickels to rub together. The only ones who would talk to me were her uncle Holler Lee and Anger's aunt Becka.

Holler was a wino who lived in a shack behind the house of an ex-wife, Malley. Malley let him stay there because she was the one who broke off the marriage.

If I brought Holler a jug of cheap wine, he'd talk with me until passing out. Anger was never close to him and certainly wouldn't have told him where she'd gone. But he had stories about her that were funny and colorful. After an afternoon with Holler I'd be smiling for a week.

Becka Martin was a different case altogether. She was from Angel's side of the family tree and Anger had loved her with a passion. Becka was a church lady. Whenever I dropped by, she fed me sugar cookies and watermelon juice.

I made it a point to visit her every other week or so for sustenance of body and soul. I devoured those cookies, and Becka was the only one I knew who had correspondence with Anger. She'd receive a postcard every once in a while and share the contents with me.

One time Anger had written that she got work as a maid on a riverboat. She'd met Louis Armstrong there. On another occasion Becka told me that Anger had had a baby and named him Ezekiel for my heroism. This made me both jealous and proud.

Becka never let me read the postcards, nor did she share where Anger made her home.

Then, less than a year before I was conscripted, I was sitting in Becka's den, eating sugar cookies. She sat next to me on the divan and leaned in close. She didn't say anything but reached into the pocket of her calico apron and brought out a postcard. It was a zoo card with a picture of a mama panda and her two cubs on it.

Hi, Easy,

Aunt Becka said that you been comin round askin
bout me. I been all over since we knew each other. For
a long time I was in Lake Charles and now I'm up
north. I am sendin you this note to say that I will
always care for you but I will most likely never see you
again.

Best Regards
Anger Lee

I was a twenty-two-year-old man at that time, but still tears
came into my eyes. It didn't bother me that her words were so
blunt, maybe even hard, at the end. Anger came from a hard
place in life, and I loved her for that.

"Anger told me that you could read," Becka said, beaming
with a maternal smile.

"That's why we became friends in the first place," I said, trying to keep the tears out of my voice. "I was readin' this book
called *Tom Swift and His Motorcycle* down in the park on Myrtle
Street. She come up and told me that she thought I was pre-
tendin' and so I read a whole chapter out loud to her."

Becka caressed my hot cheek with her soft hand.

"Get on with your life, Ezekiel," she said.

Chita Moyer's house was a block from Mission Beach. A medium-
size two-story Tudor home. It was already dark outside, but the
streetlamps showed that the home was painted light and dark
green. On the right side of the front wall was a very large multi-
framed window that looked in on the living room.

The light was on, but I couldn't see anyone. Then I went to the front door and rang the bell. There were eight notes to the ring. I'm pretty sure that it was the tune to the Tennessee Ernie Ford song "16 Tons."

I was feeling patient. There was a bright peephole in the upper-middle part of the door. For a moment it darkened and then filled with light again. Half a minute after that she opened the door.

Tall, elegant, and at least seventy, she wore a dress that was opaque because of the many layers of gossamer pastel-green fabrics it was made from. The dress was full and fluffy, but the woman underneath was slender, you could tell. Her skin was golden and her eyes ebony under thick dark brows. Behind her rose an impressive stairway.

"Yes?" I could hear the Spanish accent in just that one word.

"Yes, um, my name is Easy Rawlins, are you Miss Chita Moyer?"

"Mrs. Moyer," she said. "My husband died some years ago. How can I help you, Mr. Rawlins?"

Before I could reply, a familiar voice called out, "He's not here for you, Eata. Mr. Rawlins is here for me."

Harrison Fields was descending the stairs, ambling with the gait of a much younger man. He wore a dark-yellow suit over a midnight-blue shirt and an almost neon-yellow tie. He was smiling. A man without a care in the world.

"Drink?" he offered.

There was a games table set up next to the large window in the living room. The three of us sat there, leaving the one empty chair with its back to the street. Chita had made vodka martinis. I had mine with an olive, while they had twists of orange rind in their drinks.

"So, Easy," Harrison said after we'd been served by Chita. "How the devil did you find me?"

"I'm a detective."

"A damn good one. Eata is unlisted, and my brother doesn't even know her phone number."

The elder was smiling as he spoke. He had the patience of Buddha.

"I guess the LAPD has a better phone book."

Even the mention of the police didn't seem to bother the Ohioan.

"Must be something important to go to all that bother."

"Have you talked to your people?" I asked him.

"You mean Alastair and Winnie?"

"Your brother and sister-in-law."

Leaning back in his chair he said, "Not since I came down here."

It seemed as if he was and yet was not the man I'd met a few days before. There was something both confident and aloof in his manner.

"Then nobody told you about Curt?"

"They found him?"

"He's dead."

"Oh." That was Chita. "Oh," she said again, rising to her feet.

"How?" Harrison asked. He wore a proper frown and even had some compassion showing on his lips and forehead.

"Somebody shot him in the head."

"I, I'll go make us another round," Chita said, as she went about retrieving our glasses.

"Who did it?" Harrison demanded. "Did they catch him?"

"The police don't know. They're investigating."

"Curt was a good kid. He didn't deserve that," Harrison said to the tabletop.

Chita bustled out of the room, carrying our empty long-stemmed glasses in one hand and a silver-plated tray in the other.

"Are you looking for the men did it?" Harrison asked.

"Tryin' to make sure Amethystine is safe."

"You got anybody you're looking at?"

"He was staying at a place that Purlo controlled."

"Ron?"

"That's his name," I said, meaninglessly.

"So do they think he killed Curt?"

"I don't know. That's why I got the cops to find Chita's address. After all, you're the one that told me about Purlo. Can you think of any reason he'd have for killing your nephew?"

"No." The elder dandy frowned again. "I mean, Ron worked with gangster guys, but he never went in for the rough stuff."

"Could he have had somebody do it for him? Maybe Shadrach?"

"Nah," Harrison said with a sneer. "Shad's just a weak sister with long teeth."

The image he conjured made me smile.

"Tell me something, Harrison."

"What's that, Mr. Rawlins?"

"You came down here right after I told you about Curt being missing."

"I already knew he was missing."

"But you didn't know that Amethystine had hired me to look for him."

"I was happy you were helping."

Chita came back in with the silver platter holding three drinks: two with orange twists and one with a green olive. This she placed at the center of the table.

"It seemed kinda sudden," I said.

"Chita called me and said that she was selling her house and leaving the country. I worried that some unscrupulous real estate agent would try to take advantage of her, so I came down to help."

"Oh," I said thoughtfully. "I thought that it might have had something to do with a guy named Sturdyman."

I don't know what I expected, but I hoped to get a rise. Instead, Harrison smiled and said, "That's what Purlo calls me."

"I heard it that Purlo pushed Sturdyman out of the Exeter Casino deal."

I took up my drink and sipped it.

"I was never really in the deal," Harrison said. "I mean, I helped him connect with Curt, and he promised to get me a job. But I didn't want to move to Vegas. Too hot in the summer and too cold in the winter."

"Would you like something to eat, Mr. Rawlins?" Chita asked.

"No, thank you, ma'am. Where you movin' to?"

"Argentina. I have a son down there."

"Are you going too?" I asked Harrison.

He took a drink and said, "No. After I see her off, I'll be back in Santa Monica."

"You know, Harrison," I said, taking another tack. "When you told me about Purlo and Shadrach it seemed like you hardly knew 'em."

"Yeah. I didn't want to be involved, but I still wanted to help Curt."

"Can you think of any reason anybody could have for hurting your nephew?"

"Got to be money," he pontificated. "Got to be. Money, a mistake, or maybe both."

"What kind of mistake?" I asked, feeling oddly generous.

"Maybe Giselle had a husband she didn't tell him about or maybe Purlo messed up a decimal point and thought Curt had robbed him."

I took in a deep breath through my nostrils, exhaled, and then breathed in again.

"I thought you said Purlo was a weak sister."

"I said Shadrach was." Harrison's words floated on his smile. "Shad don't go in for the rough stuff."

"Oh. Oh yeah. Pronlon. No...Ron..." I looked out the window to see a dark sedan pull into a driveway across the street. This event seemed miraculous.

Turning back to my hosts, I experienced a moment of light-headedness.

When Harrison came into focus, I said, "Why? Why you drug me, man?"

"I don't want to suffer the same fate as my nephew," he said affably.

Chita stood up and smiled down at me from what seemed like a great height.

"Are you going to kill me?" I asked, in no way worried.

"No, Easy, I wouldn't do that." Harrison's voice seemed to come from somewhere very far away.

"That's good. Good," I intoned. "You know I like you two just fine. I only came down here, down here..."

I wanted to say that I had come to protect Amethystine again, but words, all words, eluded me. While looking around for the missing gift of language, I noticed that darkness was descending from the ceiling.

33

I was standing in the colored graveyard on the outskirts of New Iberia, Louisiana. It was nighttime and all the friends and cousins, my father and half sisters, the neighbors and church members, had gone home. My mother had just turned twenty-seven when she gasped her last breath, two days before. I was only seven, but I climbed out the back window of our country shack and made my way to her by moonlight. In his eulogy the minister kept saying that Mama wasn't dead, that she was with God. That hope pulled me out of the bed and propelled me to her grave.

I don't remember ever finding her stone back then, but in the dream I got there. They hadn't filled in the hole yet and so I looked over the side and saw her. It wasn't my mother but Anger Lee lying there, naked and half-wrapped in a white shroud. She seemed to be sleeping, there at the bottom of the grave.

I knew she was dead but could not believe it. That's when she opened her eyes, smiled, and said, "Easy."

"Anger."

"Oh, baby, don't look so sad. Bein' dead ain't all that bad. There's a whole world of beauty and love beyond this place."

"They is?"

"Oh yeah. Climb on down here, honey, and I will make you feel better than you evah knowed. Bettah than evah."

I wanted more than anything to join her. It was the strongest desire I had ever felt. But the grave was deep and getting deeper. Ten feet down, then twelve.

"Jump, Easy!" Anger called. "Jump!"

Finally, I couldn't hold back. I leaped into the abyss of the grave.

"Get your black ass up, motherfucker!"

Violently, I was being pulled from the grave and my first true love. When I opened my eyes I was seated at Chita Moyer's games table. Then I was dragged to my feet. There were at least three uniformed policemen with their hands on me. Sunlight blazed through the big window.

"What's happenin'?" I called out.

"Breaking, entering, and trespass," one of the cops yelled back.

"No! No! This is Mrs. Chita Moyer's house and I'm her guest."

"This house is vacant," another cop added, "uninhabited."

Someone else rabbit-punched me and I went down on my knees. Then I was kicked in the side, making me fall over on my back.

"Get up!" a cop demanded. I think it was the same one that kicked me.

The only thing I could do was hold my hands out with palms up.

"Turn over on your belly," the highest-ranking uniform commanded.

It took a great deal of faith to turn my back on men who had already struck me twice with no provocation. But I did as I was told and, to my relief, all they did was cuff my hands behind me and then jerk me to my feet.

And though I was cautious, I wasn't outraged over the mistreatment. After all, I had done the same and worse to Shadrach Tellman.

Someone took the wallet from my back pocket.

"What the fuck were you thinking, nigger?" the top cop asked.

"I knocked on the door and an elderly couple invited me in. We sat at that table and drank till I passed out."

"What kind of horseshit is that?" He asked questions that denied any answer I might give.

He was a big man and obviously easy to anger. But I figured that the truth, or near to it, was all I had.

"Hey, Sarge," a guy behind me said. "It says here that this guy's a PI from LA."

"A PI?"

"Yeah."

"Let me see that."

The wallet was passed over and the big angry sergeant scowled at it.

"Where the fuck you steal this?" he asked.

"It says Ezekiel P. Rawlins," I replied, more or less respectfully. "If you look at my driver's license, you'll see that the picture is me. And if you take out the card behind that you'll see that it's for Captain Anatole McCourt of the LAPD. He knows why I'm down here and who I was here to see."

This was not the script that these peace officers had studied for the entirety of their professional lives. Obviously guilty, I was supposed to beg and lie or curse and threaten. I was supposed to make claims that they could pick apart. Something that would make them have to punish me.

But mentioning a police captain's card as a reference met none of their expectations. Even a white crook wouldn't try that.

I was dragged out of the Moyer house and shoved into the back of one of the patrol cars. I sat there a good forty-five minutes. The young officer they left to guard me stood outside the vehicle, next to the back door I was closest to. This sentry was reedy and redheaded. From the bravado of his scrawny posture, I believed that he saw himself as some kind of invincible warrior.

When the sergeant and another cop returned they installed themselves in the front seat.

"Powell," the sergeant called out of the passenger's-seat window.

"Yes, sir," the reedy redhead replied.

"Go up to the front door and keep people away. We'll send somebody from the station to relieve you."

"Yes, sir."

The ruddy boss then turned toward me and said, "You say you were drinkin' in there?"

"Yeah."

"What kinda liquor?"

"Vodka martinis with green olives or twists of orange rind."

I worried that he was going to spit on me. From the twist of his lips, I was sure he wanted to.

We traveled downtown to a fair-size police station. There I was put into an interrogation room. They didn't take off the cuffs or offer me water but, then again, they didn't beat on me either.

The room came furnished with a straight-back chair and a

metal table with a Formica top. No carpeting. No extras at all. I sat on the tabletop because it was more comfortable than the chair, considering the disposition of my hands. I didn't do much thinking. Again, it was one of those interim periods where a second-class citizen had to wait, in hopes that his papers would be validated.

It was a long wait.

When the door finally opened, the reedy warrior, his ruddy boss, and Anatole McCourt came in.

I have to admit that when I first saw Anatole there was an expanse of joy in my chest. Then I remembered who I was and where. If it served his purpose, the LA police captain could drop me in a hole.

"Take the bracelets off," McCourt said to the kid.

I stood up and turned my back.

"I have some questions," the sergeant said to me.

"What's your name, man?" I asked, cutting him off.

"Sergeant Carr. Now—"

"Listen, Brother Carr. I got to take a hard piss, either in a toilet bowl or on your shoes. Dig me?"

Carr didn't like me and I didn't care. What I wanted was a toilet, some water, and coffee for the drug-induced headache that had been pounding on my skull for hours.

Once these needs were met, I acceded to the San Diego cop's demands.

Nearly an hour later I had explained to the SDPD sergeant all about Curt Fields, his missing uncle, and the reasons I ended up unconscious in the window.

"So you think this Harrison Fields is somehow involved with the death of his blood nephew?" Sergeant Carr asked.

"He knows all the players and so could be a source of great intelligence having to do with his nephew's death. I came down here to get that information."

"But instead, you let the old man drug you."

"Fuck is wrong with you, man?" I didn't quite ask. "I already had one clean drink and the woman made it."

"You don't talk to me like that in my house," Sergeant Carr warned.

Rising to my feet I said, "Fine. Let's get the fuck outta here then."

The sergeant rose to meet me. It might have been a brawl if Anatole hadn't stood too.

"Come on, Sergeant," McCourt said. "Let's go take a look at the house."

The only furniture in Chita Moyer's house was the games table downstairs and a queen-size mattress in the master bedroom on the second floor. In the kitchen there were two plates, two sets of cutlery, along with a cocktail shaker and four martini glasses.

"We figure they probably got a real estate agent to show them the house and then moved in," Carr told McCourt.

"No," I said.

"What?" Carr managed to make that one-word interrogative sound like a threat.

"He was provided with the address by my office," Anatole said. "That means the home must have belonged to her."

"I mean," I said as if I were finishing Anatole's explanation, "why the fuck did you people even arrest me? How'd you know I was there?"

Carr looked at me, considered a curse, but then snagged his lower lip with an upper canine.

"We got a call. She said she was a neighbor and that something looked hinky at this address, said there was a Negro sleeping in the window."

The rage I felt was both new and old. Older than the oldest man who ever lived and new like when you fall in love for the first time.

With clenched fists I said, sarcastically, "And you think I let somebody drug me?"

Carr understood the criticism, maybe he even agreed with it.

Whatever it was, he turned his anger on the LA cop. "Why would you be working an operation down here without telling us?"

"We just wanted to talk to them, Sergeant. Neither one was suspected of a crime."

"Well," Carr said through a sneer. "I don't know what to tell you."

"No kidding," I replied.

34

"Why you want to provoke that man?" Anatole asked.

We were standing on the curb in front of the empty house. Sergeant Carr and Patrolman Powell had already gone.

"You let somebody sock you in the head, kick you in the ribs, and then sit you down in handcuffs till your bladder 'bout to bust. Do all that and then let me dare to ask you about provocation."

Anatole took it. He knew the procedure. So instead of arguing, he asked, "Where's Commander Suggs?"

"You talked to him. Didn't he tell you?"

"No." The word passed his lips like a kidney stone.

"You didn't trace the call?"

"Anything I do about Mel is off the books."

"Then I can't help you."

"We need to bring this problem to a conclusion, Rawlins."

My car was parked ten feet away. I considered jumping in and driving off without engaging the cop-out-of-water. But, like it or not, I had to work with the Irish fashion plate.

"Did Laks talk to you directly about the trouble Mel was in?" I asked.

"No."

"Who did?"

"I can't tell you that."

"Why not?"

"It was a confidence."

"It was a lie."

Anatole's beautiful blue eyes bored into me, looking for the meaning of this accusation.

"Come on, man," I said. "He told you there was a warrant out on Mel but there wasn't, was there?"

Anatole's whole demeanor halted, like an engine with a gas tank full of sand.

He balled his left fist, held it up to his lips, and said, "I have to look into this for myself."

"What you got to do is pick a side."

This was my day for stumping law enforcement. Everything I was telling him he knew to be true; the only thing was, the answer I offered felt to him like betrayal.

"Look," I said. "Laks had Tommy Jester killed. There's no question about that. You can bet your pension he'll do the same to Mel."

"I thought you didn't know Jester."

"Slipped my mind."

"Even if you did know who he was, how can you possibly know that Laks killed him?"

"I found out that Jester sometimes had secret films made of his more affluent and powerful customers."

"What kind of customers?" he asked, knowing full well what I meant.

"Them that buys their pussy."

Anatole pulled his head back like a dog that just got a whiff of wolf.

"One of them was Laks," I added.

"How do you know?"

"I saw it. And it was what they call graphic."

"I don't believe it."

I chuckled and said, "I work for a living, Captain. No pension, no paid vacation, no office that somebody else pay the rent on. I'm my own man and I do what I know to be right. Mel haven't done one goddamned thing wrong and Laks wants to destroy him. Are you good with that? 'Cause if you are, you can go back over to Clifton's and drink your scotch. I'll be out here on the street helpin' my friends."

He stood there looking in my direction but seeing something altogether different.

Back then, men like McCourt lived lives of unquestioning trust. People like that had faith in the companies they worked for and the bosses who represented those companies; they trusted the newspapers they bought on street corners and the government that sent them and their children off to war. Anatole was like that. He trusted his betters to do what was right, just like he expected me to be dishonest, deceitful, double-dealing, and treacherous. Now all that was turned on its head.

Right then, on that Mission Beach sidewalk, Anatole McCourt realized that the people he trusted were no better than those he despised. I could see that in the rare uncertainty of his eyes.

Then those eyes hardened.

"I hear what you're saying, Easy, I do, but I can't give you that information." He raised his hand as if swearing a half-hearted oath.

"You doin' a whole buncha shit you cain't do, man. Like comin' down here and gettin' me outta jail."

"I have to think about this."

By the time I was back on the road to LA, my plans had been laid.

The first stop was John's bar.

It was late afternoon and so there were maybe seventy-five revelers drinking and laughing, hugging and dancing. "It's Your Thing" was playing on the jukebox.

"Hey, Ease," John greeted from behind the crowded bar.

"John."

"You here to see your boy?"

"Oh yeah."

"I got him out back in the blue room. He got pretty good manners for a man in his profession."

"Takes all kinds."

Tossing me a key he said, "Go on. I'll talk to you later."

At the far end of the bar was a metal door painted red. I used the copper key on the lock and entered a long hallway that had four doors on either side. At the far end was a fire exit.

The blue room, so named for its blue door, was the third on the left.

I knocked.

"Who is it?" came a gruff voice.

"Easy."

The door opened, revealing Melvin. He wore black trousers

and a teal-green T-shirt, no shoes or socks. He was still clean-shaven and appeared to be sober.

"You gonna let me in?" I asked.

He took a full step backward, allowing me to pass through.

It was a large room, maybe as much as seven hundred square feet. The bare floor was dark wood and there was a queen-size bed against a far wall. A very long pine table under a large window looked down on an alley behind the warehouse. On the table was a double hot plate and a mini refrigerator along with various dishes, cups, and canned goods.

"Not bad," I said.

"Place is okay but I'm about to crawl outta my skin."

I strolled over to the table and pulled out a chair made of bamboo woven around a metal frame. Melvin just leaned against the table.

"How's it goin'?" I asked, hoping to prime a conversation.

"That man Mirth was sent to murder me."

"Sit down, Mel. Let's talk."

With a harrumph he hopped up on the table.

"I don't know what to do," he said. "I can't go out and kill Laks. I want to. I do. But that wouldn't get Mary out of Dutch."

"No," I agreed. "It's us gonna save your bride."

"How we gonna do that?" he asked.

"She'll tell us something and we'll use that to figure out what's what."

"Sounds like fun, but I don't see how it gets us anywhere."

"Not until you call Anatole and get him to give you the information on the man told him you were about to get nicked."

"Why? What could we do with that?"

"When Laks got this demolition rollin', he got somebody to

tell Anatole about the blackmailers and that he was about to bring you in. I'm bettin' that whoever that was is involved in this thing. Did he tell you?"

"No." Mel propelled himself off the tabletop, pulled out a bamboo chair, and sat down hard. "I got the feeling that whoever talked to him about Laks was sticking their neck out and wanted to stay, you know, anonymous."

"We need whoever that was to lead us to the guy they say can produce the gun Mary used. That's all they got, and we know the evidence hasn't been presented to the chief or the prosecutor because then they'd have both you and Mary arrested. They wouldn't have warned you neither."

"And you want me to ask some upper-level cop about that?"

"Ask him hard," I agreed.

"But he's, he's probably..."

"Not some niggah you grab up off the street?" I suggested.

My question had an answer, but not one that Mel could say aloud.

"I don't know, Easy."

"It's either that or we go after Laks."

Suggs made a face that said there was a bad smell somewhere. He shook his head.

"I ever tell you why I'm not a big team sports fan?" I asked.

"What's that got to do with anything?"

"You see, if you on a team then you have to trust e'rybody, all your teammates. But you and me both know that's not how it works. We know that in life it is human nature that tells us we need to look out for ourselves, that you can trust but you have to question too. And that question, that's what makes us honest, that's what tells us the truth."

For a moment there I thought the commander was going to
vomit. But then he broke out into a broad grin. Then he laughed.

"You're a good man, Rawlins," he said. He looked down at his
bare feet, looked up, and asked, "I ever tell you where I come
from?"

"No, sir."

"I was born in Sacramento. My father died before I was two and
my mother, Mariette Suggs, left me off with her parents when I
was five. I felt bad about her leavin' back then, but later I realized
that it was probably for the best.

"My grandparents were Baptists and they dragged me to
church every goddamned Sunday. I hated it. But Gram and
Daddums didn't care what I wanted. They just sat me between
'em and pinched my arm whenever I closed my eyes.

"One day I asked my daddums why I had to go to church
every week. I mean, they said the same shit in every sermon. You
know what he told me?"

"No," I answered brightly, glad that he was being open.

"He said, 'Every man, woman, and child has to come before
the Lord once a week. Not to be forgiven. Not so that he could
hear their prayers. Not even for them to learn from the sermon's
claptrap. No. We got to get down on our knees before the Lord
so he can judge us and we can be judged.'"

Sitting there in John's blue room, Mel was considering his entire
life: from being an orphan, to getting bored in church, to accepting the sins of his lover.

He exhaled mightily, so that his cheeks puffed out and his lips
flapped.

"Okay," he said. "I'll try and find out who spooked me. Either I'll get that from Annie or somebody else."

He stood and held out a hand.

I mirrored these motions.

"I know he's on your team," I said. "But don't tell Anatole where you're at."

"Okay. When do I get to see Mary?"

"Let me give you a phone number."

35

I drove straight to Studio City from Watts. It was a sleepy town at the dawn of the seventies, with houses that were little more than bedrooms for aspiring middle- and lower-middle-class workers.

The Gaynor apartment building was on Porga Lane, in the heart of the suburb. It was a monolith compared to the one- and two-story businesses and houses that comprised the rest of the neighborhood.

I was studying the directory in the vestibule when a middle-aged white woman was coming out. She wore a dark-blue dress suit that was almost military with its straight lines and cuts. The hem of her skirt came down to the middle of her knees.

She studied me for a few seconds and then said, "She's in one-A."

"Who is?" I asked.

"The colored girl you're looking for." There was a shrug in her delivery. "Go straight ahead to the end and turn right."

"How do you know I'm not looking for, umm…" I said, scanning the list of names. "Colonel Hatton on floor three?"

Blue Suit threw up her hands and said, "Have it your way." Then she walked out the front door of the little lobby.

I was angry, but I didn't have time to worry about that woman. She actually helped me.

Through the second set of doors, there were halls either to the left, the right, or straight ahead. Following the woman's directions, I came to a glass wall. Behind this transparent barrier was a dense and beautiful garden crowded with rosebushes, slender trees, bamboo, and flowering vines. I grinned at the beauty and then turned right, passing apartments 1F, 1E, 1D, 1C, and 1B on the right. At that point the hallway abruptly turned left. Before me was the door to apartment 1A.

I knocked and waited.

After a minute I heard, "Who is it?"

"It's me, Mary, Easy."

Mel's Lilith opened the door, considered me, and then smiled. Barefoot like her husband had been, she wore tight coral slacks and a bright-red blouse that revealed her midriff.

Behind Mary stood Amethystine Stoller. She wore a dress that was pretty much shorts and a T-shirt sewn together. Her hair was slicked back and she was sporting a smile that I couldn't quite read.

Mary took me by the arm and walked me to my client, who took my other arm. The ladies escorted me into a living room where one entire glass wall looked out upon the garden. There was a glass door built into the far right of the wall. The contained, and verdant, wilderness could have been Eden or a tiger's den — maybe both.

"I like your friend," Mary said, letting me go.

Amethystine stepped back from my other arm and I sat down on the velvety buff sofa they'd brought me to.

"Oh?" I said. "Why's that?"

"Because she's a complex girl," Mary replied, putting an arm around Amethystine's waist.

I noticed that my client didn't complain about being called a girl.

"That's the way it has to be for me," Mary continued. "Girls like us are just a long list of secrets, while men are straight shots, predictable even when they explode."

"Then what about Easy?" Amethystine asked, still sporting that smile.

"He's the exception."

"You mean all men other than me are open books?" I asked, realizing we had to do this play before getting down to business.

"Of course not," Mary said, still playful. "But most men with knotty natures are either con men or dogs."

Amethystine laughed with all the potential her wide mouth had to offer.

"Sis," came a youthful male voice.

"Yeah, Garnett," Amethystine called.

At a doorway at the far end of the living room stood a young Black adolescent. He was tall, his sister's skin color, and no more than fourteen.

"Can I make a sandwich?"

"Sure. How about your sister?"

"She takin' a nap, but I'll make one for her too."

"Before you do, com'on out here and say hello to my friend—Ezekiel Rawlins."

Up close the young man contained equal parts beauty and awkwardness.

"Good to meet you," he said, holding out a hand.

"Good to meet you, Mr. Rawlins," his sister corrected.

After he made the proper adjustment I asked, "You play basketball, Garnett?"

He grinned and nodded.

"Go on and make your food," she said. Then she turned to Mary and asked, "You wanna go outside?"

I'd never been plagued by allergies before, but the wealth of pollens, floral scents, and the pregnant earth of that garden started my nostrils to tickle.

Mary led us to a round marble table that had two semicircular benches, one on either side. I took one bench and the ladies settled on the other.

"This is nice," I said.

"Jewelle knows her properties," Amethystine agreed.

"Anybody else out here?"

"No," said Mary. "There's only four apartments with access, and your friend Jewelle told me she keeps them for special clients like you."

I nodded, looking around to ensure our privacy.

"Okay, Easy," Mary said, "let's have it."

"Maybe you wanna talk to me alone?" I suggested.

"That's okay. I trust your Amy."

"You don't trust anybody but Mel," I amended.

Mary smiled and then turned to kiss Amethystine on the cheek. I was a little surprised at the flash of jealousy I felt.

"There was a reason you sent her here to me, Mr. Rawlins."

"And what, pray tell, was that?"

"She knows the rules. I mean, why else would you dare to send her here?"

"I just thought that since you're both smart, and Mel and I

were working together, that having you in the same place would be a good thing."

"Let's have it," Mary said again.

"I have that film clip you sent me after."

"That's all we need, right?"

"I don't know. He's already killed Tommy Jester and he sent the same hitter after me, Mel, and Fearless."

"Where's the hitter now?" Mary was suddenly still.

"Nowhere near here."

"Mom . . . I mean, Sis," Garnett called from afar.

"I'll be right back," Amethystine said to us both. She laid a hand on Mary's shoulder and then rose.

Watching her skip off toward their apartment, I understood what it was when people would say they lost a part of themselves.

"Are we in trouble here?" Mary asked.

"No."

"Are you sure?" she insisted.

"Yes. And that's all you get."

She took a moment, to trust, and then said, "Then Laks has to think that Mel will be after him, and so he'll be after Mel."

"And you."

Mary's smile actually showed some tooth.

"Hi," Amethystine said. She'd come back all in a rush, hurrying back to her seat. "You have to teach boys everything."

"Easy says that there will be no peace with the assistant chief."

"Oh?"

Turning back to me, Mary asked, "What about Mouse?"

"Who's that?" asked Amethystine.

"A friend'a mine," I told her. "He knows people. Dangerous people."

"You think he'd help us?" Mary asked.

"I was under the impression that you wanted to stay with Mel," I replied.

"Don't tell him."

"This is Mel we talkin' 'bout. By smell alone he can tell when a quart of milk will go sour next week."

Nodding, Mary leaned back on the backless bench.

"Okay," she said. "What's your plan, Mr. Rawlins?"

"We need Melvin here, where we can talk it out."

Mary's chin rose and her eyes smiled.

"Okay," Amethystine accepted. "Then what about me?"

I glanced at Mary, somewhat reluctantly.

"You want me to leave while you guys talk?" Mel's wife asked.

I was wondering how to say yes politely when Amethystine said, "No, honey, you can stay. My problems are probably over by now anyway."

I shrugged and went into the story about the work I'd done for her. That just went to prove what an odd mood I was in. Most of my life I never told anybody anything that mattered. That's why Fearless didn't know about where I lived. It was an unspoken creed among my people that the more anyone knew about your business, the more you were likely to lose.

But I didn't care. I told the ladies about Shadrach and Purlo, Chita and Harrison, leaving out the bit about Harrison being Sturdyman.

"You left Shad tied up in a closet? Really?" Amethystine laughed like a schoolgirl.

"I wanted to kill him."

"I'm sorry, Ezekiel," Amethystine said, the merriment gone in an instant.

"Sorry for what exactly?"

Before my client could answer, a telephone rang from somewhere.

"That's our phone," Mary said, her laughing eyes now wary.

"I didn't give it to anybody," Amethystine told us. "I don't even know the number."

"It's for Mr. Rawlins," a girl called out.

I was on the phone maybe fifteen minutes before returning to the women. They were drinking chilled white wine and laughing again.

"Who was it?" Mary asked.

"Mel."

"You gave him my number?"

"Yeah."

"What did he have to say?"

"He'll be here as soon as he can."

Mel arrived just over half an hour later. Maybe six minutes after he got there, Mary took him off to her room to *get reacquainted*.

Amethystine and I wandered back out to the marble table in the Studio City Garden of Eden. We sat side by side. The first few minutes were spent in silence.

"You're an odd one, Ezekiel," Amethystine said at last.

"In what way do you mean?"

"Even the way you ask me that. I mean, most people I've known would be a little bothered by bein' called odd."

"Yeah," I said. "I like you too. It would have been better if we met under a different cloud. I wish I could have saved Curt."

She took a moment to let the pain subside and then asked, "Do you have any idea who killed him?"

"Not for a fact."

"What about for maybe?"

I showed my palms in mock surrender and said, "Shadrach and Purlo had a lot invested in the casino deal goin' through. Maybe, somehow, the knowledge Curt had was a threat to that. Or . . ."

"Or what?"

"Maybe Curt, or somebody he knew, realized how much was to be made off the deal. I mean, if you had the money and the muscle, an investment like that could be worth millions, tens of millions. More money than most people could imagine."

"Is that what you would do?" she asked. "Sell the deal to some mobster guy?"

"Would you?"

After a long pause, and through a soulful stare, Amethystine uttered, "Maybe."

"What about Curt?"

"What about him?"

"Would he take that kind of risk?"

She concentrated on the question, sneered at it. Then she shook her head and shrugged, telling me, wordlessly, that she didn't really have an answer.

"Your brother had something wrong with his intestines. Tied up or something. Now he doesn't, and Curt wanted to take you to Paris."

"So?"

"Maybe he thought if he could make enough money, you could save Garnett and give Curt another chance to be interesting."

"Ron wanted me to entertain some of his better customers," she said, as if in answer. "I told Curt that I would kill either him or myself."

"Was your ex going to make enough for the operation and to cut you free?"

"Enough to be broke after."

"But he was talkin' about Paris."

"He wanted the chance to work again and for me to let him believe that we could be together."

"And what did you want?"

"I don't need nobody to pay my bills, Ezekiel." She was talking directly to me, not about Curt. Not about some casino/oasis out in the desert.

"Who is Sturdyman?" I asked.

"I don't know."

36

Amethystine and I, sitting there, side by side, could not have been closer or farther apart. The lies she told didn't bother me any more than pillow talk. It just meant that if I wanted to get to the truth, I'd have to make it there on my own.

"Mr. Rawlins," a gruff male voice called out.

"Commander Suggs," I hailed.

The boss cop looked better than he had when he arrived. Half an hour with Mary had reinvigorated the beleaguered warrior.

"Okay," he said. "Let's sit down and make us some plans."

Amethystine took the twins down the street to a park where they could play tennis on an inside court. Mary, Melvin, and I parked ourselves at a small dinette table set off from the large kitchen.

I started off by asking Mel, "So, did you talk to Anatole?"

"I did indeed. He says that the source was Fyodor Brennan, the chief's attaché."

"Brennan? Guy used to be a homicide detective?"

"I think it was homicide," Mel replied. "That was before my time."

"I need all his numbers. Address, phone, and anything else you can get."

"I got it all. Annie didn't want to give me it, but he could see that was the only way. He made me promise not to kill him, though."

"He wouldn't be any good to us dead," Mary explained to the absent Anatole.

"Brennan almost always has these two cops with him," Mel said. "We call 'em Frick and Frack, but really they're Sergeant Dennis Haines and Patrolman Jesse Tran. The three of them together are called Dirty Tricks. Frick and Frack stay by his side all the time except at night, when they drop him off at the Sash and Tail."

"The strip club?" I asked.

"You know the place?"

"Yeah."

"Yeah," Mary added. "Bjorn Firth's bar."

"I figure all we need is a girl willing to take our boy home," Mel announced.

"You know anybody works there?" I asked my coconspirators.

"We can't do it that way," Mary said.

"Why not?"

"Because, Easy, I don't mind if something goes wrong and we have to kill the cop, but if that does happen, we'd have to do something about the girl too."

Melvin and I locked eyes. Neither one of us had ever been on a job with Mary. Intellectually, we understood that she was one of the most dangerous people we knew, but this was the first time I'd experienced the actual menace.

"I told Annie that I wouldn't kill the guy," Mel said.

"How many times have you arrested guys for murder, and they told you that things just got outta hand?" Mary asked her man.

"Yeah," I agreed so Melvin wouldn't have to.

"What about Amy?" Mary offered. "She's gorgeous and knows how to talk with her eyes."

"No." That was me.

"Come on, Easy," Mary cajoled. "You didn't send her here for window dressing."

"Like you said," I argued. "It could be dangerous."

"We know where he lives."

"Suppose he takes her someplace else?"

"He takes her home," Mel assured. "Or maybe someplace else, she says she needs to call her baby sitter, tells us where to go, and that's it."

"What if he tries to do something to her?"

"Never been nuthin' about that with him. No complaints or rumors."

"That don't prove a thing and you know it, Mel."

"Hey," Mary said and then jumped up.

She dragged her chair over to the sink beneath a high cabinet, got up on the seat, opened a cupboard door, and rummaged around.

"I got these."

She brought the booty back and dumped it on the table.

It was a dark-brown glass bottle and a very neat derringer about the size of the palm of a child's hand.

"Knockout drops and a pocket pistol," the career criminal announced, almost gleefully. "She could drug him or grab Little Caesar here from a pocket."

"Grab what?" Amethystine was standing at the door to the kitchen.

"Where's the kids?" I asked. Anything to change the subject.

"They stayed playing tennis."

"You got bored watching?"

"I asked the instructor at the courts to look out for 'em. She's pretty nice."

Wanting to get ahead on the discussion I said, "Mel and Mary want you to take home a horny cop from the Sash and Tail."

The newly minted tennis mom raised her chin a quarter inch and considered. She was beautiful, but even if she weren't, I think my heart would have caught.

"Who's that?" she asked.

"A guy named Fyodor Brennan."

Amethystine looked as if she was considering the proposition.

"I'd be willing to try," she said, seconds later. "But doesn't a woman need an invitation to go into a place like that solo?"

"I know a girl could get you in," Mary said.

Something clicked in my head, and I asked, "How about a cop?"

"What?" Mary asked.

She brought her chair back to the table while Amethystine took the one empty seat.

"You said that you were interrogated by a cop after the thing with your goddaughter. Can you remember anything about him?"

Mary's eyes were searching the contents of her memory and then: "Graham. Um . . . Detective, Detective Derrek Graham."

"What about him?" Mel asked.

"He was the cop who came and questioned me, you know, after."

"Graham's a good cop," Mel said. "Real smart. How'd the interview with him go?"

"It was at a court apartment in West Hollywood. He asked me questions and I gave him answers. He asked about an alibi I had but never even checked up on it."

"He had access to the evidence," I allowed.

"If he had any idea of who you were, he'd have to suspect you," Mel concluded. "So he very well could have held something back."

"You're saying that he might've been playing a shell game?" Mary asked.

"Maybe still is," Mel offered.

"What kinda guy is this Graham?" I asked Mel.

"He don't give in or give up. You couldn't break him, and you'd be a fool to try."

"And Brennan?"

"Smart enough to fold with a weak hand."

"Then we know what link we got to break," I said.

"It'll be okay, Ezekiel," Amethystine assured me. "We outnumber him four to one."

After that the planning was mostly on Mary and Amethystine. Mel's wife explained the knockout drops and the double-triggered pistol, which carried two .30-caliber shells.

By the time Garnett and Pearl got back, the adults were in the living room, sipping red wine.

We visited for a few minutes with the kids. Then Mary and Amethystine went to Mary's bedroom to discuss clothes, hair, and makeup.

Mel went out shopping and returned to prepare dinner.

Garnett stayed in his room, leaving his twin sister, Pearl, adrift in the living room.

"Got any games?" I asked, taking pity on the fourteen-year-old's boredom.

"You play Scrabble?"

"I do."

* * *

We took her board out to the marble table in the Garden of Eden.

She was a good player and knew all kinds of sophisticated, unusual words, like *aphasia* and *schizoid*. I was a little better at getting multiple word and letter scores and so the game was pretty even.

"Your sister seems like she takes care of you guys pretty well," I said when the board was getting filled.

"She's great. Um…" Thinking about spelling. "I mean, me and Garnett don't have to worry about nuthin' really. And Amy's real smart."

"So you're happy with her?"

"Shoreline," she called out triumphantly, laying out the letters connecting two columns of already placed words. "And a double word score too."

"Dinner!" Melvin called from the glass door.

He made angel-hair pasta with hot Italian sausage simmered in a red wine and tomato sauce. Along with the entrée he served garlic bread and a green salad.

I don't know about the others, but I loved it. There's something about a cook you haven't experienced, who knows what he's doing, that makes food new and interesting.

I loved looking at Amethystine too. Her short dress was loose and bouncy. It had a red-and-blue floral design over a cream-colored background, leaving much of her form up to speculation. Her hair was pulled tight with a round ponytail at the back. Her lips were a toned-down red and the liner around her eyes was barely visible, ending in metallic gold flecks at the far end of each.

After dinner Amethystine talked to her siblings about staying inside and not opening the door for anyone.

"Where you goin'?" Pearl wanted to know.

"Just out for a drink," her sister said.

"Could you bring back a dessert?" Garnett asked.

Amethystine kissed him on the forehead and said, "Of course. But we might be so late that you'll have to have it for breakfast."

After that we were off for a night of kidnapping, maybe torture, and, according to Mary, even murder if we weren't careful.

37

"That was unfair, Ezekiel," Amethystine said on the drive to West Hollywood. We were alone in my car.

"What was?"

"Talking to my sister like that."

"Like what?"

"I could tell by the way she was sitting that she was telling you all my little secrets."

"Isn't getting to know your family a good way to know you?"

"And why would you want to do that?"

"I like you."

"Don't." She sounded as if she weren't kidding.

"Why not?"

"This, what we're doing, is just a job for you. You'll do all your little detective things and figure out who killed Curt, then you'll be off on some other case."

"What if I don't want to be off?"

"The Sash and Tail is on the next block, on the right. Let me off on the corner here so nobody sees you."

I pulled to the curb and she got out, making it a point not to look at me. I might have wondered more about this strange behavior, but the night was filled with other activities.

* * *

Mel and Mary had taken a room at the Hills Motel, two blocks up from Sunset Boulevard. When I came to join them, Mary decided to go out and get a pint of Jim Beam.

"She's something else," I said to Mel when she was gone.

"Yeah," he said contemplatively. "More than I ever imagined."

"Must make you wonder about bein' a cop."

"What makes you say that?"

"Come on, Mel. You broke your oath for her. You walked away from the job for her. Hell, you left her, for her."

The way Mel was looking at me, it seemed like he was ready to fight. Luckily the liquor store was next door and Mary's key was already sounding in the lock.

She came in and looked at us, the question in her usually unreadable eyes.

"What?" she asked.

"You bring Dixie cups?" Mel wanted to know.

As long as I was talking with Mel, concentrating on him, I felt okay—even with the threat. But when it was the three of us, I started worrying about Amethystine. Sending a woman out to seduce some man, a potentially dangerous man, was contrary to my upbringing. But even dealing with these feelings I knew that Niska was right—the world had changed.

"Don't worry," Mary said, reading my fears. "Amy's gonna be just fine."

"How can you be so sure?"

"She got knockout drops and a derringer in her clutch. If one don't get him the other one will."

"How come you had all that stuff with you?" Mel asked her.

"I hope you don't think that I would go out unprotected in this dangerous world, Mr. Suggs."

We played penny-ante blackjack on one of the two beds for nearly two hours. By that time Mel had won $1.27. Mary and I had each paid about half of that.

That's when the phone rang. I nearly jumped up.

"Hello," Mary said into the receiver. After a few moments she said, "Uh-huh, okay, twelve thirty. Okay. Got it." She hung up and said, "Twelve thirty Ringgold North."

"That's the address McCourt gave me," Mel said. "So he took her home."

"Was she okay?" I asked.

"She sounded good."

Lit by two streetlamps, the house's high arched roof was covered with dark wood shingles that came together in sinuous lines reminiscent of flowing waters. Mel drove up into the driveway and we all got out.

"You sure she sounded all right?" Mel asked Mary.

"She sounded fine."

"And you're sure it was her?"

"Come on," she said. "It's fine."

The front door was recessed inside a flat porch-like area. When the door came open and light flooded out, Amethystine called, "Come on in."

I walked right up to her and we kissed as if it was the most natural thing in the world. That was our first kiss, and I will never forget it.

She brought us down a short hall that led to a spacious sunken living room. Fyodor Brennan was laid out on a burgundy-carpeted floor.

The furniture was heavy and dark. On the wall above Brennan's unconscious body was an oil painting of some medieval castle. It didn't look like a knockoff.

Mel turned the attaché over for us to get a good look at him.

He was a small guy in a light-gray suit with dark-blue pinstriping. His mustache was razor-thin and his cologne was the strongest thing in the room.

"How did it go?" Mary asked Amethystine.

"Easy. I talked to him in the bar about the great gin fizz I made. I said it was the best anyone ever tasted. So, when we got here, he wasn't suspicious at all. After he finished the drink, he played try to kiss the girl for a few minutes and then got woozy. When he realized what was happening I bear-hugged him from behind until he passed out."

The women's conversation was quite pedestrian. Like discussing a recipe or how to discipline an unruly child.

"How long will he be out?" I asked.

"We'll have enough time to search the house, I think," Mary surmised.

Mel organized the search. After being a lead detective for a decade, he was the most qualified. He had me go through the bedroom, where I found the gun. It was taped to the underside of the bottom drawer of a green metal filing cabinet. I had to yank the drawer off the track to find it. I'd looked everywhere before that. Under rugs, in pockets, and at the back of closet shelves. I threw the mattress off the bed and raised the frame to look under the stack of nudie magazines he hid there.

All that and it still felt too easy. I would have taken that gun and buried it somewhere in the desert. Or maybe I would have given it to a good friend like John the bartender, asking him not to tell me where to find it. But, I supposed, Brennan felt invulnerable.

"Mary," I said as she and Amethystine were searching the kitchen.

"Yeah?"

"Wanna come with me over here?"

She accompanied me to Fyodor's bedroom, where I showed her what I'd found.

"Is this the weapon?" I asked Mary, holding the .22 pistol in a white handkerchief I always carried with me.

Mary didn't reach for the gun, just leaned forward, peering at the piece.

"Can you turn it over?" she asked.

Using the hand under the silk, I flipped the gun.

"I can't believe it," she said. "That bastard took it."

"You're sure?"

"It had the same red paint stain on the butt."

I wrapped the gun in silk and shoved it into a pocket.

"But why would Graham keep it in the first place?" Melvin asked when we were reconvened in the sunken living room.

The still-unconscious Fyodor was tied up with electrical tape I'd taken from Shadrach's house. Waste not, want not.

"I bet I know," said Mary.

"What?" That was Amethystine. She hadn't actually seen the pistol. I was trying to protect her but there she was, deeply involved.

"It was when he questioned me," Mary answered. "That's it.

He had brought my file to the bungalow. They had been investigating me over a thing I was doing with this Yugoslavian diplomat guy."

"Doing what?" Mel asked. He couldn't help it.

"Guy's name was Stefan, Stefan Davidovitch. He had a contact in South Africa who was moving diamonds. They wanted me to help with sales in America; thought that selling them here would cause less trouble. So when Graham asked me about Stefan, I figured if I just said I knew the guy it wouldn't hurt. But I guess he saw something."

"So he held on to the gun for leverage," Amethystine surmised.

"Then why didn't he ever use it?" I wanted to know.

"Stefan died from a heart attack a month or so after that," Mary told us.

"Then," I said, "years later, Laks goes to Brennan and offers him Mel's job, and Brennan finds out that Graham had once been on Mary's tail. Only question is, why Laks do all that?"

"Me bein' a bulldog," Suggs admitted. "It wasn't just the time I saved your ass, Easy. I didn't like Laks, and I pulled the rug out from under him every chance I got. I heard it that the chief was gettin' tired of his vigilantism. Maybe he planned to use me to get him out of office."

"Maybe?" I asked.

"There was a couple'a meetings. But I said I wasn't interested in being underhanded. If they wanted him out, they should'a fired him."

Remembering these events, I'm most aware of the fact that I wasn't in my right mind. The worst thing that a man in my situation could do would be to work with career criminals, cops, or strangers. I was working with all three. The mistake that most people made was thinking about right then. That night we were friends with goals that benefited us, mutually. But I know, from experience, that friends often turn into enemies. Sometimes your best friend will wake up in the middle of the night realizing that you could turn on him — or her.

Criminals, cops, and strangers.

Even then, in that dark wood-shingled house, I knew that I was setting myself up.

At that moment I turned and started walking from the room.

"Where you goin'?" Mel asked.

"To see if your boy got some tequila."

38

Fyodor had Cuervo, limes, triple sec, salt, and just the right glasses for a classic margarita. I'd finished making and serving the third round when Brennan started making moaning noises like he wanted to wake up.

It was nearly 2:30 in the morning and we were at peace with our cactus libation. Our attention was on the captive, but he was taking his own sweet time. Amethystine got bored waiting and so went into the kitchen and came back with a pitcher filled with water and ice cubes.

This she poured down the back of Fyodor's midnight-blue shirt.

He lurched awake, struggling against his bonds. At first, I don't think he was aware of our presence.

"Hey, Fyodor," Mel said.

The attaché stopped thrashing around and looked up to the voice.

"Suggs? Why you got me like this?"

Mel took out the murder weapon, saying, "Either you gonna explain this gun or I'm'a choke you."

That was when the police chief's aide looked around the

room. We must have seemed like a serious group, a lynch mob. He knew Mary and was at least aware of who I was.

"Cut his left hand free, Easy," Mel said. "And pour the motherfucker a drink."

I did as asked.

Fyodor gagged on the first swallow, but that didn't keep him from the second, third, and fourth.

"You know you can't get away with this," he said to us all. When nobody trembled in fear he said to Mel, "You helped Peter Barth beat a grand theft charge."

"Yeah, about that," Mel agreed. "Evidence got lost but Master Sergeant Creaque located it just today. A new warrant's out on Barth right now. So, Fyodor, you don't have a card to play."

"Laks'll kill me."

"Laks won't be a problem," I said.

"What do you know?" my prisoner asked dismissively.

"I know about that film Mirth killed Tommy Jester tryin' to get."

"The chief'll see it first thing tomorrow morning," Mel added.

We had him and he knew it.

"You don't have anything on me," he announced to the general populace of the room.

"We don't need to," I said. "'Cause you better believe Laks'll take you down with him."

"I didn't do anything wrong," Fyodor said loudly and yet unconvincingly.

Mel tensed. I put a hand on his bulging right biceps and he eased up.

"Look, Fyodor," I said. "I know you can see what's going on

292 • WALTER MOSLEY

here. Laks is gonna be out on his ass and somebody's gonna have to oversee the investigation. Mel tells me that it'll most likely be you, especially if you're the one hands over the film of Laks to the chief. The girls' names are on the inside of the box."

It was way too much information for the attaché. Fyodor had to wonder about what happened to Mirth. If Mel knew that he had anything to do with the cop assassin coming after him, what would he do in retaliation?

Fyodor's eyes darted back and forth among the four of us. Finally he vomited—violently. Margarita and something like half-digested pastrami went down his dark shirt and onto the maroon carpeting below.

He was pathetic. Defeated and weakened, he slumped, his head hanging down.

Amethystine, the volunteer mother, went to the bathroom and returned with a dampened washrag and a bath towel. The latter she spread over the dampened rug. Then she pressed the cool washrag against Fyodor's forehead.

He sighed in momentary relief.

When Amethystine moved away I pulled a chair up to face the errant cop.

"Look, man," I said. "You're torturing yourself thinking you have to make the right decision. But there's no decision to make. Tomorrow morning Mel will be back in his office and a copy of the film clip will be in your inbox. You're going to take that film to the chief and he's going to take it from there."

"Why, why, why doesn't Mel take it?"

"I like being in special projects," Commander Suggs said. "I don't want or need to be an administrator."

"Why me?" Fyodor asked.

"Because," Mary interjected, "you're in this shit up to your nuts and that makes you a loose end. And loose ends either get tied up or cut off."

Seeing Mary in the role of inquisitor was yet another novel experience. She went right to the heart of the attaché's problem; you could see it in his eyes.

"We're, we're good if I do this?" he asked Mel.

"Solid."

"But remember," I put in. "We have other copies of the film. If you give it to Laks, then all bets are off."

I had no compunction about lying to him.

He tried to nod, but his face looked most like a quivering leaf.

"With that one hand, it should take you five or six minutes to get yourself free," I told him. "Don't forget what we said."

"That's right," Mel added. Then he hit our prisoner with an honest-to-God haymaker. Fyodor was unconscious before hitting the floor, the chair shattering beneath him.

"What's the chief gonna think about that black eye?" Mary asked her man.

"I don't give a fuck what he thinks."

The four of us drove back to the Hills Motel. After saying good-bye to our confederates, I drove Amethystine to Studio City. Once there I parked out in front of the building and we sat for a few moments in silence.

"You wanna come in?" she offered.

"I gotta get home to my own kids before they forget what I look like."

"You live a very interesting life, Ezekiel," she said.

"Not as a rule. Most of the time I work alone or maybe with

one helper. For that matter, most often, I take on just one case at a time."

"I know. I don't want to pester you, but have you figured out who killed Curt?"

"No. And before I go any further, I'll put you in touch with Mel. He's a good cop and he owes both of us."

Then she leaned over, gave me a long, soulful kiss, leaned back to smile and study, then kissed me again.

"Is that a goodbye kiss?" I asked her.

"Only if you need it to be."

I got back to Brighthope Canyon and Roundhouse a couple of hours before sunrise. Fearless was sitting on the outer patio beyond the koi pond, smoking a cigarette. There looked to be a little creature trundling around his feet.

When I approached, he said, "Hey, Ease," without turning to see me.

The creature yipped and jumped at me playfully. It was all black with soulful yellow eyes.

"Another dog?" I asked.

"Told you I was gonna get you a guard dog."

"Guard dog? This just much a toy as the other two." I reached down to scratch behind the puppy's ears.

"Toy that's gonna get up around a hunnert eighty pounds."

"What breed?" I took the seat opposite Fearless and the guard puppy jumped into my lap.

"A few. Bull mastiff the dominant one, though. When he's grown this niggah here could kill a lion by hisself."

"Mastiff, huh?"

"He will love you and yours and take down anybody you point at."

"An' why you think I need somethin' like that?"

"You gettin' old, Easy, you know you need a edge."

"Maybe." I considered the little creature. There was something feral even in the way he played.

"Everything work out?" my friend asked.

"Some of it. Mel'll be back in his office tomorrow morning, and if everything works, Laks'll be out by the afternoon."

"What's the rest of it?"

"Amethystine."

"I thought the cops were gonna work that case."

"There's only so much they can do."

"What's that s'posed to mean?"

"I'm'a go up to bed, Fearless."

"If you don't need me no mo', I'll probably be gone by the time you get up. Feather and Jesus know what to do with the dog."

"Okay. Drop by the office to get what I owe ya."

39

I awoke to the sound of a child crying. Looking down I saw that a sunbeam was shining on my left foot. Little Essie wailed loud and long from the kitchen floor, reminding me of air-raid sirens in the night. I had every intention of going downstairs and comforting my granddaughter, but instead I turned over in the bed, falling back into a deep bunker of sleep.

The next thing I heard was Essie and Jesus playing downstairs. The sunlight had moved up to the wall. Jesus's laugh was more rare than the prehistoric shrimp that hatch after a deluge in the desert once every decade or so. My son's laughter was the hard-earned humor of a man sentenced to hell and then saved on a whim.

The beauty of that guffaw washed over me, returning the sleep to my eyes.

"Daddy?"

Two seconds after the wake-up call I felt the blunt paws of the guard puppy on my chest. I knew it was him because the other two dogs were lighter, bouncier.

"What?" My eyes were still closed.

"It's Niska."

I hadn't heard the phone ring. At least I hadn't distinguished it from the sirens blaring in my dreams.

"What's she want?"

"I don't know. It's after three."

I opened my eyes. The sun was shining somewhere else.

"She says it's important," Feather insisted.

"What time is it?"

"I just told you, three."

"And Niska's on the phone?"

"Uh-uh. She wants you to call her back."

"Where's Jesus and them?"

"They went to Pismo Beach for a picnic. They wanted me to come, but I had to stay and take care of Prince Valiant."

"Who?"

"That's your dog's name. I named him that because he reminds me of Fearless."

"The two'a you get outta here and let me get dressed."

I remember her kissing my forehead and the puppy's nose on my cheek.

"Hello?" she answered.

"Hey, girl," I said.

"Hi, Mr. Rawlins. You sick?"

"Naw. Just catchin' up on my sleep. You got somethin' for me?"

"I think so. A woman called for you. She said her name is…"

Niska gave me a phone number. I called it, got what I needed, and fifteen minutes later I was dressed in proper gray trousers, black leather shoes, a black T-shirt, and a yellow sweater buttoned up to the diaphragm. When the phone rang again, I decided not to answer but Feather didn't know that.

"Dad!"

"Hello?"

"I expected you to call me by now, Rawlins."

"Hey, Mel, what's up?"

"When I called at noon, they told me you were asleep."

"While you were on holiday in the mountains, I was workin' night and day. And I'm about to go out now. You need somethin'?"

"Laks is in the wind."

Those five words, as the hipsters used to say, definitely interfered with my flow. It was like sitting in the cabin again, suddenly aware of a possible assassin in the bushes.

"He left home at four in the morning after getting a call," Mel continued. "Told his wife that he had an emergency at the office. Half an hour ago they found his car at LAX."

"That don't mean a thing." Another five words.

"No. Fyodor must'a called him the minute he was free."

"What about him?"

"Fyodor?"

"Yeah."

"He's in his office. Probably waiting for that film clip."

"You didn't send it?"

"I did . . . to the chief."

"Wow. Laks must'a had more bones in his closet than we knew about."

"Must be."

There was little more that we could say over the line.

"I'll talk to you later, Mel."

"Talk to you then."

Feather and I played with the new puppy for a while. She told me what Fearless had explained about training a guard dog. After that I headed for the door.

"Where you goin', Daddy?"

"Out to find somebody."

"Okay."

My destination was Brown's Hotel, on Olympic, downtown.

The man at the front desk was tall, gaunt, and white-ash-colored, in a gray suit. He asked how he could help me in such a way that he might as well have said, *Get the hell outta here.*

"Chita Moyer," I replied brightly.

"Yes?" he asked.

"Could you call her room and tell her that Mr. Rawlins is here?"

"For what purpose?"

"She's the one called me, man. You could ask her that question if you want."

The concierge turned half away from me to make the call. I couldn't hear what was being said but there seemed to be some kind of disagreement. Finally, he cradled the phone and faced me.

"You can wait in the lounge," he said.

There were two turquoise-colored, high-backed, lightly padded chairs sitting next to a tall and slender window that looked down on Olympic. Set between and before the chairs was a round wooden table with a high-gloss top.

Upon the little table lay a folded-up copy of the *LA Examiner*. I amused myself, reading about things that may or may not have happened.

There was a brief description of the death of Curt Fields on page twenty-four. He was shot in the head and the authorities suspected that he had at least two partners. They had broken into the 2120 Building in order to steal valuable equipment. One of the partners, Aaron Oliver, of Reno, Nevada, was found in the stairwell outside and a floor down from where Curt was found. The police were looking for the partner or partners who committed the murders.

"Mr. Rawlins."

I looked up and then stood, holding out a hand, which she took after only a moment of hesitation.

"Please sit," she offered, and we both settled in our moderately comfortable high-backed chairs.

"Mr. Arkady said that he didn't want to send you up to the room because you were being belligerent. I thought I explained over the phone what happened in San Diego."

"You did," I agreed, "and I wasn't being anything to Mr. Arkady. I'm here because you asked me to come. I don't think it was right for you to drug me and then call the police. But those are small issues, all things considered."

"That's good. I never meant you any harm."

"Okay. Now what is it you want?"

"I need you to do something for me."

"That's what you said over the phone."

It was her turn. She hesitated a bit before taking the plunge into cold water.

"Last night," she said, "Harrison went out, for a smoke he

said, and never came back. When I looked for your card in my purse, I found a great deal of cash."

"How much?"

"Around thirty thousand dollars."

"That's a great deal, indeed. Why would he do that?"

"As I told you on the phone, Harrison had me drug you because there were people after him and he couldn't be sure that you hadn't joined forces with them."

"You didn't tell me who was after him."

"Gangsters." She shivered as if a cold breeze had found its way to her shoulders.

"Could you be a little more specific?"

"Las Vegas gangsters."

"Oh."

"He didn't tell me very much about them. He did say that they might have wanted to kill him to keep him quiet. Do you know what he was talking about?"

"Maybe, but could you tell me something first?"

"Certainly."

"If your boyfriend thought I might be trying to kill him, then why would you call me?"

"He changed his mind about you," she said. "That's why he didn't, you know..."

"Didn't what?"

"Didn't kill you in the house. That was the plan, but talking with you, Harry was pretty sure that all you wanted to do was help poor Curt's ex-wife."

It was an odd feeling, thinking of this frail elder woman as my executioner.

"I think the people after Harrison, if anybody really is after

him, would be men called Shadrach and Purlo. He met them at
a poker club in Gardena, and Curt was, somehow, working
for them."

"Did they murder Curt?" she asked.

"I don't know," I said honestly. "Now, let me ask you something else."

"Okay."

"Do you believe Harrison?"

Chita seemed very small in that towering chair. A lovely
woman of a certain age, alone in the world and looking at me as
if I were the embodiment of that question, as if I were an indict-
ment of her entire life.

"Yes," she said at last. "I wanted to go back to South America
for many years. But my resources had dwindled, and he was a
gambler, usually down on his luck. Then he called a few days
ago saying that he'd had a windfall. He got into a high-stakes
game and won."

I was enjoying her tale.

She hunched her shoulders and continued. "I knew he was
lying."

"How'd you know that?"

"Harrison is two things: bad luck and a good time. I knew he
was lying, but..." Gazing across the lounge, she stopped talking
for the moment.

"So, what do you want from me, Mrs. Moyer?"

"I want you to find him and tell him that I'm not afraid."

"I don't understand. Didn't you just tell me that he was lying
to you?"

"You asked if I believed him. And maybe I don't believe him,
but I do trust him."

My expression said that I didn't understand the nuance.

"A few days ago, James Carnaby from Royalty Cruises' main office called me," she said. "He's the man who sold me and Harrison passage to Buenos Aires. James told me that a man had been asking about me, about when I was leaving. When I asked who it was he said he didn't get a name but the man looked rough and had a scar over his lip. Harrison tried to play it off. He said it was probably some insurance agent wanting to sell me a useless policy. But after that he was very worried. And then you showed up at our door."

"You two came here," I concluded. "And he left in the night."

"I want you to find him and to tell him that I'm not afraid," she reiterated.

When she lifted her pocketbook, I considered grabbing it away from her. But, I thought, she probably wasn't reaching for a pistol, and Mr. Arkady had been eyeing us from the front desk. I didn't want to spend another night in jail.

Chita came out with a fat envelope.

"Five thousand dollars," she said, and laid the pregnant letter on the round table.

I became aware of my hands. They were resting on my thighs, not reaching for the parcel.

"Why would you trust me?" I asked.

"Because Harrison said that he believed you were a good man. He really does have a good feel for people."

"Then why did he drug me?"

"I've already explained that. We drugged you just in case he was wrong."

That moment felt like a perfect little example of life: someone I shouldn't trust asking for my help, money that I shouldn't take lying there in front of me, and a man behind the front desk staring from his post, preparing to pounce if I did anything wrong.

"Will you help me?" she asked.

"I don't see how. I don't know how I'd find him."

Chita leaned forward, gazing into my eyes.

"There's a young man named Paul German," she said.

"Okay."

"Harry taught him how to play cards. It's funny, Harry couldn't win if his life depended on it, but if he came across someone with talent, he could make them rich. Paul might know how to get in touch with him."

"Have you called this Paul?"

"I don't have his number."

"Look him up."

"I tried. He's not listed. He lives in a studio apartment in Westwood, on Astral Lane." She gave me the address.

"Why don't you go there?"

"Harrison always said that there was no trust among gamblers, just hard knocks and brass rings."

"So Paul might be one of the people who want him dead?"

"I'm an old woman, Mr. Rawlins. Go there for me. I'll pay you five thousand dollars up front, just to deliver a message."

"Okay," I said. "All right. You'll be here?"

"I'm paid up through the next five days."

"Okay. You can keep your money. I'll go talk to this guy German and see what he has to say."

40

I was at the Studio City hideout by a quarter to eight. Mary answered the door.

She was wearing a gray sharkskin one-piece button-up that was open at the throat. On an extremely thin gold chain necklace there hung a bright-blue opal.

She noticed me noticing.

"Mel give me it," she said on a real smile. "He was just so happy to be together again."

"He in?"

"Uh-uh. I guess a lotta problems piled up while he was away."

"How about Amethystine?"

"That is so cute."

"What?"

"How you say her whole name like some priest calling out for the Father, the Son, and the Holy Ghost."

"Are you Catholic, Mary?"

"Amy's not here. Took the kids out to a cousin in Riverside, I think. You wanna come in and wait for Mel?"

That night was Harvey Wallbangers. I must have had six of them. They tasted like anything but vodka.

"I wanna thank you for saving my Mel," she said upon serving the third round.

"You helped too."

"All I did was provide the list of ingredients. You did the shopping, the cooking, and the serving too."

"You think my prints were on that gun?" she asked midway through the fourth round.

"I dunno," I said with a wave of my hand. "But I'm positive that it never got tested."

"Guess I'm lucky that it wasn't Mel or Anatole that was the detective on the case."

Looking up from her tall glass, Mary considered me.

"You know, if you and Mel weren't friends I'd do you right here on this rug," she said. "Fuck you hard enough that you'd still remember it on your dying day."

That sentiment set me up straight on the couch. We stared at each other for a while until I said, "Woman, go make us another drink and think of something to say won't make me feel like I'm about to get shot in the back'a my head."

She laughed loud and long. In my inebriation I could see that allowing herself to get drunk, alone with me, was the most intimate thing she could accomplish.

Mel showed up around 11:00.

"You guys been drinkin', huh?" he said from the entranceway.

"Like barracudas at the bottom of the ocean," his wife verified.

"What took you, Mel?" I asked as he settled down next to Mary.

"Laks killed himself."

"He what?"

"Bullet to the brain and all his troubles were gone."

"Where'd they find him?"

"Motel on Hollywood Boulevard. Been dead for hours. Nobody heard the shot."

"Killed himself," I said, as if trying to commit it to memory.

"I would'a done it myself if I could," Mary announced.

"Don't say that," Mel said.

"Motherfucker was tryin' to destroy you. Hell if I wouldn't'a done the same to him." Both rage and confidence shone in her eyes.

It struck me that over the whole time of Mel's problems she never showed any fear for herself.

"He was a brother and we drove him to this," Mel told his wife. "That's wrong."

"What about Fyodor?" I asked, partly to defuse the tension.

"He's out. After I talked to the chief he told Brennan to clean out his desk."

"Hi, everybody," Amethystine hailed. She'd taken Mel's place at the entrance to the living room.

She wore a bright-blue blouse and her hair was tied up into a tight ball at the back of her head.

"Hey, Amy," Mary greeted. "Let me fix you one of my famous Harvey Wallbangers."

"No, honey. All I need is some sleep."

She came into the room and sat down on a chair next to my end of the couch. She reached out and pressed my hand for an instant.

"Why are you men so serious?" she asked.

Mary told most of the story, scaling back on her glee in deference to Mel.

When she finished I asked Amethystine if she'd mind giving me a ride home.

"I'd love to," was her answer.

"I got people on those guys Shadrach and Purlo," Mel said as I got to my feet. "Looks like both of them have disappeared, though."

My client nodded but didn't ask or say anything.

"This is bad," I said to myself as she navigated our way toward Brighthope.

"What is?"

"It's the second time in a week I needed somebody to drive me home."

"Nice work if you can get it."

"Maybe I need a vacation."

"Where would we go?"

That turned my head in her direction.

"I thought you said we'd stop seeing each other when I finished my investigation."

"I did."

"But now we're going on a vacation?"

"I said that, you know, because I didn't want you to think I was using you."

"Using me how?"

"I don't know. But I still want to see you."

The only thing I could think to ask was, "Why'd you take Garnett and Pearl to Riverside?"

"The apartment was gettin' kinda crowded and I didn't want them eavesdropping on the things we were talkin' about."

"That's such a good answer," I mused.

"What?" she queried, still with a smile on her face. "You think it sounds made-up?"

"No, no, no, no, no . . ."

Those were the last words I remembered saying until she and I were walking and stumbling on the blue-brick path to Round-house.

Feather answered the door and Amethystine introduced herself.

"I'm one of your father's clients," she said. "We were celebrating the end of the case and he had a few drinks too many."

I was less than half-aware, but I could still register how enchanted my daughter was with Amethystine.

"Hi, honey," I said.

"You smell drunk, Daddy."

"Really? That's good. I thought I might'a stepped in somethin'."

When I awoke, Amethystine was sleeping next to me. We were both naked and half-covered in the sheets. I sat up and looked down at her. Her eyes opened, and she gave me a wide grin.

"Don't worry," she confided. "I didn't take advantage of you."

"You ever hear of a guy named Paul German?"

"No pillow talk for you, huh?"

"He's a friend of Harrison's and a gambler. I thought maybe he knew Curt."

Giving up on flirtation she said, "There was a Paul guy used to come to the club sometimes. I don't remember his last name but he was bald and in his forties."

"No. This is a young guy. A good player."

"I don't think so," she said, and then she kissed me.

What went undone the night before we accomplished that morning.

By the time we came downstairs, Feather was long gone to school.

I made us a simple breakfast of scrambled eggs and toast, fresh grapefruit and coffee.

"What are you doing today, Mr. Rawlins?"

"I have an appointment I got to keep."

"Doing what?"

"I just need to get a few answers."

"Not about me, I hope."

"Why not about you? I thought you still needed answers."

"Curt is beyond help and Commander Suggs said that Shadrach and Ron have gone."

I heard the words, but it was the strength of character in her tone that arrested me. It hadn't been since the days of Anger Lee that I felt so enamored.

"No," I said. "I mean, yeah, yeah, Mel got the gangsters covered. This is another case. A woman whose husband deserted her."

"So you've moved off from me," she flirted.

"You know that's not true."

"You need a ride?"

"No. I keep a few old cars in the parking lot downstairs. I don't think I'll be gone that long."

41

Up on the roof I sucked down a deeply needed cigarette. After that, all I had to do was get dressed and show Amethystine where she might find a bathing suit in Feather's chest of drawers.

"Do you think she'll mind?" the ex-wife, almost ex-client, asked.

"Not a bit," I said, before kissing Amethystine goodbye.

The address on Astral Lane was a boxy seven-story hollow structure with walls one apartment wide on every side. The hollow center of the building had outer stairways leading upward to the various floors and abodes.

The mailbox on the first floor told me that Paul German lived in 4C.

Noonday sun and shadows cascaded down through the maze of stairways as I made my way to his door.

I pressed his button, heard a buzzing in the distance, knocked, and buzzed again.

"He's out of town," a man said.

The voice came from behind me, across the atrium.

I turned and said, "Yeah. I heard that he might be out in

Atlantic City but I'm only in town a couple'a days, so I decided to drop by and knock."

"I don't know about all that," the man said, coming out of his door. "But I haven't seen Paul in weeks."

The neighbor's Caucasian skin had seen a great deal of sun in his sixty-some years. He carried a fairly large and empty canvas bag, telling me that he was probably going off to some grocery store.

"Yeah," I said meaninglessly. "A guy told me that Paul might have come back. That was an older gentleman called Harry."

"You got me." The shopper hunched his shoulders and began making his way down the stairs.

If he had gone back into his apartment, I would have been the one taking the stairs, worried that he might be watching through some peephole. If he did that, he would have seen me trying the doorknob of 4C and finding it unlocked. When I passed the threshold of German's apartment, the midday shopper might have been compelled to call the police.

I didn't have to go far. Ohioan, math enthusiast, and lucky in love if not cards—Harrison Fields was dead on the bare pine floor of the tiny living room. Dressed in a herringbone jacket and dark-green pants, his right eye was open wide while the left had been shot out. Lifeless lips bore an insincere grin.

I took out my traveling gloves, my breaking-and-entering gloves, and donned them like a doctor preparing to perform an examination or maybe a coroner looking for the cause of death. When I knelt down next to the dandy, I got a scent, a pleasant smell that was at odds with the situation. Then I went through the dead man's pockets, looking for anything that might explain why he was there and, also, why he died there.

His wallet had seven dollars in it and also a driver's license that had a picture of Harrison under the name Mark Melon. There was some change in a front pocket. Mixed in with the quarters and dimes was a five-dollar poker chip from the Exeter Casino. There was a single key in the other front pocket.

The only thing I kept was the poker chip.

The door opposite the front led to a bedroom. The bed was made. An old leather suitcase stood upright in a corner. Next to the travel bag was a blue satchel that turned out to be filled with cash.

Without opening the suitcase, I sat on the bed, reached for the phone on the nightstand, and once again called Anatole McCourt.

It was pretty much the same routine as at the 2120 Building, with fewer players. Four uniforms showed up first. This time they knew my name and merely asked me to stick around. Five or six minutes later a detective in a dark suit arrived. His name was Holder. The senior officer sent the uniforms out to canvas the seven floors of the hollow-hearted building.

While Detective Holder looked around, I took a seat in the kitchen. It was pretty neat in there. An orderly line of tiny ants was making its way to and from a crack in a cabinet door below the one-basin sink. They seemed so peaceful following a path that was millions of years old, that was so much more civilized than any punch-drunk civilian walking the streets of Los Angeles.

"What's it look like?" I heard Anatole ask from the living room.

His voice got me moving.

"What you see is what you get, Captain," Holder, a white man of early and hale middle age, replied. "Single shot to the left eye."

When I emerged, Holder gestured toward me and said, "He was here like you said. Told me the door was unlocked. And, oh yeah, there's a blue bag in there with a whole fuck of a lot of money in it."

"Carry on," McCourt told Holder. Then he turned his gaze on me.

That was one of the memorable moments of my career because he held out a hand for me to clasp.

"Thank you, Mr. Rawlins," were the words he used, but it was his heartfelt tone that arrested.

"Nuthin' to it, Captain. Just doin' my civic duty."

I don't know what Holder made of our restrained lovefest. I'm pretty sure that the detective considered me a possible, maybe even probable, suspect. He'd never know that I solved a case that even Anatole couldn't take on.

"You're going to have to give a witness statement," Anatole informed me.

Two uniforms were coming through Paul German's front door.

"Sure," I said to Anatole. "But I have an appointment downtown. Could I do it later on?"

"Certainly. I'll walk you down to your car."

When Anatole and I got out on the landing, someone shouted, "That's him! The Black one!"

It was the shopper from across the way, his canvas bag now filled with vegetables, cans, and small boxes. He was talking to one of the uniforms at the door to his apartment.

* * *

"I suppose this has to do with the missing person case you were working on?" Anatole asked when we had reached my blue Pontiac.

"I heard that the guy lives here had studied poker under Curt's uncle Harrison. I sure didn't expect to find the old man dead."

"What's with the false ID?"

"I don't know. Maybe he was afraid of being found out."

"Found out about what?"

"I'm really not positive, but I think he had somehow double-crossed the gamblers."

"What about Chita Moyer? Where's she in all this?"

"I really don't know."

"And why were you looking for the old guy?"

"My client, Amethystine Stoller, Curt Fields's ex-wife, wanted to know what had happened. I thought Harrison might have some idea."

"You get this address from the guy we found in the closet?"

"Yeah, yeah."

Anatole knew that I was holding back. I could tell that by the way he looked at me. But I had a get-out-of-jail-free card from helping Mel and exposing the plot against him. He wasn't going to lean on me — this time.

"You got any idea who killed the old man?" he asked.

"No," I lied.

When I got home, Feather was already back from school. She and Amethystine were laughing next to the grotto-like pool that Feather practiced in. They jumped in and started swimming back and forth in the Olympic-size pool. In between laps, Feather gave Amethystine pointers to make her movements more proficient.

Orchestra Solomon, the owner of the mountain upon which stood Brighthope Canyon, stood at the side of the water watching the younger woman and girl. Orchestra, also called Sadie, loved the energy and abilities of women. She often came out to watch Feather swim. Tall and elegant, down-to-earth and regal, Sadie was the richest woman west of the Rockies, it was said.

"Hi, Daddy," Feather called when she saw my approach.

Jumping out of the rough-hewn pool, my daughter ran into me, her arms thrown around my neck. I knew this meant that she was happy with the presence of my latest client.

"You havin' a good time?" I asked.

"Yeah. Amy's great. She could be a really good swimmer if she worked at it."

Amethystine joined us.

"I'd try out for the Olympics if I could only start ten years ago," she said.

"Do they have a senior Olympics?" I asked.

"One day, probably," my daughter allowed.

"You find your missing husband?" Amethystine asked me.

"Oh yeah. I always get my man."

Our eyes locked for a moment, and then Orchestra came up to us.

"You know, Easy," the sixty-something multimillionaire said. "Ever since you and Feather came to live here I've been much happier."

"That makes three of us."

"And Amy," Orchestra added, "she's so beautiful. Have you ever been to Madagascar?"

"Can't say I have. I was in North Africa in the war, though."

Looking at Amethystine with almost hungry eyes she said, "Amy is lovely like they are there. And those women are the most beautiful on earth."

After making this pronouncement, Sadie Solomon walked off, headed for her home. I watched her go, thinking that the world she lived in was somehow different than the one I and mine inhabited.

"Mrs. Blue gave me the day off," Amethystine said from behind me, shattering the trivial reverie.

Before I could turn, a human-size splash indicated that my fish of a daughter was back in the water.

"…but I'm going in to work tonight," our guest concluded.

I reached out to touch her shoulder. It felt real.

"You want a ride to your car?" she asked.

A few months after my stint at Nuremberg, I was stationed in Paris as squad leader of a troop of Black soldiers that participated, almost daily, in marches down the ancient boulevards, celebrating Allied victory.

During that time, I made friends with an older French guy named Gaston. He lived in a doorway down an impossibly slender alley about a block away from our temporary barracks. I used to bring him bottles of wine along with cheese and baguettes.

Having been raised among the French-speaking people of Louisiana, I could communicate, in a limited way, through that specialized dialect. In the war my language skills improved so it was easy for the Frenchman and me to converse.

"I was a middle-class man before the war," he told me one

318 • WALTER MOSLEY

afternoon while we passed a bottle of red wine back and forth. "I lived in a fourth-tier flat of an elevator building."

"That sounds very nice, Gaston," I said.

We were sitting on wooden crates, getting high, remembering times before the slaughter of millions.

"Do you know what we used to say back then?" he asked.

"No, sir, I don't."

"If someone came home and took the lift to their floor and then pressed the button for the lobby, we would say, 'That is someone who knows how to send the elevator back down.'"

"I'd love a ride," I said to Amethystine.

She was someone who lived the life that Gaston had been talking about in the twilight of war. That didn't mean she was good or virtuous, just that she was a comrade, no matter what.

42

"You're so quiet," Amethystine said after maybe fifteen minutes on the road.

"I am? Guess I'm a little played out."

"You are a beautiful man."

"Old man," I corrected.

"Not quite yet."

Joe South was on her radio advising Americans to "Walk a Mile in My Shoes."

"I had a real heart-to-heart with your friend Shadrach," I said at song's end.

"He's no friend of mine," she replied.

"Acquaintance, then."

We were coming up on the outskirts of Studio City. Amethystine pulled her car to the curb on Coldwater Canyon Avenue. She turned in the driver's seat to face me.

"What did he say?" she asked.

"That Harrison was Sturdyman."

"Oh? I didn't know that," she claimed.

I smiled. "You know, you get more charming when you lie."

Her dark face took on a different kind of darkness.

Forging on, I said, "The first thing I noticed about you was your perfume."

"It was? What about it?"

"It's very pleasant but not really sweet."

"You like that?"

"Garnett needed an operation. He needed it and you borrowed the money from Shad. He turned around and sold your debt to Purlo, who planned to use you, in a carnal way, with his big players."

Everything about her right then was remote, maybe even calculating.

"I already told you all that," she said.

"That's where Curt came in. He offered to do a secret job for Ron P. that would enable him to pull off the Exeter Casino deal in Vegas. Curt took the job to save you. Maybe he thought you'd come back to him. You'd fly off to Paris and he wouldn't be so boring anymore. The only problem was Harrison. Curt was still a kid. He wasn't sure of himself, so he asked his favorite, funny uncle for advice. Harrison saw the possibilities. He probably thought that he was helping you guys."

"Helping?" She couldn't keep the hatred out of her tone.

"Yeah. He made contact with someone, a bigger crook somewhere, and made the deal to sell Curt's work for a sizable down payment and probably a piece of the action. Finally, after a whole lifetime of being a loser, Harrison Fields was gonna come out on top."

She was as still as a cat that had come across potential prey. I think she might have hated me for talking about Curt's uncle with a trace of empathy.

Then she sat back, took a breath, and relaxed.

"I don't care," she said.

"No, you don't."

"What's that supposed to mean?"

"Why didn't you take the money?" I asked.

"What are you?" she condemned. "Like a trained seal show-ing you can balance a ball on your nose?"

"Come on, girl, answer my question."

Instead, she said, "It's because you came up so poor, huh? My mother was like that. We'd be somewhere in Dallas and she'd put a hand on my shoulder and say, 'Child, we gotta get outta heah. They's trouble.' And when I'd ask her how she knew, she'd say, 'I can smell it.'

"Just like you smelled my perfume on Harrison. I, I hugged him because I didn't want him to suspect why I was there."

That turned me, a little bit more, in her direction.

"I didn't take the money," she said, "because I was there for Curt. When I read him saying that Sturdyman was out, I knew that Harrison had fucked up and pulled Curt down with him."

"You could smell it?"

She smiled despite herself. "I don't know how he tricked his way into where Curt was, but that note told me that he did. He killed that man Oliver outside the room Curt was in and then . . ." She took a breath to contain the grief. "I'd been to Paul's place a few times—to ask him if he knew where Harrison was. The last time I went, before seeing you in Studio City, Harrison was there alone. Paul had left him a key if he ever needed a place to stay. When I pulled out Mary's derringer, he broke down. He said that he didn't mean to kill Curt, that he brought the gun to give to him—"

"He admitted killing him?"

"Yes. He said Curt didn't want to run with him. When Harrison pushed, Curt said that he had to tell Purlo what Harrison was doing in order to save me..."

"And what, exactly, was Harrison doing?"

"It's like you said. He sold Curt's reports to mob guys he knew in Cincinnati. Then, then, then he said that he did it for me too."

"Huh?"

"Yeah. He said that Purlo would still own my debt and he was sure to kill Curt when they were through. He said that killing Curt would mean that only one of us would die instead of all three."

"Is that when you shot him?"

Instead of answering she straightened up in her seat, turned the ignition, and pulled away from the curb.

When we merged into traffic I said, "I hope you wore a pair of gloves."

"I'm no idiot, Ezekiel."

We got to the apartment hideaway and Amethystine pulled up behind my parked car. There was a ticket under my windshield wiper.

We sat there for a moment in labored silence. I wanted to forget everything I knew, to start over again.

Maybe Amethystine was a mind reader, maybe she just knew me that well after only a few days, because she asked me, "Can't we just get over it? Start over again?"

"You murdered that man."

"He killed Curt...for money."

"I got to go."

"Will you call me?"

I wanted just to say *no,* no I wouldn't call, but the words that came out were, "All I can say is, fare thee well, Amethystine."

"That sounds final."

An hours-long conversation whittled down to a few sentences. Just the beginning of a talk that might have gone on for years.

"One week," I said in explanation, "and one way or another, I was involved in five killings. Five dead men. Five."

Amethystine didn't speak because there was nothing to say.

"Shadrach and Purlo might be added to that list," I said.

"What would you have done?" she asked, her subdued tone filled with passion.

"That's different."

"In what way?"

"I know me," I said. "At least that far I do."

Her smile was the right response.

"I," she said and then paused, considering the words she was about to say. "I don't want to lose you."

"We ain't nevah had each other," I said, once again that teenage boy looking for Anger on the streets of the Fifth Ward.

"Are you going to tell Mel?"

"No. I'm not gonna tell anybody, but you already know that."

"Then why farewell? Do you think I'm a danger to you and your family?"

"Maybe to me."

"I'd never hurt you."

"I can't," I said, an unexpected sob welling in my throat.

She put a hand on mine.

"I'll tell you what. I'll give three months for us both to think about it. I'll be here. I will."

* * *

I don't remember leaving her car or driving back home.

It was twilight by the time I got to Brighthope. Feather and three of her girlfriends were laughing by the koi pond. Jesus was making dinner while Benita played with Essie.

I said my hellos and went up to the roof with a triple shot of Jack Daniel's.

I'd finished the drink before Jesus came up to join me.

"How you doin', Dad?"

"It's been a hard week."

"Is it the case you're working on?"

"Cases," I corrected. "And no, everything worked out the way it was going to."

"Is that good?"

"It is what it is."

"You got a cigarette?" my son asked then.

"You smoke?"

"Every once in a while."

I took the pack from a pocket and shook out a Lucky for him and one for me. I lit us both up. He took in a deep drag and then let the smoke out.

"Feather said that you really like that woman, the one who stayed over last night."

"Feather liked her."

Sometimes at nightfall in LA the darkness seems to roll in, in waves. It was like that, that night.

"Do you like her?" Jesus asked.

"She's young."

"Like you always said, Dad, we all just people. And you need somebody to keep you company."

"I got a family."

"You need more than that."

"I do?"

ABOUT THE AUTHOR

WALTER MOSLEY is one of America's most celebrated writers. He was given the 2020 National Book Award's Medal for Distinguished Contribution to American Letters, named a Grand Master of the Mystery Writers of America, and honored with the Anisfield-Wolf Award, a Grammy, a PEN USA Lifetime Achievement Award, the Robert Kirsch Award, numerous Edgars, and several NAACP Image Awards. His work has been translated into twenty-five languages. He has published fiction and nonfiction in *The New Yorker, Playboy,* and *The Nation.* As an executive producer, he adapted his novel *The Last Days of Ptolemy Grey* for AppleTV+ and serves as a writer and executive producer for FX's *Snowfall.*